INSIDE A MADMAN'S MIND

Everything seemed to be spinning out of control. He realized he was spending too much precious time covering his tracks. *Unorganized.* He was puzzled that in a city of millions things were closing in so quickly on him. He had thought it would be so simple to lose himself in a metropolis—now he felt naked, vulnerable—people seemed to discover his mistakes so quickly. Bad luck that some fool computer expert had decided to become a hero by tracking down the woman from Florida. And now the man had a reporter working with him. The two of them were in his very own apartment complex, inexorably closing in on him, trying to piece together an impossible set of clues.

His life had become so complicated, so complex. He had to get some rest. Had to plan what he was going to do. Didn't want to kill the woman on his balcony. Senseless to do that. He thought of her sister. A waste to have killed her, waste to kill this one. . . .

(Cover photograph posed by professional model)

SAFETY CATCH

JARON SUMMERS

LEISURE BOOKS   NEW YORK CITY

A LEISURE BOOK

Published by

Dorchester Publishing Co., Inc.
6 East 39th Street
New York, NY 10016

Copyright © 1985 by Jaron Summers

All rights reserved. No part of this book may be reproduced or transmitted in any form or by any electronic or mechanical means, including photocopying, recording, or by any information storage and retrieval system, without the written permission of the Publisher, except where permitted by law.

Printed in the United States of America

SAFETY
CATCH

1

Southern California was settling in for a blistering day and by nine a.m. the tiny waiting room in the parole office was a sauna. David Cursore, in keeping with the stipulations of the court, arrived for his weekly review and took a seat on a splintered oak chair. After a moment he noticed a mouse peering at him, eyeing the remains of an apple core, from behind a wad of paper. Using his toe, Cursore nudged what was left of the fruit toward the creature. The rodent twitched grey whiskers and nibbled at the offering, then suddenly scampered away as heavy footsteps approached.

Parole Officer Gwilliam waddled in. He was overweight, out-of-shape, and Cursore had the feeling that the man might have been a lobster in another life. Beady black eyes protruded from blanched skin and hands resembling claws flapped at Gwilliam's sides. His elbows and knees were swollen to such an extent that Cursore expected them to suddenly break open without warning and splatter soft pulp on the stained carpet.

Ignoring Cursore, Gwilliam ordered his secretary into his office. The girl wore an imitation silk dress several sizes too small that strained against her enormous breasts.

Cursore could hear the hum of a window air-conditioner in Gwilliam's office and through a frosted glass partition he could see the silhouette of the two. The secretary left and returned shortly with a steaming cup of coffee. The fresh aroma clashed with that of the cheap cigar Gwilliam sucked on. David overheard Gwilliam relate a joke about a black Polish farmer. His secretary did not laugh, which mattered little to the parole officer who *haw-hawed* in falsetto at his own humor. David continued to wait, watching the ponderous outline of Gwilliam talk on the phone, pick his nose and scratch his rubbery neck.

At 10:30 the secretary apologized for Mr. Gwilliam's hectic schedule.

Half an hour later she ushered Cursore into the cubicle. He sat down across from Mr. Gwilliam who seemed extremely busy scribbling notes in a large green binder. The secretary scowled and left. The heat made her blouse even tighter or perhaps it was all the Diet Dr. Peppers she was drinking, pumping her body up, flinging it against taut fabric. After several minutes, punctuated by Gwilliam relighting his third foul cigar, the parole officer looked up and considered David Cursore as though he were a newly discovered species of cockroach.

"Irony. Life is filled with it, isn't it, Mr. Cursore?"

"Yes. It is." Must be very careful not to agitate him, thought David. Careful.

Gwilliam sported a plastic ballpoint pen guard in his shirt pocket to keep ink stains off the polyester material. Today he wore five different colored pens in his shirt guard. He glanced down, past his flappy chin, at the varied colored pens, carefully selected the red one as though it was a medal of valor and held it daintily in his pudgy fingers. Then he brought out a news clipping that he unfolded and patted flat on his desk. Gwilliam's bulging eyes focused on the article. He chuckled to himself. He circled several lines in red. "See, Mr. Cursore, it says here that the computer industry has *cursors*. Little rectangles of light, like pointers on tv screens. Don't you think that's funny?"

"I guess there's some humor in it."

Gwilliam interlaced his stubby fingers and slipped them behind his bald head. He leaned back. "Goddamit, for a smart college man you sure are slow on the upbeat! Your surname is Cursore. You got two years in the slammer and two years on probation for a computer crime.

They're making computers with cursors. You got your ass in a sling for using computers the wrong way and your name is Cursore. Pure irony."

"Right. I was accused of making computers do things and a computer made me."

"Now you got it. 'Cept of course you were more than accused. You were convicted. Right, Cursore?"

"Right."

"And like all felons, you were innocent, weren't you?"

They had been through this before so David Cursore said nothing.

"Been keeping your nose clean, Cursore? Cursor. Chriiiist—what irony!"

"Yes."

"Still paying the rent in that fancy Marina del Rey apartment?"

"Yes. I'm still employed at Integrated Electronics."

"Still working nights, are you?"

"Still am."

"I don't like my people working nights. Too much temptation, if you know what I mean."

"Yes."

"Have you made any unreported trips out of the state?"

"No."

"I mean," said Parole Officer Gwilliam, "a man making your kind of money, he might want to fly off to Vegas for the afternoon. I'd hate to see you go back to the slammer for something as dumb as that." Gwilliam with great show withdrew a blue pen, then flipped through several dogeared pages in a blue binder. He inhaled his soggy stogy and let the smoke trickle out of his wide, flat nose. "I'm going to give you a warning about your dress."

"My dress?"

"Jeans. You're thirty-eight years old, Mr. Cursore. Not a kid no more. Jeans are for teenagers. Or someone who hangs around them. You got no tie. You're wearing cheap running shoes. You need a haircut."

"I'm sorry."

"Sorry, bullshit. Look, there's bums that come in here better dressed than you. See, I don't care what *you* think of me. It's the office I stand for that counts. You understand? I wear a tie, dress pants, a suit coat. You? You act like you're some smart-ass teenager. I don't have to tell you what happens if you get caught around girls under age, do I?"

"No."

"No, what?"

"No, sir."

"Why do you dress that way?"

"The jeans are clean. My shirt is laundered. I paid seventy dollars for these Nikes. I feel comfortable in them."

"Comfortable. Like you felt comfortable last week when you came in ten minutes late? You beginning to get the idea our schedule is set up for our convenience, not yours?"

"Yes, sir."

"That's good. How's it feel to have to wait ten minutes for me? You didn't like it, did you?"

"I was here at nine."

"I told you to be here at 10:20. Don't you recall that? I wrote it on my calendar last week."

"Sorry, sir."

"On Friday we'll get together at seven p.m. Your place."

"I'm planning to visit a friend and..."

"You be at your place *at* seven p.m. You understand?"

"Yes."

"Go and sin no more, Mr. Cursore."

"Thank you," said David. He stood and moved toward the door.

"Just a second."

"Yes."

"You hate my guts, don't you?"

"No."

"Yeah, you do. But you just remember that the prisons of California are doing you a very big favor by turning you loose. And any time you don't like dealing with yours truly, we'll be delighted to let you finish out your prison term behind bars. So next time we meet, you smile. I don't like dealing with people who sneer when I'm talking."

"I didn't think I was."

"I could tell you were thinking about it. Go."

Without looking back, David Cursore left the office.

As he drove from the interchange that led from the San Diego Freeway to the Marina, the tension started to leave his stomach. Over the ocean, the sky was blue and he could already smell the fresh air.

After David parked his car, he went to the health club in the apartment complex. He worked out on Nautilus equipment for half an hour, then swam twenty laps of the Olympic-sized pool. He took a hot steam, then a sauna and shower. For five minutes he let the needle-hot water massage his scalp until all the cigar smell was washed from his thick hair. Usually it was an interesting combination of black and white. Salt and pepper. But in the shower his hair glistened black. He dried off, slipped on his swimming trunks, then found an empty lounge on the sun deck that opened on to the harbor. A thousand sail boats bobbed gently on the sea. He watched the wind tease their sails. He felt normal again.

A blonde woman in a green and blue bikini moved past him, temporarily blotting out the sun. She sat down on the next chaise longue and started to rub coconut butter tanning oil onto her long legs.

"Hello," he said.

"Hi." She half smiled and the tiny crinkles at the corners of her eyes became delightfully mischievous as though she were thinking of some private joke.

As the sun fluttered out from behind a cloud, she lay back on the chaise longue and took a deep breath of ocean air. Her breasts rose and fell, gentle waves of delight.

"I'm always uncomfortable approaching strange women."

"You don't seem very uncomfortable," she said without opening her eyes. Those mischievous crinkles around her eyes were back.

"That's because you're no stranger." He closed his eyes, letting the sun's heat sink into him.

"We know each other?"

"Your name is Dusty Bleudell. You went to the University of Florida. You love water skiing. You teach grades four and five in Miami. You were married until a year ago."

Hazy emerald eyes opened and she propped her head on her wrist. "You're David!"

"You ruined it. I was about to tell you that you've got the University of Florida look. I was going to say I could tell by the shape of your toes and the callouses on your insteps that you're a water skier."

"Callouses on my instep? Mary Lou

was right about you. Said you loved to tease."

"A little. How do you like her apartment?"

"It's great. Never guess she was a senior citizen."

"You're not mad, are you?"

"No. Not mad. I'm a bit of a tease myself, Cursore. You don't mind being called Cursore, do you? Mary Lou said that's what she called you. It's a real interesting name. Where'd it come from?"

"England. I don't mind being called Cursore, if you don't mind having dinner with me tonight."

"Well, as long as Mary Lou recommended you so highly . . . How about around eight? It's apartment eight-fifteen. Oh, you must know . . ."

"Right, Dusty. By the way, do they call you that?"

"Rhymes with lusty." Her green eyes sparkled in the sunlight.

"I'll be at Mary Lou's at eight," he said.

"OK." She closed her eyes and savored the sun like a young cat stretched out on a private verandah. "Actually, I looked up the meaning of cursor. It's Latin and it means runner."

"Sounds like you've done your homework on me."

"Mary Lou made you sound so interesting. You a runner, Cursore?"

"Sometimes." He got up. "I'll drop by

before eight."

"Wonderful."

Cursore picked up his athletic bag and rode the elevator nineteen floors up to his apartment. He was thinking about something Mary Lou had said about Dusty: " . . . She's like Everest. Never really been conquered. Occasionally, I think she tolerates a temporary success. Treat her gently, Cursore."

Okay, he'd treat her gently.

Inside his three bedroom penthouse with its orderly arranged teak furniture, he sat down in an overstuffed chair. He was grinning. Then he sniffed and frowned. In his athletic bag he found the jeans and shirt he had worn to the probation office. They reeked of Gwilliam's stale cigar smoke. Cursore carried the clothing into the hall, opened the garbage chute and stuffed the jeans and shirt into it. He heard the jeans' metal rivets rasp against the aluminum chute.

He had eighteen more months with Parole Officer Gwilliam. Five hundred and forty days.

He walked back to his balcony and looked down at Dusty. She was swimming easily, languidly in the pool. He had seen sensual bodies from various angles, but for the moment no body and no angle compared with hers. The day was going to be a winner after all. *Treat her gently*. He promised himself he would.

Cursore turned from the view and picked up a book on fly fishing. He started to read it. A few minutes later there was a soft knock on his door.

It was Dusty. Water glistened on her suit. Her green eyes met his. He started to speak but she placed her forefinger on his lips and gently pressed. He retreated into his apartment. She followed, sliding her finger down his throat, across his collar bone, then downward to the button on the top of his swim trunks. She tugged and the button broke.

He almost said something again. Again she pressed a forefinger to his lips. All right, if she wanted him to be quiet, he would be quiet. He watched as she slipped out of her suit. Sunlight seemed to rustle against her naked body. She stepped toward him and peeled his trunks from him. He could feel her wetness against his body. He could smell her.

And then they were making love. *She's so beautiful,* he thought. *Like a fashion model.* Fashion to passion, he thought. She must have sensed his mind was somewhere else because she started to move urgently against his body and he could not stop himself from exploding.

They lay together on their backs, spent. He moved his head toward her; he wanted to satisfy her, really wanted to. Wanted to make her abandon control.

She pushed his head away. "We don't

have time now," she said. "Be my turn tonight."

Silence.

"I have this theory," she said. "All great affairs begin with a lie and end with the truth. So don't say anything. Then maybe we'll have a chance."

He watched her tug her suit back on, then she reached into her purse and shook out a white shirt. She slipped it over her smooth shoulders. On the shirt, above her left breast was a sentence written in small letters: "Being easy isn't pretty."

He started to chuckle. She laughed and the sounds merged, became one. When she was gone, he wondered if perhaps everything had been an illusion. No, it hadn't. He could still smell her scent and the carpet was crushed where she had lain on it. No. Wasn't an illusion at all.

2

Jon Andrews seemed perfectly normal. He was thirty-four years old with wide, muscular shoulders. He spoke with the easy midwestern accent of someone who had been raised with love and understanding. He usually wore a matching handkerchief and tie. His Roman nose was large but not obtrusive, and he was always clean shaven except on Sunday mornings when he stayed home and watched football. The Jets were his favorite team.

You would be hard pressed to find anything about Jon that did not seem normal. But there were things. For example, he thought that five times five was twenty-nine. Twelve times four was sixty-one. Nine times nine was five. Also, Jon dreamed in Ukrainian, his native language.

The problem with multiplication had started when he was twenty-five. He had been abducted by the Chinese in Hong Kong. They had discovered he was a Russian field agent. For the better part of a year they had kept him in solitary confinement between interrogations. Jon's weight dropped from one hundred eighty-five pounds to ninety. He was left alone for weeks at a time, and, sitting or squatting in a black, soundproof cubicle, he had started to go mad. So he had invented a game. He spent days reciting the multiplication tables and then to amuse himself he would change things around. A five became a thirteen. A nine became a zero. Then the next day, or what seemed like a day, he would reassign fresh values to old numbers. As a result of these elaborate mind games, he stayed more or less sane. The problem was, he had worked so hard reprogramming his brain he had actually convinced it to accept a ridiculous series of mathematical conclusions. Better that than losing his sanity.

Jon Andrews completed swimming the length of the pool and pulled himself out, then lay down in the sun, not far from Dusty Bleudell. He had been watching her earlier and he wanted to have sex with her. He studied her when she had taken the chaise longue next to David Cursore. He had heard almost everything they had said and it had made him feel sad because Dusty was a *safety.* A *safety* was a word that Jon Andrews had invented to describe certain individuals he needed in order to survive.

He waited until Dusty got in the water one more time, then took the elevator to the eighth floor. He moved casually to room 815 and using a pass key that he had stolen a year ago, let himself into Mary Lou's apartment. It was a two-bedroom corner unit with thick shag carpets, chocolate brown. There was a lot of brass. Especially lamps. He found rubber gloves in the sink. He put them on, then wiped off the door knob. Jon noticed Dusty's photograph. He opened the fridge and noted several six-packs of Coors, and a pound of bleu cheese neatly wrapped in plastic. The cupboards were haphazardly stocked with canned foods. He found a rack of Swiss cooking knives and selected one of the larger ones. In the master bedroom, he discovered three hundred dollars in cash behind a copy of An American Gothic. There were rings in a jewelry box, A necklace featured a gold Canadian Maple Leaf $100 piece. Jon pushed out the $100 gold coin and slipped it in his swim trunks. He heard Dusty's key in the lock and quickly stepped to the side of the door. She entered the room, then closed the door behind her and locked it.

She saw the butcher knife in his hand, she saw his cold grey eyes. She saw that he had no fear.

"What do you want?"

"How much cash do you have?"

"I have one hundred and thirty dollars in my purse."

"Get it."

She walked to the bedroom and opened her purse. There was only ninety dollars in it. "I forgot. I bought some things."

"What things?"

"Stockings and cosmetics."

"How long you planning on staying in Los Angeles?"

"A couple of days."

Jon slapped her hard. She fell backward onto the bed. "If you lie to me again, I'll hurt you seriously."

"I'm staying ten days, maybe two weeks."

"Then you're going back to Florida to teach school?"

"Y-yes."

"What about money?"

"I have an account in California."

"I saw your savings book. You've got over five thousand dollars. You're thrifty."

"I was going to buy some paintings from a California artist."

"If you try to get away, I'll kill you. Understand?"

"Yes."

He found some adhesive tape and tied her to a chair. Then he quietly let himself out. He came back in five minutes. He was dressed in a pair of slacks and a brown sweater. He carried a bird cage. It had a furry hamster in it who stared at the world with myopic black eyes.

"I'll give you the money if . . ."

"Don't talk. I want to show you something." Jon broke open a capsule that contained some white powder. He sprinkled a few grains in the hamster's mouth. Then he opened a beer and slowly drank it. He kept the transparent rubber gloves on. A minute later, the hamster squealed, went into frothing convulsions and died.

Jon picked up the remains of the powdered capsule and moved it toward her mouth.

"Please don't—I'll do whatever you say!"

He jammed the capsule in her mouth, pressed the knife at her neck and said, "Swallow."

She did, choking for breath. He cut the adhesive from her arms and legs. "You'll be dead in forty minutes if you don't get the antidote. If you do exactly as I say, I'll give you the antidote, and you'll be fine. Won't even have a tummy ache. You going to do what I say?"

"Where's the antidote?"

He showed her a red pill, then slipped it back into his pocket. "Get dressed and come with me. Do one thing you shouldn't and I'll run away. You'll never see me again. And you'll die."

Fifteen minutes later, he walked her into the Bank of America where she had her account. Since it was Friday, the bank was open late. Dusty withdrew $5,040.00, leaving $10 in her account.

She walked, as instructed, quickly back to her car. They got in and drove along Pacific Coast Highway. She looked at the clock radio in her rented Mustang. Her green eyes flashed at him. "I feel sick . . ."

"Not yet. Here's the pill I promised you." He handed it to her, then opened the canned soft drink he had brought with him. She swallowed the pill, washing it down with the soft drink.

"Who are you?"

"A Russian agent on the run."

She started to laugh but then the convulsions hit her. Her spine arched and her head snapped back and she was dead.

He swung the car off Pacific Coast Highway, then drove down a narrow road. At the end of the road was a manhole cover. He pried the lid back and dropped her body into it. He heard it thud softly at the bottom of the shaft. There was not enough light to see the sea water gurgling in the drain bottom but he could hear it. He knew that the bootleg drain which fed into the Malibu sewer system would carry her body two miles out to sea. For a moment, thinking of her green eyes, he was sorry that she had been a *safety*.

He got into her car and drove to Santa Monica. He parked by a meter, got out and walked several blocks. He dropped the rubber gloves into a trash can, then took a cab back to the Marina Surf Towers.

He regretted not having sex with her but he consoled himself with the thought of her money. And, more important, the poison was perfect. Quick and deadly. He had used only three grains in the sugar powder. Three grains, each grain smaller than a fleck of salt. A part of Jon Andrews regretted killing Dusty Bleudell. But it was a very tiny part of his soul. He thought about the word "soul." He did not believe human beings had souls. Nothing had a soul.

3

They walked in the dark from the Washington, D.C. mall to a restaurant called "Food for Thought" on Connecticut Avenue. They were old friends and old enemies. Ivan Tornof had been posted with the Russian Embassy in Washington for the last nine years. Ivan, growing bald, still walked with the energetic step of a man much younger than fifty-five. Dr. Alan Wolsey was CIA but during his frequent visits to Moscow his passport listed him as a business man. Dr. Wolsey taught political science at Georgetown University. None of his students realized what the heavy-set, middle-aged man was all about.

The American knew Ivan reported directly to the Second Chief Directorate (KGB) in Russia. And the Russian knew who Alan's superior was in the CIA, and who that superior reported to—and on and on.

They found a table at the back of the restaurant and ordered soup and hot dogs. "They're nitrate-free," said Alan.

"In my country, we have bun-free,

meat-free, and mustard-free hot dogs. In short, no hot dogs at all. Mother Russia does her best to protect her loyal comrades."

"No wonder you look so trim, Comrade."

"I wish. My wind is not what it used to be. I have trouble sleeping. I'm going to have to get dentures. It's a pain in the ass to grow old, Comrade."

"I know. Dotty says she'd trade me in for a new husband except she couldn't handle a newer model."

"How are Paul and Jeannie?"

"Paul is doing well with his law practice in California. Jeannie is doing OK with her second marriage." The American crossed his fingers and smiled a weary smile. "Your wife?"

"She's sad we'll have to go back to Russia. She's gotten accustomed to nylons that come in those plastic eggs and twenty-seven different kinds of corn flakes. And she adores the reruns of 'Three's Company.'"

"Why don't you defect? I can get you political asylum."

"Thank you, my friend. I'm too young to defect and far too old to be a martyr."

Their soup came and they ate it slowly. "Is this as good as the borscht we ate in Leningrad?" asked the American.

"Better."

"I think not."

"We were both hungrier then." Ivan

picked up a paper napkin and wiped a smudge of soup from his neatly trimmed moustache. "We have a problem, but of course, we are not going to have a conversation about it."

"What are we not going to talk about, Comrade?" Alan considered his old friend over the brim of the coffee cup that held a brown liquid guaranteed not to contain caffeine.

"We are not going to talk about Jon Andrews."

"A nice American name. One of your people?"

"You have heard about him?" The Russian scowled.

"No, but we would not be silly enough to call one of our operatives Jon Andrews." The American thought about it for awhile. "But, then maybe we would."

"There is a photograph of him. It will arrive in your mail in a brown envelope. The postmark will be Buffalo."

"And where is this Jon Andrews?"

The Russian shrugged.

"And why are you 'not' telling me about him?"

"If you or I do not catch him and kill him soon, then he will be a great embarrassment to both our countries."

"One of your men going off the deep end? Hasn't happened often." The American sipped some more coffee. "Why was he brought here?"

"To kill Queen Elizabeth."

The American gagged on his drink and the Russian passed him several paper napkins to stifle his fit of coughing. "It was craziness, hatched by some fool committee of Smersh. I stopped it before it could happen, except—well, except in order to stop it I had to have one of my operatives kill Jon Andrews."

"And your man failed?"

"There was a fire. The papers said he was burnt up. I think not, though. It is hard to kill one's countrymen in a foreign land. Everything else went wrong. In the end Queen Elizabeth did not even show up."

"If Andrews is alive, would he know your people tried to kill him?"

The Russian nodded his head, turned to watch a man in a black sweater standing in the doorway. "One of your agents, Comrade?"

"No," said the American. "He works for the Japanese."

The American paid for the meal; after all, when he had been in Russia Ivan had always paid. Fair was fair.

Autumn permeated the night air and crinkled leaves scraped across the dark sidewalk. Women were starting to wear their furs. The air had a nice crisp flavor and neither man said anything for several blocks.

"What cover did Jon Andrews have?" asked Alan Wolsey.

"Investment banker."

"So he had a lot of money?"

"He had access to a lot of money. Developed a wonderful taste for your bourgeois possessions. Of course when he went for ground, we cut off all of his financial resources. I think we did rather well."

"But he still likes champagne?"

"Yes, and it must be French," said the Russian. He undid a roll of mints, offered one to Wolsey. Wolsey, caught up in thought, shook his head. The Russian sucked on his mint as they walked on—a pair of anachronisms, a brace of spies on opposite sides of a spinning coin.

"Hobbies?"

"Women. He's crazy about women. He likes sailing. Possesses an incredible knowledge of small arms."

"I think you're right. He could be very dangerous."

"He is a sociopath of the first water. We made a terrible mistake when we missed killing him. Terrible."

"He might have slipped into Canada or Mexico," said the American.

"No. Loves possessions too much. Loves owning things. Besides, he feels no compunction about taking them from your countrymen. As a matter of fact, he enjoys it."

"Why?"

"Hates all Americans. His father was supposedly an American sailor who more or less raped his mother after he got her drunk. Then, when Jon was seventeen, his mother was killed in Paris. He thought it was an American."

"I bet you gave him that idea, Ivan."

"Yes. We do bad things, don't we? Anyway, we sent Jon to Hong Kong on assignment. But as luck would have it, he encountered a group of Chinese agents working for your people. They caught him and tortured him for almost a year before I could do a swap. He obviously had no use for Americans by then."

"And how long has he been loose in this country?"

"Over two years."

"Perhaps," said the American, "he'll fade into the woodwork?"

"No," said the Russian. "Twice I have almost gotten him. Twice he has slipped away. His method of survival will change. We trained him to maintain his cover through careful and selective small crimes. These crimes would not even appear to be crimes."

"Unreported burglaries? That kind of thing?" asked the American.

"Yes. But since Jon Andrews realizes we'll find him again, I feel he'll attempt a major extortion. And since he cares nothing about the lives of your citizens . . . well, it could get messy . . ."

"Maybe we should talk soon about Jon Andrews . . ."

"Yes. I was hoping you would say that . . ."

They stopped near a parking lot. The American beamed. "Hey, have you seen my new Nissan? What do you think . . ." Then, Alan Wolsey did a peculiar thing. He tried to breathe and couldn't.

"Oh, my God," said Ivan Tornof. He caught the American in midair, laid him down and started CRP. Wolsey started to breathe.

The ambulance came quickly. Since the Wolseys lived only a few blocks from the hospital, his wife was already at the emergency entrance when the ambulance screamed to a stop. Green smocked hospital attendants wheeled Alan out of the ambulance; Dotty held her husband's hand. An intern temporarily kept Wolsey's heart going. A nurse, with electric defibrillation paddles, stood by.

The Russian watched.

"Dotty, thank you for the best years of my life. You know what I liked the best?"

"Don't talk that way, Alan."

"Liked it best when you said I was a great dancer. Oh, yeah. And a great lover. Thank you." He was gone.

The Russian tried to keep the tears from coming. When he finally left the hospital, he felt like a one-sided coin. Be no fun now without his friend, the American. Crazy years they had together. Ivan considered telling another American operative about Jon Andrews. But he couldn't trust any of them. Moscow, with its miles of bureaucratic twisted corridors, thought Andrews was dead. Better to let sleeping dogs lie. What a funny expression, he mused to himself. God, how he would miss Alan.

4

David Cursore made a dinner reservation at El Torito's in the Marina. The receptionist remembered him and promised him a window table overlooking the harbor. Cursore reread a proposal he had written for Integrated Electronics. The report outlined how tiny computer switches could be synthesized from inorganic chemicals. If the theory worked, it would eventually be possible to "grow" computers like mushrooms. Cursore was convinced such a breakthrough was years away but it was fascinating research. He had time for his favorite shower—cold, hot, cold. During the hot phase he shaved. He took his time toweling off his lean body and rubbing dry his closely cropped hair. He walked into his bedroom and pulled on a white pair of jeans and silk shirt. He found some moccasins made from calf skin, and as he wiggled into them, he strapped on an inexpensive digital watch. It chimed eight p.m. as he pulled his hallway door locked behind him.

He tapped gently on Mary Lou's door.

No answer. He rapped again, harder. Perhaps Dusty was in the shower. He listened at the door. All was quiet. Puzzled, Cursore waited for a few minutes, then knocked again. Still no answer, so he returned to his apartment and called Mary Lou's apartment. He let the phone ring ten times, then hung up and poured himself a finger of Scotch over cracked ice. He thumbed through a copy of BYTE magazine and tried to keep his attention on an article describing why computers would revolutionize the eighties and nineties, but an uneasy feeling kept nuzzling the back of his mind. It was something Mary Lou had told him. "Dusty's fun and loves kids and you can always depend on her. Just 'cause she's got blonde hair and a stupendous figure, don't make the mistake she's a bubblehead, Cursore."

He closed the magazine and thought about Mary Lou. He and Mary Lou were old friends, especially by California standards. Their relationship was going into its second decade and they always remembered each other's birthdays. Every Friday, Cursore cooked Mary Lou dinner while on Sunday she would do the honors. Her specialty was fried chicken with thick gravy and dumplings. His was trout. A relationship based on food and wit. What more was there? Mostly Mary Lou employed her wit to assess the current lady in Cursore's life. "That redhead'll cheat on you, the first pair of pants that comes along . . . that little gal from Dallas, she'll split with the first sailor who chugs by in a yacht . . . and that gal who thinks she knows everything about running a law office? Hell, I'll bet she's still married. Doesn't have enough sense to get herself out of an entanglement with her own husband."

Mary Lou had been unerringly and delightfully accurate.

"How do you know so much about women?" he had asked.

"Don't know a thing about women. But *you*—I know plenty about you."

"Come on, I think you must be psychic."

"Nope."

"Then how do you do it?"

"Look, Cursore, after seventy-eight years of shuffling around this planet you get a nose for decent breeding stock in both men and women. You're top quality but you have some kind of compulsion to fall for losers. Go for quality. And speaking of top quality, wait until you meet Dusty. She's just getting over a marriage to a real jerk. So go easy on her. She'll make hellish good breeding stock."

"Breeding stock? You never had children."

"Profit from my mistakes, kid," Mary Lou had said. "Profit."

Two more blank phone calls, and half an hour later Cursore cancelled the reservation and scrambled some eggs. He watched the last half of "Casablanca" on his Betamax, then called Mary Lou's again. No answer. It was eleven when he realized it would only be eight in Honolulu. He called Mary Lou at her brother's.

"What's the matter? You get lonesome for me, Cursore?"

"Always lonesome for you."

"Did that damn parole officer give you a rough time today?"

"Yeah."

"Keep your cool?"

"Yes. Just like I promised." God, what a sweet woman. How many other people bothered to care like that?

"Meet Dusty yet?"

"Yes."

"You're calling to thank me. Right? I told you she was out of this world."

"I met her by the pool and we had a date. She stood me up."

"Dusty wouldn't do that. Unless of course you weren't a gentleman. Were you?"

"Absolutely."

"Maybe you got the time mixed up. You know how you do that."

"No. It was eight o'clock. I even set it on my watch."

"Is her car next to my Cadillac?"

"Dunno."

"Well, check it, dumb-dumb," said Mary Lou.

"Good idea. What does she drive?"

"It'll be a rental car. I told her she could drive my Caddy but she said no—doesn't like to borrow people's cars. Told you she had class."

"OK. Anything I can do for you?"

"Just keep watering my little bonsai elm. You have to water it every day or—"

"—it'll die. I know."

"OK. Love you kid and good luck."

"Me, too. Say hi to your brother and be good, Mary Lou, OK?"

"At my age what's the alternative?"

"Bye." Cursore hung up, slipped on a sweater and took the elevator down to the garage. Next to Mary Lou's metallic blue Seville was an empty space. There were a set of tire tracks in the dust next to the Caddy. Cursore went back upstairs to Mary Lou's apartment, and after knocking several more times, let himself in.

"Hello, Dusty, it's me. David Cursore. You okay?"

No answer.

Feeling like an intruder, he glanced around. Light spilt across the chocolate brown carpet from the table lamp that was connected to a timer. He switched on the lights in the kitchen. A false plastic ceiling hid half a dozen long fluorescent tubes. Bright light bounced off the spotless white tile. He could hear the fridge gurgling as its ice maker churned out cubes behind the freezer door. A lemon smell from some detergent hovered above the sink. Still feeling like a trespasser Cursore padded down the hallway to the guest bathroom. He snapped the light on. Spotless. The shower was clean enough to make a salad in. He moved down the hallway and checked the master bath. Somebody had splattered a bit of water on the mirror over the marble sink. There was a pair of bedroom slippers by the waste basket and a large plastic bag crammed with perfumes, powders and creams. Obviously, the cosmetics belonged to Dusty.

He checked the master bedroom. There was an open suitcase on a velvet-covered bench next to an oak chest of drawers. A soft white dress hung on a hanger on the back of the bedroom door. Cursore touched the material—so smooth, like expensive silk. It had the bouquet of Joy perfume—light and fruity.

He checked around for Dusty's purse but did not see it. He was beginning to feel sheepish. She had simply gone out. Took her purse and gone. He wondered what he would say if she walked in— maybe with another guy.

"Oh, hi, Dusty. Forgot to water Mary Lou's little bonsai elm. I'll be out of your way."

Dusty would give him a look and maybe her date would give her a look.

Cursore realized he was probably misreading everything. Maybe she had forgotten, or maybe she'd thought nine o'clock and when he hadn't shown up.... Nope. He had phoned and hammered on the door. Someone called up at the last minute? She must know some people in Los Angeles. Everyone knows somebody in Los Angeles. That somebody had a car and it was broken down? Nope. Why would anyone call her from the freeway? Didn't make sense. All right. A friend calls up and says: "I've got this acute pain and my doctor said to go to the emergency room at the nearest hospital." So Dusty, being a nice thoughtful woman, would race off to take the sick friend to a hospital. Or how about—Dusty had gone to buy something and gotten lost or had an accident? Maybe she was stumbling around the city with amnesia. Anything could happen in Los Angeles.

Cursore found Mary Lou's red kettle with the broken whistle, filled it with water and doused the tiny elm on the balcony. Tomorrow, when Dusty told him what happened, they'd have a laugh.

He was careful not to overwater the miniature elm, didn't want the black soil to spill out of its pot. He wiped off the spout and carried the kettle back to the kitchen and set it down next to Mary Lou's rubber gloves. Oh-oh. There were no rubber gloves. Mary Lou had eczema and always wore rubber gloves to protect her hands. Always. Heaven help the individual who moved her gloves from their sacred spot by the tea kettle. Cursore looked under the sink for them. Not there. He glanced in the trash can. Not there. He walked to the bathroom and looked around, then tried the laundry closet. No gloves. He had seen them the morning before. Now why would Dusty even use the gloves? She hadn't had time to do the dishes. The maid had been in Wednesday. That's why everything was spotless. Maybe Dusty had eczema, too. No. If she did, she'd probably carry her own special pair of rubber gloves. If that were the case, they'd have been in her luggage. No way Cursore was going to get caught rifling through Dusty's lingerie. That would end any chance of a relationship. He could hear it now:

"And then this weirdo I'd met by the pool was dipping into my luggage when I got back to my friend's apartment . . . honest to God, he had a key and everything. Right out of 'Psycho.' He said he was looking for my rubber gloves. Don't ask me what he wanted to do with rubber gloves on our first date. Talk about fruitcakes . . ."

Cursore caught his reflection in the hall mirror. He was smiling as he scribbled a note that said: "Dusty— Came by to pick you up at eight. You weren't there. Give me a call at 856-5400.

Maybe we can do something tomorrow evening. Hope everything is OK. Cursore."

He'd slip the note in the crack along the doorjamb and be on his way. Then he noticed the chair. Mary Lou had four captain's chairs in crushed velvet that were always neatly arranged around the stained oak living room table. The chair closest to the credenza had been pushed against the wall, making it impossible to sit without being flush against a blank wall. Why would Dusty move a chair like that? To change a light bulb? No light overhead. Maybe she wanted to do some kind of exercise? Cursore walked over to the chair and saw the strip of adhesive tape around a rung on the back of it. White adhesive tape. Had she broken the rung, then taped it together? He pulled the tape away. The rung was OK. He thought about moving the chair but that might frighten her when she returned. She obviously thought she had the place to herself. He rolled the adhesive into a ball and tossed it into the trash with the rest of the adhesive. Bingo. More adhesive. He reached into the trash container and took out several strips of adhesive—each was an inch wide, several feet long. Bits of crushed velvet clung to the sticky side of the tape. There were also short blonde hairs.

Someone had gotten into the apartment, someone had tied up Dusty with tape. Someone had taken some rubber gloves. What else? Stop! Warning bells started to clatter in his mind. This isn't my job. Isn't my territory. Isn't my responsibility. Call the police. That's the right thing to do. Just call the police and tell them what's going on, and they'll ask me who I am and I'll tell them. And then they'll do a make on me and they'll find out I'm on probation and they'll ask me more questions.

He could hear their questions now—"Is it your habit to inspect strange women's quarters before you date them?" Goddamn Gwilliam would have a field day with that.

Only one thing to do. Walk away from it. No one knew he was here. No one had seen him come in. Fine. Just walk away from it.

Then he saw the dead hamster in the bird cage. Blood seeped from its nose and mouth and ears. He almost reconsidered his decision, but he locked Mary Lou's door behind him and took the stairs back to his apartment. No one would ever know he had been there. A moment later he was leaning against his door, breathing heavily. He did not want to see the inside of a jail ever again. Under any circumstances. Ever. A dead hamster! What the hell was going on? Maybe Dusty had a hamster—and it got sick, so she had gone to the vet's.

Then he remembered Dusty's face.

The green eyes. The blonde hair. The way she spoke. The images flooded through his mind. Mary Lou was right. Dusty was just hurting, just starting to come out of her shell. A vixen peeking around a tree. "Don't," he warned himself, "don't call the police. So she's in trouble. It's not your fight. She got into it, she'll get out of it."

The two horrible years he had spent in jail undulated across the images of the green-eyed blonde. He never wanted to go back to those echoing corridors and those cold roller coaster nights and soggy potatoes that were reheated five times. Especially, he did not want to have to deal with the low lives who sifted through the prison yards. The child abusers and kidnappers and the extortionists. There was Peter the Pimp. He'd gotten twelve years for pouring acid down the throat of one of his girls who testified against him. And there was Mr. Bell—he'd used razor blades on luckless women he trapped in phone booths.

He realized that if he called the police, he might find himself in a lot more trouble than he wanted. If he got involved, if the police thought he was pulling something, they'd throw him back in prison. End of his parole.

Cursore never wanted to go back to prison—he hated the freaks and sickos who infested the cells. They were evil. Cursore asked himself why he should stick his neck out for anyone—especially a woman he had met for three minutes? Jail was such a terrible place to go back to—a sewer that you had to understand in order to survive. And that, Cursore realized, was why he was going to call the police. He had found out first hand, eyeball to eyeball, the kind of scum that dwelt on the planet. He didn't want Dusty to have to deal with such scum. She was too clean, too innocent. Didn't really matter if he'd known her three minutes or three centuries. He called the police.

5

It was slightly past midnight when Sergeant George Dartwell arrived at Cursore's apartment. Dartwell was from the Lennox Station of the L.A. Sheriff's Department. Each man knew enough to be wary of the other. "So, what can I do for you, Mr. Cursore?" asked the sergeant. He was a large man with rugged ears that hung against his skull like a pair of tiny koala bears. His hair was trimmed close to this massive head and his shoulders looked like they belonged to an N.F.L. lineman. He had biceps the size of fire hydrants and fingers the diameter and texture of fat dill pickles.

"I appreciate your coming over, Sergeant."

The sergeant glanced at his watch and nodded.

"I'm looking after a friend's apartment down on the eighth floor."

"Have as good a view as this?"

"Yes."

"What's this pad set you back a month?"

"The company I work for supplies it. I'm not sure."

"It's more than I make in two months. So what happened? A robbery while your friend was away?"

"I met a girl who's staying there. She disappeared."

The sergeant glanced up at the oak beam ceiling for guidance but found none. "I've had a helluva day. What do you mean disappeared?"

"We had a date tonight. She wasn't at home when I showed up."

"Tell me about this broad." The cop sighed.

"Dusty Bleudell is her name. About 25. Blonde. Teaches school in Florida. Flew here to buy some art, and according to my friend she's totally dependable."

"She good looking?"

"Very."

The cop leaned forward, resting his fire hydrant arms on his knees. "Did you actually see anyone grab her? Or was there a note or anything..."

"Nothing like that. But when I checked her apartment..."

"You went in?"

"Yes. I have a key so I can water some plants for Mary Lou, the lady who owns it. There was a chair in the middle of the room with white adhesive tape on it. I found a bunch of balled-up adhesive tape in a trash can in the apartment. The adhesive tape had blonde hairs and paint from the chair sticking to it."

"Anything else?"

"Some rubber gloves were missing. There was a bird cage with a dead hamster in it."

"A dead hamster. You call the Humane Society, too?"

"I didn't want to bother you but if something happened to Dusty..."

"Let's go water the plants in your friend's apartment."

"Pardon?"

"You got a key. You been asked to water a plant. You invite me along. I don't need a search warrant. Use your head, Mr. Cursore. Didn't you learn anything in the slammer?"

Inside Mary Lou's apartment the cop noted the collection of silver coffee spoons. Mary Lou had scrounged them from around the world. There were several silver dollar coin collections in picture frames on the wall. There were some small petitpoints on the wall in a variety of reds and greens. One said, "Less is better." Another said, "Cleanliness is next to a psychosis."

"How old is this Mary Lou?" asked George Dartwell.

"Eighty."

The sergeant picked up an ivory letter opener and considered its weight. "I would think a robber might grab those silver dollars. Where's the chair with the adhesive?"

"By the table."

"I thought you said it was next to the wall."

"I must have moved it."

The sergeant peered at the rungs along the back. "I don't see any tape on here." He got down on his knees to inspect it.

"Most of it's in the trash can."

The cop followed Cursore into the kitchen. Cursore turned on the light and swung back the lid on the trash container. Sergeant Dartwell peered in. "I see nothing. Clean as a whistle."

Cursore looked in. He frowned.

"Maybe this Dusty came back home and emptied the garbage can. You ever think of that?" asked the cop.

"Somebody emptied the trash."

"Yes, they did. Probably threw out the dead hamster too. Anyone else got a key to this place?"

"No. I guess you must think I'm out of it," said Cursore.

The cop looked at his watch again. "Apartments in the Marina are giant boxes of granola. Full of nuts and flakes and fruits. Give this broad some time. She'll probably show up. Probably got sidetracked at a party. It's Friday night and I bet there's fifty of them going on."

Cursore went down to the garage with the cop. Sergeant Dartwell slid into his black-and-white sheriff's car and rolled down the window. "Look, I'll give you another *fer instance*. This blonde, you've never met before, right? A real looker—who's to say she's not a bit kinky?"

"I know this sounds thin but Mary Lou vouched for Dusty. Mary Lou has a sixth sense about people."

"Don't go on what an eighty year old woman says about a twenty-five year old girl. Or what that twenty-five year old fox tells an eighty year old broad and what she really does. Now, *fer instance*, this Dusty hits on you, makes a date, then maybe she hits on another guy. She takes him up to the old broad's apartment for a little fun and games. Maybe into a little bondage, a little S and M. So they get it on and she takes off for his place. What do you think?"

"I think you've got a dirty mind."

"No question about that, Mr. Cursore. But that's what makes me a good cop. Got to think just as dirty as the creeps. No offense. White collar crime like you go for—don't make you a creep. If you were a creep, you would have thought dirtier and then you wouldn't have gotten caught. You want to think dirty? Look what you put together from a couple of hunks of adhesive tape and a misplaced chair? I gotta go." He tooled off into the night, merging with the endless haze of lights on Lincoln Boulevard.

* * *

In his penthouse Cursore stripped down to his shorts and got on his stationary rowing machine. With long strokes he started to pull on the aluminum handles, and after a few moments, sweat dampened his brow. He could feel the muscles in his gut smart but he continued rowing for another twenty minutes.

He showered and made himself some peppermint tea, then turned out the lights and looked down at the harbor. The sliding glass door was open and the sound of a girl laughing drifted up through the black night air.

After he finished the tea, he set his alarm for six a.m. and went to bed. He waited for sleep to come.

It didn't.

He thought about taking a sleeping pill. Dumb idea. Finally, he slipped on his jogging suit and called Mary Lou's number. Nothing. He took the elevator to the garage. Dusty's car was still gone. He went back to Mary Lou's apartment and knocked. No answer. He let himself in, called out her name. No answer.

What does a person do when she comes in from sex and swimming? Has a shower. Cursore went into the master bath and slid the glass door open. There was a step-down shower/tub in white and pink tile. He felt the surface of the tub around the drain. Dry. Maybe Dusty was fastidious. Maybe she had polished the tub off with a towel. Maybe the water had simply dried. There was always hair around the drain. No hair. Dusty was either a very neat person or she did not believe in showering after swimming and oiling her body down with tanning lotions. He had seen her slipping through the pool like a beautiful porpoise. OK. Where's her damp suit? Don't people toss their suits in the shower? No suit in the shower. He checked the other bathroom and the laundry room. No suit. He hunted through the closets and the drawers in the bedroom. He found two of Mary Lou's bathing suits but not the green and blue one that Dusty had worn.

Why would she leave her swim suit on? Maybe she went down to the sauna but then why take her purse? He went back to the master bedroom. He sensed exactly what it felt like to be a cat burglar as he carefully checked the half dozen dresses she had hung up in the closet. He felt two things—guilt and excitement. Each dress was covered in cellophane from a Miami dry cleaners. There was one empty bag—obviously it had contained the dress Dusty was now wearing. Why would she wear it over a damp swim suit? Hell, he told himself, I'm crazy. Maybe Dartwell was right. She met a guy, threw on her dress and took off with him for a ride to God knows where. Probably it was an old friend, an old lover. A new lover. A set of lovers.

Who could figure out anything in the middle of the night in the Marina?

There must be a hundred rational reasons why she had stood him up. Nevertheless he carefully sorted through her belongings. There were two leather cases plus a garment bag. The smaller one contained more cosmetics and personal items. The larger had been packed with sweaters and underclothing. If she walked in on him now! He found a small folder. There were several envelopes in it. One envelope said "California Art Buying Expenses." It contained half a dozen receipts for plane tickets, meals, Polaroid film and parking lot tickets.

Another envelope was crammed with clippings of Southern California galleries. Dusty had scribbled some notes on pages torn from art catalogs.

The third item was an envelope from a bank in Florida. There was a copy of a transfer to the Bank of America in Southern California. The transfer was for $5,050.00 and included a savings account number at the bank.

The rest of the folder overflowed with Xeroxes of selected pages in art books showing photographs of California artists. In neat, precise writing, Dusty had jotted down telephone numbers and comments on phone conversations she had had with gallery employees or the artists.

There was no bank book. Maybe she had left that back in Florida, had simply forgotten it.

Cursore copied the numbers from the Visa and Mastercard receipts as well as the information on the cash transfer.

It was after three a.m. when he returned to his apartment. If Dusty did not show up by noon Saturday, Cursore knew what he was going to do.

If he got caught, he wouldn't have to worry about putting up with Parole Officer Gwilliam. Parole Officer Gwilliam only dealt with people on parole. Cursore was going to take a chance on going back to jail. That was the only way he had a chance of tracing Dusty. Back to the slammer, he mused, it would be for a lot longer than his last stretch. And this time if he went back to prison, he'd deserve it. Never again could he insist he'd been framed.

As he lay in bed, aware of the distant waves, Cursore wondered if Mary Lou could have been wrong about Dusty. Maybe Sergeant Dartwell was right. What Dusty told Mary Lou about herself and what Dusty was really like could be totally different.

Finally around five a.m. Cursore fell asleep. He dreamed of Dusty. Green eyes, flowing blonde hair. Green and blue suit clinging to her slender figure. She whispered: "I'm never conquered—occasionally I tolerate temporary success." Then he heard her laugh in his dream and woke up. He was alone in his apartment.

6

Jon Andrews' favorite time of the week was Saturday and Sunday. These were his days to relax, days to let his guard down. He never bothered with *safeties* on the weekend. After he completed his one hour exercise regime at the apartment's health spa, he walked several miles to the Omelet Parlour in Santa Monica. Although it was not yet eight a.m., a number of the regulars were already sitting on benches in front of the restaurant, waiting to get tables. The scent of eggs and fried potatoes was a comforting aroma for Jon. It summoned back the memories of his childhood—his mother preparing breakfast while his father shaved and dressed in heavy coveralls and hummed in their tiny one-room apartment. His father had been a pipefitter with a passion for opera. Jon's childhood mornings overflowed with snatches of Ave Maria and Nessum Dorma. Then a kiss from his mother. The thin carpet next to his bed was always icy to the touch of his bare feet. He savored the memory. A good childhood.

His father's tenor voice. The bouquet of sizzling eggs, cold floors and then cozy homemade socks. And through a tiny window, his city coming alive—the sunlight shimmering on the turnip-shaped dome of the mutlicolored Greek Orthodox church, a block away, where he had been christened.

He was twelve before he discovered that the man who sang operas in the morning was not his father. His real father had been an American serviceman who had a one-night stand with his mother. It was at that moment of discovery Jon had started to despise Americans and for a long time had refused to use his English name.

"We're getting to be regulars, aren't we?" said a voice beside him, jarring him back to the present.'

"Pardon?" asked Jon. He looked at a svelte black girl. She was in her mid-twenties, sparkling teeth set in an oval face. She had the trim body of a dancer; he remembered seeing her wearing a T-shirt with a silk screening of Pilobolus, the dance company. This Saturday she wore running shorts and a bright jerkin with the name "Donna" stenciled on one sleeve. "I said we're getting to be regulars." She grinned. "You OK?"

"Oh, sure." The fact that a part of his life was giving way to routine saddened him, for he could not afford the luxury of predictable patterns.

"Great. Doesn't the air smell wonderful?"

"Sure does. I don't know how anyone can live anywhere else than the beach." He realized she was drawing him out. Her attention made him feel good.

"Suppose they're existing on a shoestring and finishing graduate school at UCLA?"

"I see you around here all the time," he said.

"Just on Saturdays. You live around here?"

"About two miles away."

"Can you see the ocean from your place?"

He nodded.

"You need a roommate?"

"Maybe." And he thought to himself that when he completed his major plan, he would enjoy being with such a woman as this Donna.

"Why don't we just get married? That would make it simpler."

"Simple things in life are best. And also the most complicated. And also the most scary." He realized he was telling her too much about himself. Yet, he wanted to tell her everything. He needed to have someone, just one person in his life understand him. Share his world. He realized this was a weakness but it was a part of what made him a person. He was so tired of denying his weaknesses.

They had breakfast together and afterward browsed through a nearby antique and junk shop. Donna found a two hundred year old porcelain pitcher and basin set. Tiny gold angels frolicked on the lip of the pitcher.

"Would you like me to buy that for you?" he asked.

"Too expensive."

"Money is no object."

"It is to a good relationship," she said.

"You studying psychology?"

"No. Actually I'm a linguist."

"You're kidding."

"No. Take you, for example. Your speech patterns give you away."

"What are you talking about?" He smiled at her and picked up an old English walking cane with a heavy brass head. If she were an agent, sounding him out, he'd have to . . . He glanced in an antique mirror. There were several other customers meandering through the store. The shopkeeper had his back to them. With luck he could cave her skull in with the head of the cane and disappear out the back door before anyone realized what had happened.

She picked the pitcher up and turned it in her hand. "This is very good quality. Not a chip in it." She glanced at him. "A second ago you said—'simple things in life are best.'"

His fingers tightened around the black shaft of the cane.

"Well, you pronounced the words

correctly. No accent at all. Kind of midwestern. But you left out the articles. Most Americans would say—'*the* simple things in life are *the* best.' "

"My grandfather was from the old country," he said.

"Russia?"

"The Ukraine."

"That explains it." She set the pitcher down. "Did something you ate upset you?"

"No."

"Good, you seem a little unsteady."

"Maybe it was the omelet." He was relaxing now. If she were testing him, she would never have been so obvious. His people knew how dangerous he was. If she were working with them, she never would have left herself so vulnerable. Unless, of course, she was very good at what she did. Stop it, he told himself. Too paranoid. I ran into her by accident. If my people suspected me, they wouldn't have waited weeks to spring the trap. I would have been dead an hour after they discovered me.

"Maybe you're coming down with a touch of the flu. There's a lot of it going around. I'll give you a lift home if you don't mind squeezing into an old MG."

"I don't mind. How do you know I don't have a car?"

"I saw you jog here. My car's fifteen years old—and held together with Crazy Glue and prayers. First thing I'm going to do when I make some money is have it restored."

After she drove him to the Marina Surf Towers and parked in the adjoining garage, he invited her into his apartment for a look at the harbor. For a second she was reluctant, then agreed. Donna was impressed with the view from his penthouse, with his leather bound collection of old classics and with the computer terminal that linked him to the stock market exchange. She seemed particularly taken with his mirror top coffee table. It was at least three feet by seven feet. The sides were Moroccan red leather. The surface of the mirror was polished to perfection and reflected the exposed wooden beams of the ceiling. There was nothing on the surface of the glass, not even an ashtray. He showed her how to move around the room and see the clouds that drifted over the ocean in the surface of the table.

"That table gives you a real different perspective, doesn't it?" she asked.

"Totally unique."

"I've never met an investment banker before. Do you like it?" she asked. She moved further back from the coffee table; sun caught the edge of the mirrored top, sending a flash of light through her black hair.

"It's OK."

"But it sounds so exciting."

"What you do is exciting."

"You kidding?" She held her hand over her face to shield her eyes from the sun sparkling off the coffee table, nearly blinding her.

"No. You could join the CIA."

She laughed. "What would they do with me?" She stepped into the shadows of the room.

"Make you a spy catcher."

"How could I possibly catch a spy?"

He poured some cognac for them. "You figured out that my grandfather was a Ukranian. What if I'd been a mole?"

"Mole?"

"That's a person from a foreign country who lives in an enemy's country among its citizens for ten, twenty years. Then when the two countries go to war, the mole is in place—ready to kill, blow up bridges, poison the water supply. That kind of thing."

"How horrible. Could you imagine living with people for most of your life and then suddenly starting to kill them? I don't think many people are capable of that."

"People are capable of almost anything. The only thing they need is the opportunity," he said. As soon as the words were out of his mouth he regretted them.

"I think the world of banking has made you a trifle cynical."

"Not really." He had already told her

his name was Dennis Baron. He wondered what her reaction would be if she realized he had killed a woman eighteen hours earlier eleven floors below them. He could turn her into a cynic, given a week or two.

"Do you like to bike?" she asked, noticing his ten-speed Peugeot on the patio.

"Love it."

"Me, too." She glanced at her Timex watch. "I guess I better be going."

"OK." He swirled the amber brandy in his tumbler. The aroma was soothing. He saw her distorted reflection in the snifter. It is a pity, he thought, that she will be leaving, for he had felt himself becoming aroused by her. For reasons that were difficult for him to fathom he was more attracted to black women than white. "Please stay."

"I'd love to but I've got so much to do. I'm really behind in everything. Saturday I have to do my laundry and clean up my apartment and try to get my bills paid." She set her half-finished brandy down.

He smiled gamely. "Let me walk you to the elevator." He set his brandy snifter down, and as he did so, he deliberately let it slip. It broke against the red tile of the wet bar counter. He grabbed for it and deliberately cut his finger. It happened in less than half a second and she gasped.

"Oh!"

"It's fine. I'll put a little peroxide on it and it'll be as good as new in a year or so."

She giggled and hurried to the sink, turned on the water. "You'd better rinse it out."

"OK. Look—what I said about people being capable of anything. I didn't mean that. I've been in kind of a negative mood what with the Middle East mess and watching that report on crime on Channel Seven every night."

"The news is really depressing. I hardly ever watch it anymore."

"Look, you have to go. I can bandage this up. It's not very bad."

"I'll get a bandage. Where do you keep them?"

"In the bathroom off the bedroom hall."

With the grace of a dancer she fluttered down the corridor. He wrapped a paper towel around his finger and followed her. As she was looking through the medicine cabinet he walked into the bathroom. Their eyes encountered each other in the mirror. "Did you cut yourself just so I'd stay?"

"No."

"You're fibbing. But you get A for effort. You must be awfully horny." She took his hand and kissed it. She bandaged his finger. "I don't like the looks of that cut. I better examine you completely. You don't mind disrobing."

She led him into the bedroom.

"I don't mind."

She helped him take his clothes off. "My, but it's warm in here. You don't mind if I slip my clothes off, do you?"

"Would that be ethical?"

"Absolutely," she said.

When they were both naked, she pulled the lambskin spread back from his oversized bed. "You'd better lie down and rest. That cut could develop into something nasty."

"You're quite right."

After they had made love, he cradled her head gently in the crook of his arm. She was breathing quietly. "I still think you'd make a great CIA agent," he said.

"No. I only know one trick for catching spies."

"What?"

"Spies can learn our language, our customs, all of our idiosyncrasies—but there is something they can't do." She picked up a cassette tape of an old radio play called 'The Shadow.'

"What?" He put the cassette tape in the player.

"Nursery rhymes. Only children learn nursery rhymes. Lots of spies were caught in England in World War II that way. For example, if I said to you, 'Mary had a Little Lamb, Its Fleece was White as Snow—and everywhere' . . . what would you say?"

"Pardon?"

"What's the rest of the nursery rhyme?"

"I don't know."

"Don't tease me that way."

He picked up the roll of adhesive tape that he kept next to his bed and started to unwind it.

"Didn't I bandage your finger right?" she asked.

"You did a great job, doctor. You're very smart."

"Why are you pulling off that tape? Hey, hey—I'm not into bondage—if you are that's OK but we can have a lot more fun other ways."

He broke off a length of the tape.

The old radio drama of a Shadow episode started to play. Goosebumps appeared along the black woman's thighs as she sat up in bed.

7

Integrated Electronics occupied four city blocks and was two stories high with narrow windows eighteen feet above the ground. One entrance and one exit served all of its employees. On the weekends, if the Southern California weather was poor, there might be a dozen people working on computer hardware design. An equal number might be puzzling over new software programs. But since it was Saturday and there was a brilliant fall sun in the sky, only ten employees were at Integrated Electronics. Integrated Electronics designed the most sophisticated security systems in the world and these systems had been installed in the plant; one guard was technically all that was required for the weekend shifts. (As a matter of fact, the security systems would have functioned without any guards).

To be on the safe side five guards were at their posts in the monitor rooms. Closed circuit television showed them exactly what was happening in the building. On the east wall of the monitor room were a dozen, tiny television sets. Ten of them scanned empty corridors and offices. From time to time these flat images changed to other empty laboratories and corridors as a random program switched from camera to camera.

On one monitor, a man in his late sixties dictated letters. He was dressed in a three-piece blue suit and white shirt. He wore a navy blue tie with small white dots on it. His name was Buff Tallons and he was the president and chief executive officer of Integrated Electronics. He worked twelve hour days, six days a week. On Sundays he worked from seven in the morning until noon. This drive, coupled with an MBA from Harvard and a command of six languages, was the reason Tallons had been able to build IE from a fabricator of circuit boards to one of the largest and most successful computer companies in North America. IE's current sales were over three billion dollars.

The twelfth monitor was focused on David Cursore as he sat behind a computer keyboard. He had been hunched over the keyboard for most of the afternoon.

One of the guards opened a Coke and started to unwrap a bologna sandwich when a soft electronic buzz went off. A second later a keyboard in front of another guard printed out the following message: "Unauthorized entry into Alpha codes. Contact B. Tallons only. Do not take any other action." This message repeated itself.

The guard picked up an interoffice phone and spoke to Buff Tallons.

A few minutes later, Cursore glanced up from his keyboard as Buff Tallons entered the room. Buff and Cursore had been friends for most of their adult lives. Cursore couldn't understand Buff's preoccupation with capitalism; Buff had a hard time appreciating Cursore's fascination with Zen.

"Putting in another long day?" asked Cursore.

"I get paid for it."

"A billion here and a billion there. I guess it adds up."

The chief executive officer sank into a leather chair opposite Cursore and closed his eyes. "How long we known each other? I don't want to think about it. When I consider long periods of my life, it reminds me of my mortality. I don't want to die just yet. Too much to do."

"You'll live another half a century."

"Then I'll be the first president of a five hundred company to break one hundred ten. I pay you enough?"

"More than I'm worth."

"No. I pay you what you're worth. There are many people who can build hardware systems and there are many who can design software systems. But not many who can do both like you." The older man picked up the phone and called the guard room. "This is Mr. Tallons. Switch off surveillance to this room."

"Yes, sir," said a voice.

Tallons replaced the phone in its cradle. Cursore waited for the president to start talking.

"Cursore, I'd be up to my ass in alligators if some of the stockholders realized I'd hired you. As far as I'm concerned, that problem we had with Pan Pacific Electronics is over. Hell, I know you—you wouldn't tamper with security transfers. Not your style. You said you were framed. I bought it then. There's not a dozen other people out of the nine hundred employees here who have your security clearances."

Cursore knew what was coming but nodded his head. "I appreciate your confidence in me."

"Then why are you requesting information on our Alpha codes?"

"I could lie to you, Buff, and tell you I wanted to run some test programs on bank transfers, but the truth is I'm checking out the balance in a savings account that belongs to Dusty Bleudell."

"Did she ask you to?"

Cursore shook his head negatively.

"That's the kind of thing that got you in jail. How far have you gone?"

"Just found out the current balance of her bank."

"Why?"

Cursore recounted what had happened between Dusty and himself. Buff Tallons interlaced his fingers and closed his eyes and listened. When the younger man finished talking, the president of Integrated Electronics said: "You only met this woman for what? Half an hour?"

"That's not important. I knew all about her, and a couple of days ago she had $5,050.00 in her account. Friday she took it all out except for ten dollars."

"Suppose she didn't take it out? Suppose there was a computer mistake? Suppose the bank starts hunting? Suppose they find out we've been tapping into their central computer."

"Since the Alpha codes aren't supposed to exist, who's going to find out anything?"

"I don't care what's supposed to exist and what isn't. Those codes could be used to destroy several banking systems."

"I'm not going to do that."

"I know that and you know that, but you have been convicted of misappropriating funds with a computer. What do you think would happen if someone found out?"

couldn't . . ."

"Stop playing word games with me." The older man ran his slender fingers through his thinning hair.

"I'm sorry. You're right," said Cursore.

"Dusty is obviously special, and from what I can figure out, you must believe something terrible happened."

"Yes."

"I can think of one hundred reasons why a woman would cut a holiday short. Suppose she had to go home because of a death, or a friend was in trouble? Also, from what you said, she was going to buy some fairly expensive paintings. Maybe she got a deal, bought the art, and is now on her way home with it. Or getting drunk with the artist. You could be overreacting a bit—couldn't you?"

"Maybe I'm reaching . . ."

"Rubber gloves that aren't where you left them. Dead hamster that disappeared? Some adhesive tape. Look—what if she had a sore knee from jogging and taped it up herself? You couldn't find her swim suit. Maybe it was torn and she tossed it down the garbage chute. Her bank account? Was it a money transfer to a different account or did she personally withdraw the cash?"

"As far as I can figure out she just withdrew it."

Buff found a package of mints in his jacket pocket and ate one. "Cursore, I don't want you hacking around anymore with Alpha codes. OK?"

"I guess I have an overactive imagination."

"If you didn't you couldn't do what you do with computers. You wouldn't be all that interesting and people wouldn't want to interview you."

"What are you talking about?"

"There's a girl from *Business Week*. Jasper Larner or Harner or something. She called our PR department about you. Wants to do an article. They referred it to my office."

"What'd you tell them?"

"I said I'd talk it over with you."

"I don't think an interview would be a wise thing," said Cursore.

"My first reaction. Then I got to wondering how it would look if we refused to let her talk to you. I can see the headlines now—'Integrated Electronics hires man accused of computer theft.' Wouldn't look very good. On the other hand, if she were to talk to you, and the gist of the article had to do with how you, as a reformed computer freak, are helping us build systems that can't be accessed, well . . ."

"I get the feeling you've already decided what the strategy is."

"Cursore, I'm sorry. A lot of people consider you a top risk. But if we can work that angle to our benefit we'll all come out smelling like a rose. What could be more logical than hiring an ex-hacker to help us beef up our security systems?"

"Just a minute ago you said you felt, you *knew*, I wasn't guilty of any computer crime with Pan Pacific."

"Right."

"If this reporter does a story like you're suggesting, then it'll look like I'm an ex-con."

"No, it won't."

"I never broke any laws, Buff. You know that..."

"Hold on. You just broke a dozen laws by dipping into this Florida girl's bank account. And God knows how many times you've done similar stuff. You may not have transferred money or ripped anyone off but you've broken the law. Because I know about the Alpha codes and allow you to use them illegally, I'm breaking the law. In the eyes of any court in the land we're criminals. This reporter is going to write about you as an ex-criminal. But if she knew the truth—"

"—we'd both have alligators snapping at our asses."

"True."

"The fact is," said Cursore, "that article is going to brand me as an ex-criminal or felon or jailbird and you're going to end up as a model citizen."

"Good point."

"It's not fair."

"What is? Look at it from my point of view. We either handle this story in a positive way or we have to cut you loose. I've got to answer to stockholders and directors of the board and the press and the government."

For a moment Cursore considered handing in his resignation. Be too dumb. He had an incredible position considering his record. Didn't matter if he was guilty or innocent of computer crime. If he resigned now he could kiss his apartment, his car, his tailored shirts, his sailing, and maybe more importantly, his computer research goodbye. Kiss it all goodbye. He had a price; Buff knew what it was. That's why Buff was the toast of Wall Street.

The older man dusted an imaginary speck of fluff from his pin stripe suit-coat. Buff knew what Cursore would do. Like a good attorney, Buff never asked a question unless he knew the answer. Do your homework. Plan ahead.

Cursore thought of Parole Office Gwilliam. "I'll do what you say, Buff."

"Thanks." Buff got up and headed toward the door. "And remember—no more hacking bank computer systems. Alpha system is just something that's in our competitor's imagination."

"Sure."

An hour later as Cursore was getting off the elevator next to his apartment, he remembered Mary Lou's bonsai. He glanced at his watch—might as well do it now before dinner. After he ate he was going to have a shower and go to bed.

As he finished sprinkling water on the tiny elm, Mary Lou's phone rang. He decided to let it ring. On the eleventh rasp he picked up the phone and said "Hello?"

"Is Ms. Dusty Bleudell there?"

"No."

"This is California Car Rentals. Her car was found abandoned in a no parking zone in Santa Monica. She can reclaim it at the Santa Monica Police Impound Yard. Or we can do it."

"Is there a charge if you do it?"

"Thirty dollars plus fees."

"What are the fees?"

"Probably fifty dollars for towing. Another twenty-five dollars a day for impounds."

"I don't know what to tell you," said Cursore. "I haven't seen her."

"Well, if we haven't heard from her by ten a.m. on Monday, we'll take care of it, but the additional fees will be added to her charge card."

"Thank you."

The clerk left the phone number of California Car Rentals and hung up.

Cursore walked back to the master bedroom. Her suitcase and clothing were exactly as he remembered them. He looked in the trash can again. No adhesive tape. He clearly remembered the white tape with bits of blonde hair and flakes of paint clinging to it. Remembered it as well as his name. He looked for the rubber gloves. Still gone. The green and blue swim suit was gone. Five thousand dollars from her account had disappeared. The hamster's body had vanished along with the bird cage it was in.

The only thing that had been found was her rental car.

OK. Think the worst. Someone ties her up, frightens her. That person gets her to withdraw her money. Then he gets rid of her and leaves the car. The logical thing would be to call Sergeant Dartwell and have him check the car for fingerprints. But in order to persuade the sergeant to do that, Cursore realized he would have to explain the missing five thousand dollars. And the police would want to know how he had discovered that salient fact. And if he told them, then that would be the end of his parole. Back to jail for breaking one of the prime stipulations of his parole. He had promised not to use computers for anything of a criminal nature. And as Buff had pointed out to him, he had broken about half a dozen "privacy" laws in one afternoon.

Inexplicable forces had him trapped. Had him pinned. Were pressing the life

out of him.
 It was the same kind of feeling he had felt for two years in the pen.

8

When Cursore woke Sunday morning, light rains had cleansed the decking on the boardwalk. The sun's rays filtering through soft clouds began to warm the sepia sand along the bike path that wound past Santa Monica and Venice and Marina del Rey.

From his balcony he watched fishermen and weekend sailors lugging six-packs of beer, picnic hampers and bait aboard their boats. A gaggle of Japanese tourists laughing and giggling hurried onto a sixty foot whale-watching yacht. A pod of Blues had been spotted earlier in the week. Cursore leaned against his silver balcony railing; white and blue sails billowed in the distance. Colored triangles hung above shimmering blue acres of ocean. So distant, he could not see the ships below them.

A girl sat on the boardwalk, playing a silver flute. Her flute case sparkled with coins that the breakfast crowd had tossed her way. Evil did not seem to exist at this moment. Maybe it was the sunlight or the freshness of morning or the melody of the flute against the gurgling ocean.

His phone rang. It was Mary Lou in Honolulu.

"How are you?" she asked.

"OK. You're up early."

"Been worried about Dusty. I'm flying home tonight. Can you pick me up in front of United?"

"I thought you were going to stay for another week."

"Getting antsy. Besides, something's wrong."

"You feel it too, huh?"

"Yes."

"Maybe I should call Dusty's place in Florida."

"I already have. Just got her answering machine. I'll be arriving on United Airlines at eleven p.m., your time. OK?"

"Have a safe flight, Mary Lou. Meet you at luggage pick-up." He hung up, then walked to Fisherman's Village—a collection of specialty shops hawking everything from salt water taffy to posters, a tourist trap with a couple of nice restaurants mixed in among the gewgaws. Cursore bought some steaming mocha coffee and a couple of chocolate covered donuts, found a wire-rimmed chair and sat down next to the boardwalk. Mary Lou's call added to his uneasiness. The day was becoming more beautiful, but he felt himself becoming increasingly irritable.

"That's an interesting breakfast, sailor." Cursore looked up at the husky, underslung voice. He did not recognize the lady. She would have been difficult to forget. A stunning redhead with shoulder-length hair and firm eyes that didn't miss a beat. He had the uncomfortable feeling those blue eyes could see through him. The eyes were both ice and fire. Beneath the eyes was a small nose with three or four freckles on either side. She'd made no effort to cover up the freckles with make-up; she didn't seem to be wearing any, and really didn't need to. The redhead was blessed with one of those peaches and cream complexions that most women dream about. Her body was slim except for her breasts. Full and firm. She had taken care to camouflage their size with a loose fitting blouse. The kind of person who offered humor instead of her body.

"You're right," said Cursore. "Too much sugar for me. Want one? Or maybe there's something else I can get you. My car? My boat? The shirt off my back?"

"I can resist anything but temptation, sailor." The woman sat down and started to nibble on one of the donuts. She had sparkling evenly-spaced teeth. The sunlight bounced off the brass buttons on her sailor's shirt.

"I haven't met you, have I?" he asked.

"I thought a computer wizard like you would know everyone. I hear you do to an

IBM console what Heifetz does to a fiddle. And you're a misocapnist."

"What's that?"

"Someone who hates smoking. I'm one, too."

"What else do you hear?"

"Bachelor. Footloose and fancy free. Countless ladies have succumbed to your irresistible charms."

The conversation reminded him of his meeting with Dusty. Sometimes it's fun to have the upper hand; other times, cruel. Cursore had never seen this lady with the white starched sailor's outfit before. He was young enough to have ladies "hit on him" but old enough to feel a little out of his time warp when it happened. "OK, I give up. What's your name?"

"Why do you want to know, Cursore?" Only his friends and one or two select enemies called him "Cursore." Maybe she was somehow tied to Gwilliam's probation office. Naw. Gwilliam didn't have the budget or the wit for such a stunt. He saw the twin fish dangling on her gold charm bracelet. Pisces. The birthstone of Pisces was Jasper and Buff had told him about a female reporter named Jasper. Bingo. "You're a reporter. Your name is Jasper. Right?"

"I didn't think it showed."

"If you want to make an appointment with my secretary, I'll be happy to see you. But don't follow me around. I don't like it." He pushed back from the table and headed back to his apartment.

She caught up with him. "I'm sorry. It really isn't how it looked."

"Look, if I want to be followed I'll move to Russia."

"This is terrible," said Jasper. "Guess it served me right for reading other people's mail."

"You been reading my mail?" he said, his voice laced with anger. Several people gaped at them.

"It's OK," Jasper said to a passing couple. "Just a little lovers' quarrel. Caught him going out with one of my best friends—a sheep."

Cursore could not help but smile. He slowed down as she caught up with him. "You and I live in the same complex," said Jasper. "I'm a freelance writer—makes me kind of a snoop."

"You're pushing your luck, lady."

"Will you just give me a chance to explain? I kept seeing all those exotic magazines on computer design with your name on them. The mailman even got some of them mixed up with my stuff—I get a lot of magazines too. A couple of my editors have been after me to do a story on computers, and since the biggest computer complex around here is that company you work for, I talked with Tallons and I mentioned your name and he tried to get me to talk with someone else. I got a nose for news and I found out you were in jail for a little problem with money transfers. When I found that out, your boss started giving me the royal treatment. And I don't follow you around, I've seen you at the mailbox often enough so I know what you look like. When I saw you eating breakfast, I thought it'd be fun to meet you. I'm sorry. Really."

"I'm edgy, I guess."

"Anything I can do to help? Really, I *am* sorry."

Cursore gauged her, the sunlight shimmering off her flowing auburn hair. There were things she could do for him but he didn't feel that they knew each other that well.

"I said is there anything I can do for you?" She smiled. It was a wonderful and devastating smile.

Another time, another place, Cursore might have thought she was coming on to him because he was so damn cute. Maybe. But Jasper was also a reporter who made her living by writing stories about people. He could not afford to let her under his skin. "Yeah. I'd like to read something you've written."

"Like what?"

"Maybe a personality piece."

Her fourth floor apartment was on the "bad" side of the building with a view of smog-stained L.A. freeways and black roofed warehouses. Also, Jasper was not a great housekeeper. Basically she was clean but there were piles of books and magazines and articles scattered across her small living room. She found a year old Harper's Magazine, picked up volume ten of The Encyclopaedia Britannica from a bean chair, and gestured for Cursore to sit. He read the magazine while she squeezed fresh orange juice. Her story was about migrant workers. It was lucid, thought provoking, gutsy.

He finished his orange juice and said he thought she was one helluva writer.

"Thanks."

"Where'd you learn?"

"Ever since I've been about sixteen, I've wanted to be a writer. Great novels. Screenplays. Mostly I read a lot of good stuff—Dickens, Hemingway, Camus—my parents saw to that. The problem was that I tried to write perfect stuff for a long time. Never did. Also, I had too much money."

"I've never had a problem like that."

"My father is a very successful orthodontist. So he indulged me. Then I married Rick, my first and last husband. He was a very successful land developer. He not only indulged me, he spoiled me. His idea was to make me into a beautiful, sensual companion."

"Did he?"

"I was in on the conspiracy. The problem was everything I wanted to do with my writing got sidetracked—what with buying houses and going on ocean cruises and getting my nails sculptured and planning one goddamn weekend party after another. Before our divorce I blamed him; afterwards I realized I was just as much at fault."

"So you started writing..."

"After I stopped being a bunny."

"Where you ever a centerfold?"

"I started really writing good things about three years ago."

"But were you ever a centerfold?"

"Let's talk about you," she said firmly. "Did you do it?"

"What?"

"You know."

Cursore thought for a moment. "You mean did I use my knowledge of computers to illegally transfer money from one account to another?"

"Or securities."

"I've been convicted, haven't I?"

"That article I wrote about migrant workers. The one you just read. Two of the people in it were convicted of trespassing. Do you think they were guilty?"

"There's a world of difference between what I was accused of and trespassing."

"The migrant workers were accused of being where they shouldn't have been. You were accused of being where you shouldn't have been—namely in someone else's computer network."

"You got a point."

"You still haven't answered my

question, Cursore—you don't mind if I call you that, do you?"

"My friends do. And those friends have enough faith in me to realize I never transferred anything illegally. I should also point out that I don't have that many friends."

"But the system you designed to penetrate bank computers was used to do a little crashing."

"You got the terms all down pat, haven't you?"

"It was a word your attorney used—means to juggle figures and numbers around illegally in a computer network."

"You've *read* the transcripts on my trial?"

She nodded. Her hair moved like wind blowing through soft grass. "It's all a matter of public record. I don't think you were guilty. For what it's worth."

"Too bad you weren't on the jury."

"Too bad. More orange juice?"

"Please."

He watched her and wondered if she had been a centerfold. "I wonder if your opinion of me matters that much?"

"Over the course of human events? Probably not. But I could never sleep with a man who I thought was a criminal."

"Is that an offer?"

"Depends. Have you ever had herpes or is there any reason that you may think you're carrying it?"

"I've been lucky so far. Are you making me an offer?"

She brought him a refill of orange juice and watched him drink it. "If I made you an offer, you'll have no doubt about it."

"What are you going to say about me in the article?"

"The truth. As I see it. I think you were set up. I mean the other two guys—who seem to have gotten all the money—just disappeared, didn't they? Why'd you hang around to get caught, unless you didn't know what was going on?"

"The deputy D.A. said I thought I was too smart to get caught. Thought I was smarter than most people."

"You are."

"Do you want to go sailing?"

"Sure."

He had a twenty foot ketch with sails that needed patching. The deck of the boat was crying for varnish and the auxiliary motor needed overhauling.

When they were out past the breakwaters, the wind picked up and he steered toward Catalina.

"Where are we going?" she asked.

"Nowhere."

The sea cradled them, lulled them. The sun caressed them. The salt air seeped through them. They were at one with each other, drifting.

"You said I was smarter than most people. Smart people don't go to jail.

There is a part of my mind, though, that's different than most people have. Sometimes I have this quirk that figures out mathematical problems at an intuitive level. When I'm designing computer programs or hardware, my mind jumps ahead of itself. While it's happening I don't have any real sense of time. It's a delicious feeling. You ever feel that way when you're writing a story?"

"Yes. Yes, I do."

"Maybe the process is getting lost in yourself. It's like an addiction, but a lot better than drugs. Not that I've tried that many. Once in the hospital I had morphine. What I go through is better than morphine."

"I know what you mean. Especially when I wrote poetry."

"Good. I hope that clears up your thoughts on me being smarter than other people."

She leaned forward and kissed him softly on his lips. "You are a very vulnerable person out here, aren't you?"

"I guess."

"How come you trust me with all this stuff?"

He laced his hands behind his head and stared up at the heavens. "Beats me. I guess if you wanted to you could really grind me up in an article."

"I've decided . . . The article I'm going to do on you—I won't use your real name. I'll make the main character in the piece kind of a composite."

"Can you do that?"

"Yes. I probably wouldn't have unless you leveled with me or at least tried to. I can still tell you're holding something back."

"Aren't you?"

They laughed.

He wondered how he had been lucky enough to meet two dynamite ladies in less than forty eight hours. He thought of Dusty again and felt uneasy about her. "Breeze is coming up. We better head back. It'll take about an hour."

The sea water shot along the hull. From time to time a breeze snapped the sail. She opened a bottle of wine and they drank it out of plastic cups. She had a picnic basket with sourdough bread, cheese and fresh tomatoes.

"Jasper is an interesting name," he said.

"My mother was into astrology and that kind of stuff."

"Our mothers probably would have loved to meet each other."

They didn't speak for half an hour. The waves picked up and the tide started to change. He kept the bow pointed more or less toward the breakwater.

"Did you ever notice that this boat is off course about ninety five percent of the time?" she asked.

"Most boats are when they're at sea."

"I know. But they nearly always get to

where they're going. It's too bad we can't accept people the way we accept boats."

"You mean we get upset because people are off course most of the time?"

"Yes. Especially after we start to love them. Funny, huh?"

"You're too deep a thinker for me," he said.

"It was a lot of fun, Cursore," she said when they tied up at the tiny berth.

"Nice. Even philosophical."

"I'm sorry you were preoccupied," said Jasper as they walked along the walkway.

"Did it show?"

"What's her name?"

"Dusty. I just met her for a little while the other day."

"The blonde? The one you were talking to in the pool on Friday?"

"Yes."

"She was very beautiful."

"I didn't see you there."

"I don't think you were looking for me."

"Did you see anyone talk to her after I left?"

"No. I left before either one of you did."

Cursore tossed the trash they had carried from his boat into a large metal drum. "Jasper, can I say something between you and me?"

"Sure."

"It's off the record. You won't . . ."

"No. I won't quote you or misquote you or anything."

"Dusty was visiting a friend of mine who lives on the eighth floor. Sometime between about four Friday afternoon and eight that night, she disappeared. Right off the radar scope."

"Disappeared? Vanished? Like in magic?"

"No. LIke someone abducted her."

"What?"

"I checked my friend's apartment where Dusty was staying. Something happened."

"What?"

"I'm not sure. I found strips of adhesive tape. There were some rubber gloves stolen. Some of Dusty's things were gone. Her car was found abandoned this morning. There was a dead hamster. It's gone."

"You call the police?"

"They think I'm crazy."

"There's always a logical explanation . . ."

"OK. Come up and look at Mary Lou's place with me. See if you can come up with a logical explanation."

"OK."

They waited in the main lobby for the elevator. It stopped on its way to the basement garage.

Jon Andrews was inside the elevator. He smiled at Jasper and said, "Hi." Beside him were two large suitcases.

"Hi," said Jasper.

The door slid shut.

"Very quiet guy but I guess most investment bankers are," Jasper said to Cursore.

"You know a lot of people around here, don't you?" The next elevator door slid open and Cursore held it open for Jasper. As they stepped in, Cursore pressed Mary Lou's floor. The chrome door slid shut.

In the basement garage, Jon Andrews lugged the two suitcases to his late model Jaguar. He hefted them into the trunk, then closed the lid and locked it.

He drove into the street. The warm afternoon sun played across the lid of the trunk, creating dappled designs on the paint.

Eight stories above, Cursore opened Mary Lou's balcony door and stepped out onto the deck. For a moment, earlier that day, he had a momentary feeling that evil did not exist. That feeling was gone now.

He was aware of the redhead standing beside him.

"You're pretty worried about this Dusty, aren't you?"

"Yes."

"How come you've taken me into your confidence? I'm kind of like a total stranger."

"I know. But out there on the ocean, you seemed to have an ability to handle being alone. That means you trust yourself and so I figured I could trust you."

"And you accused *me* of being a philosopher." She smiled.

9

The cinnamon sun settled through clouds that hung along the Pacific. One instant the sky was buttery yellow; the next a kaleidoscope of oranges and blues. Shafts of sun fanned out over Malibu; the Pacific Coast Highway turned grey. Traffic was light from L.A. to Malibu, but heavy in the other direction as sun lovers returned to the city.

Jon Andrews switched off his headlights as he turned off Coast highway and guided his Jaguar over the bumpy lane. He came to the manhole where he had disposed of Dusty's body. The area was hidden from the Coast highway by a stand of magnolia trees on a hillside. Working quickly, he pried back the heavy manhole cover with his jack handle. The cast iron cover ground against the rocky lane. He glanced at the nearest beach house fifty feet away. A high wooden fence separated it from the lane. One light burned in its second story. Soft music, a Strauss waltz, floated toward him. A dog barked, then Jon Andrews could only hear the sounds of the waves slurping across the beach. He opened the first suitcase and shook the contents into the hole. He heard a half dozen closely spaced splashes. He tossed the empty suitcase into his trunk, then swung the second valise onto the gravel road. He unsnapped its locks, opened the case and tipped it toward the hole.

"You, over there in the alley. What the hell do you think you are doing?" said an angry man's voice by the fence.

A dull, white cone of light found Jon as he emptied the contents of the second valise into the shaft. He closed the case and held one hand over his face to shield his eyes from the flashlight which was coming closer.

"This is a private lane. Didn't you see the signs?" asked the angry voice.

"No."

The man, late sixties, had a leathery face as the result of far too much sun; there were six inch wide liver blotches on his sinewy arms. He wore cutoffs and an old white T-shirt.

"What the hell you mean? Didn't you see the no trespassing signs? You can't dump garbage here. I saw you here the other day."

"That a fact?"

"That is a fact. Now you haul ass before I call the cops." The older man stuck a briar pipe between his yellowed teeth, touched his lighter to it and gulped a mouthful of smoke.

"Sorry to bother you, old timer," said the Russian.

"Don't old timer me. Yank that manhole cover in place and split."

Jon nodded, reached down and started to twist the cast iron cover into place.

The man from the beach house, puffing violently on his acrid pipe, leaned over the Russian's shoulder. Jon Andrews drove his fist upward and into the groin of the older man. The man doubled over, his mouth opening in pain. Before he could scream, the Russian had him by the throat, fingers closing on the loose skin. An instant later there was a soft popping noise as the man's Adam's apple ruptured. The pipe clattered to the ground; spittle from his mouth sprayed against the Russian's sleve. The Russian drove the palm of his right hand upward into the man's nose. The man's neck snapped. The flashlight had landed in a clump of weeds and its beam illuminated the Russian's face. Jon's face became grotesque, distorted from the low angle lighting. He picked up the flashlight and turned it off, then tossed it into his Jaguar's trunk. Jon started to jam the old man into the shaft, then stopped. What would happen when the old man was missed? There would be a search. They might find the body at the base of the sewer shaft. *Think*, he told himself. Suppose the body was washed up on shore after it had gone through the sewer pipe. The old man had a broken neck. Someone might remember him talking about someone dumping garbage into his bootleg sewer. Maybe the old man had already jotted down the license plate. There would be a link. And the Russian would have to chance the task of changing his identity before he was ready. That could ruin everything. There was a point in the midst of an identity change when one was exposed, at risk. So *think,* he told himself.

The Russian glanced around. Only the old man had seen him. No other lights had blazed on in the other houses. No cars had approached, freezing him in their headlights. He started to load the body into his trunk.

Didn't make sense. Why dispose of one body and replace it with another? In the distance he could hear the tide washing across the sand, almost like the steady hum of the traffic from Pacific Coast Highway. Traffic?

He estimated the distance between himself and Pacific Highway was fifty yards. By heading directly over a small ridge he could cover the distance in a few minutes.

The old body was much heavier than its slight frame suggested. Jon walked fewer than ten steps when the body slipped from his grasp. He clutched for an arm and tripped over a vine. The

Russian and the dead man tumbled into damp leaves. Jon cursed in Ukrainian, got his shoulder under the body and continued toward the haze of lights on the far side of the magnolias. The thick scent of the trees mixed with the odor of gasoline and diesel exhaust. The combination was cloying.

As the Russian attained the crest of the ridge, a car turned off the highway and moved toward him. He dropped to the ground and the corpse moaned as air escaped from its chest cavity.

The Russian watched the headlights of the car bounce along the valley. The car's wheels crunched across the gravel, moved quickly past the Jaguar; for an instant its headlights illuminated the open manhole. The car continued for sixty yards and stopped at the end of the lane where a chipped concrete stairway lead to the beach. Across the stairway entrance was a high mesh gate with a lock on it. A boy got out of the car and tried the gate.

"Can't open it. Locked."

"Never mind, I'll turn on the radio," said a girl's voice. The headlights of the car went dark.

"I can break the lock," said the boy.

"No. We'll get in trouble," said the girl. "Come on back to the car. We'll drink the wine here." A second later the sound of punk rock blasted from the two-door Firebird.

Jon got to one knee and tried to raise the corpse to a sitting position. The man's arm had become slippery in the wet weeds. Jon grabbed the dirty white shirt that clung to the body and pulled the corpse to a kneeling position. He jerked the body's arm around his shoulder and dragged it a final ten more yards to a bank above Pacific Coast Highway.

The traffic thundered by, an uninterrupted streak of blazing headlights. The speed limit was fifty five but most of the vehicles were doing well past sixty five or seventy. The Russian leaned against a tree and squinted into the onslaught of traffic. He was looking for a big truck. A Greyhound bus would do nicely.

Had anyone glanced up along the bank, he would have seen two men tottering above the traffic. One of them seemed to be drunk; the other seemed to be supporting his friend. If someone could have heard them, above the whining roar of the traffic, he would have heard the labored attempts of the Russian trying to get his breath. Then there would have been another sound— it would have been a gasp that changed into a scream.

The old man was not dead. He was alive! With the strength of the mortally wounded he seized the Russian by the throat. The Russian, winded, was caught temporarily off guard. He lost his footing and started to slip toward the highway. He could feel the hot breath of traffic as it swooshed by a dozen feet below him. The old man, his shirt stained with dirt and blood, lashed out—a wounded animal unable to speak because of a smashed larynx. Jon, at least thirty years younger, twisted and turned away. His right foot found solid footing under a gnarled root. He struck the old man in the shoulder. The old man clawed at the air. Jon smashed him again. The old man tumbled backwards into the rushing traffic, then somehow regained his balance. Out of the corner of his eye, Jon saw a semi-tanker barreling out of the darkness, its headlights erasing the black night. Locking his foot under the root, he swung at the old man's head with all his might. Had the Russian's foot not been anchored his blow would have carried him onto the highway. The blow connected.

The old man toppled backwards but his hand tore into Jon's face. Jon felt searing pain as jagged fingernails gouged his cheek.

The old man was cartwheeling, spinning, a rag doll. There was a soft thud as the one-inch welded bumper of the semi thundered into the old man.

Brakes screeched. The truck driver threw his hands up to avoid the broken windshield as the body slapped against it.

Another car traveling far above the

speed limit struck the old man.

Holding his bleeding face, trying to catch his breath, Jon disentangled his foot from the root and half crawled, half ran back to his car. Vehicles continued to screech and honk behind him on Pacific Coast Highway. There was a tremendous roar followed by flames that leapt toward the black sky as a Corvette fishtailed into the rear of a truck and exploded.

The Russian crouched a few feet from his Jaguar. The alley blazed with light as the teenaged boy switched on his headlights. To the Russian's horror he saw the Firebird driving directly at the open manhole.

In the distance he could hear sirens approaching. The teenaged driver swerved his car at the last instant and missed the gaping shaft by inches.

Eyes unaccustomed to the darkness, Jon Andrews managed to stumble to the manhole and wedge its heavy cover into place. He had a terrible fear that he would misjudge his position in the darkness and plummet headfirst into the shaft. Fishbait in a bootleg sewer. What a way to end it all. Perhaps fitting. The end of a clever spy. A man who in the end could depend on no one. Not even himself.

The cast iron lid clanged into place. Blood was pouring down his cheek. He slipped his key into the ignition, the motor caught on the first click. Thank God.

As the sirens approached from several directions, lights came on at the furthest house along the alley. Dogs started to bark.

On Pacific Coast Highway two California Highway Patrol cars screamed by. Northbound traffic was at a standstill. Jon turned south, heading for Santa Monica.

He stopped at a Mobil station at the end of Sunset. While the young attendant cleaned his back window, Jon went to the washroom. Inside, he locked the door and dashed cold water against his face. There were two long cuts in his cheek running from beneath his right eye to his chin. He was lucky that the old man had not gouged out his eye. He found some soap and washed the deep scratches as well as he could.

In the car he kept his injured cheek turned from the boy when he returned with change.

As he drove into his Marina apartment basement he caught his reflection in the mirror. He looked like he'd been out all night brawling. Although the ugly slashes on his face had almost stopped bleeding, his right eye was beginning to turn black and blue.

His clothing, which he always kept fastidious, looked like it had been slept in for a week. At least the hand he had deliberately cut the previous day on the brandy snifter was healing satisfactorily. The Russian got out of the Jaguar and limped to the lobby, rather than wait for the elevator he walked nineteen flights up the fire stairs to his penthouse. It would be better not to let anyone see him as he was.

A few minutes later he was immersed in a steaming hot bath, sipping vodka from a cut glass tumbler. There was a jacuzzi built into the tub and he switched it on with his toe. Bubbles flooded around him and he realized that he would live after all. It had been close and he could never use the bootleg sewer for disposal of *safeties* again. Things were becoming more complex and he considered running that night. Leave now, he told himself. No. Not quite ready. He was growing tired and when he ran he had to expose himself. More soothing bubbles massaged his body. He thought about the black girl—she had been delightful. He cursed her cleverness and his paranoia. The scent of her perfume tingled in his memory. Her body. Delicious. What a shame to have to kill her. But, better her than him. And then the old man. The fool should have minded his own business.

The Russian turned the hot water faucet on to maximum and near-boiling water cascaded into the tub. Felt good. Yes, thought the Russian, he would wait for awhile. He picked up a small remote device and pressed a button on it. In the next room a cassette tape started to play. It was an old radio recording of The Shadow from the 1950's. The Russian listened to the voices and the music from decades before. The bubbles seeped around his body. The Russian was at ease, relaxed, as the daring deeds of The Shadow filled the penthouse. The Shadow took chances and won, was willing to gamble all. After awhile the tape ended and the Russian considered who had been talking at the pool to the woman from Florida. What was his name? Curse? Cursing? Cursor? Something like that. The man had been talking with Jasper. Jasper, the journalist. Once the Russian had considered her a safety, but when he found out how many contacts and friends she had, he had abandoned his plans for her. She would have been missed easily; not worth the risk. That was the problem with *safeties.* Too many things could go wrong. That's why he had decided on a major plan. All or nothing.

The Russian picked up a sponge and squeezed hot soapy water on his chest. He turned off the jacuzzi and rinsed himself in the shower. As he was drying off the Russian continued to think about the man and Jasper. Suppose they started talking about the woman from Florida.

How would the conversation go?

The Russian could not remember if Jasper had seen him admiring the woman from Florida. Did it matter? Not really. Unless the man with the funny name had some strange compulsion to find the woman from Florida. And even then it did not matter. To discover what had happened, the man with the strange American name would have to be extremely clever.

Even if he were extremely clever, he would also have to be lucky. The Russian picked up the bottle of vodka and poured another tumbler of the white liquid for himself. He walked into the bedroom, drinking the vodka in short gulps. He was thinking about his Master Plan. "MP" would be his code name for it. He selected another cassette tape of an old Shadow radio play and played it. How would The Shadow carry out a Master Plan? He would be cunning. Decisive. Ruthless.

10

By midnight Sunday, the Los Angeles airport was socked in with fog and Mary Lou's flight was diverted to San Francisco. Cursore picked her up Monday morning at Los Angeles International. She was tired, sunburned and had started to smoke again.

As they drove back to their apartment complex, Cursore outlined the highlights of the weekend, his meeting with Dusty, how she had stood him up, the missing rubber gloves, the missing adhesive tape, the dead hamster that vanished, his frustration with the police.

Mary Lou lit another cigarette from the stub of one she had smoked to the filter. "I don't think the people who designed Virginia Slims thought it would be very chi-chi to chain smoke them."

He laughed.

"Look, Cursore. I haven't seen Dusty in over a year. There's a possibility she's changed. People change, God knows. Every time I see my brother it's like meeting a different person. One year he's a bartender. Then into Yoga. Then marriage. For three years a celibate. I thought he was studying to become a priest. After damn near a century of this crazy planet all I know is that you never know."

He told Mary Lou about meeting Jasper. "Not mad at me, are you?"

"Why should I be?"

"You kind of lined me up with Dusty and..."

It was Mary Lou's turn to laugh. "Look, kid, I just runs 'em by you. You takes your chances. Since we've known each other, how many foxes have I introduced you to in any given year?"

"Not that many."

"Come, come, my horny little friend. There's checkers in supermarkets. There's friends of friends. There's nieces of cousins. If you paid a dollar a head, you'd owe me five hundred bucks."

"You almost sound like a procurer."

"I felt like it after I found out what happened to some of those poor gals."

This time they both laughed—the rich, warm blend of laughter that only happens with old friends.

"What's your next step?" she asked.

"Since the police aren't going to be any help, Jasper and I are going to check out Dusty's rental car ourselves."

"I thought you said it was impounded."

"Jasper's getting the car."

"She's pretending to be Dusty?"

"Yes."

"I don't think you can pull it off."

"*Voilá,*" said Cursore, pointing to the entrance to the Marina Surf Towers parking lot. Ahead of them, a tow truck pulled a late model Mustang into the structure. Jasper, who sat beside the tow truck driver, waved.

As Mary Lou and Cursore watched, the tow truck driver expertly maneuvered the Mustang into a parking slot. Jasper gave the driver some money and stepped out of the truck. The driver grinned and drove off.

Cursore introduced the two women to each other and helped Mary Lou tote her ostrich-skin luggage up to her apartment. "Jasper," said Mary Lou, "I know reporters are clever as blazes but how'd you get the police to release Dusty's car?"

"We found Dusty's rental agreement at your place. I called the impound yard and said a woman by the name of Jasper Gardner was coming over. All they wanted was $75 in fines and towing fees."

"But you didn't have the keys . . ."

"I told them there was something wrong with the starter; that's why I abandoned it in the tow-away zone."

Cursore reached into his pocket and took out a set of keys. "I picked up a spare set from the rental agency before I met you this morning."

"You're an awfully smart pair," said Mary Lou. "I would have gotten the key first and then driven the car here. Probably saved fifty dollars in towing fees."

"We thought of it but we didn't want to disturb anything in the car," said Cursore.

"Speaking of disturb, don't disturb me for the next ten days. OK? I am beat—didn't sleep all night."

"Do you mind checking to see if anything has been stolen?" asked Cursore in her doorway.

Mary Lou glanced around her place. "Looks OK to me but I have to get some sleep . . ."

"But Mary Lou . . ."

"Let her sleep, she's dead tired," said Jasper.

"You and I will be very good friends," said Mary Lou, and closed the door.

Cursore and Jasper went to his apartment and found that a messenger had left a package. They carried the package that contained fingerprint paraphernalia down to the garage.

"One really knows where he stands with Mary Lou, doesn't he?" asked Jasper.

"That you do." He slipped the key into the locked door of the Mustang.

"Just a second. Why don't I get my Polaroid? You unwrap the stuff from the lab."

"Why do we need pictures?" he asked.

"Whenever I've covered a homicide, the I-dent team takes pictures like mad. Besides, art work will help me sell this as a do-it-yourself piece on crime prevention."

When she returned Cursore was re-reading the directions on how to use the fingerprint powder. She took several photos of the Mustang. Since the sports car was in sunshine, there was no need for a flash attachment.

They took their time dusting the exterior of the Mustang for fingerprints. Part of the car was dark blue, the other part white. On the light areas they used a camel hair brush to gently "dust" on black powder. The powder was like fine charcoal. They used a different camel hair brush to apply white powder on the darker paint.

"You got to think like a criminal," said Cursore. "If the person or persons who abducted her drove, they'd probably adjust the rear view mirror." He dusted the glass in the mirror, then the steering wheel and various dials on the dash.

They worked carefully, methodically for two hours.

"We keep getting his print again and again," said Jasper. She pressed some clear Scotch tape on a print on the chrome edge of the gear shift. When she peeled the tape back it lifted the print from the smooth surface. She applied the tape to a three-by-five card. The image was a small oval with none of the characteristic whorls or arches associated with fingerprints. On the driver's side of the car they found twelve similar prints. Jasper transferred each to a three-by-five card.

In addition to the oval print, they discovered other real fingerprints. These seemed to match each other. They lifted them from both the driver and passenger sides.

"My guess," said Cursore, "is the group of similar prints belong to Dusty. The circular ones are from the rubber gloves, stolen by the perpetrator."

"Perpetrator? You sound like a cop."

"I do? OK, let's start checking the seat and floor for stuff."

"What stuff?"

"I don't know. Blood stains. Adhesive. Dirt."

Even in the bright sunlight it was impossible to see clearly on the car's floor. Cursore left for his apartment to find a flashlight. Carefully, Jasper took the floor mats out and set them in the sunlight.

She meticulously ran her fingers over the floormats as sunlight filtered through her red hair, transforming it to warm rust.

When he returned with the flashlight, she held up a wheat-colored stalk of grass, several inches long. "I also found some sand on the driver's side," she said.

"Good."

She held the wheat-colored stalk for him to smell. It had a sweet odor.

They used the flashlight to check under the seats. "Sure is clean under there. Looks like a brand new car," said Cursore.

"Only one hundred ninety miles on the odometer. Told you I was a wonderful reporter."

"If you're so wonderful what was the reading when you left the police impound lot?"

"One hundred and eighty-two miles."

"Next we find out how far it was between the place Dusty's car was picked up and the police lot."

"Seven miles. I asked the truck driver."

"I'm impressed."

"With me?"

"No. The driver. He'd have to be pretty smart to remember all that kind of information."

"He didn't; he had to radio in. The dispatcher keeps a record."

"Now I'm impressed."

"With me?"

"Depends. Have you ever been a centerfold?"

"Would it make a difference?"

He smiled at her. "It's about five miles from here to the airport. If Dusty drove straight here, and she didn't drive anywhere else, and I don't think she did, then the . . ."

"Perpetrator?"

"Yeah. The perpetrator and she drove —let's see—how many miles did the car have on it when she picked it up at the airport?"

"According to the rental agreement, ninety."

"Mmm. OK. That would mean they drove eighty miles. Say from here to the center of LA and back. Or Malibu and back. Or . . . ?"

"Several short trips."

"Possibly."

They checked the trunk, back seat and glove compartment. "All I can find is the smell of a new car," said Jasper.

"How about the ashtray?" He pulled and found a wad of paper and unfolded it. The band had the number "$100" printed on it in black ink.

He wanted to tell Jasper about the $5,000.00 withdrawal. "Too bad there isn't a way to use your computer wizardry to check out her account," said Jasper.

"Yes, too bad. But I wouldn't want to go to jail."

"I would hate for that to happen."

They rechecked the car, then had lunch at a nearby health food store. As they finished, Mary Lou staggered in and sat down across from them.

"I thought you were going to sleep," said Cursore.

"Couldn't. You know where I hide my spare cash? Behind the picture in my room?"

He nodded.

"Gone. $300. And besides my rubber gloves, my large kitchen knife. Also the trash liner in the garbage can has been changed."

"Maybe the maid did it?"

"No. I have special trash bag liners. The maid knows about them. She was the one who bought them, come to think of it. Someone was in my apartment and emptied the garbage. I'd call the police if I thought it would do any good."

"You didn't touch anything in your master bath, did you?"

"You asked me not to. Think I'm getting senile?"

"A little. Want something to eat?"

"Not this rabbit food. I'll pick up some beer and a submarine sandwich next door. And I got shopping to do. You two can have a look at my bathroom."

An hour later, Mary Lou let herself into her apartment. "My God, you two have painted everything black and white. Will these smudges wash off?"

"Sure," said Cursore.

The three of them stood in the master bedroom and surveyed the damage. Every smooth surface, every place that someone could touch, had been dusted. The living room and kitchen looked like a raccoon with ink pad feet had gone crazy.

"We found Dusty's fingerprints on her cosmetics. It matches the only prints we lifted from the car."

"Lifted?" asked Mary Lou.

"Yeah," said Jasper. "You get a print, then you stick Scotch tape on it. Lifts right off."

"I don't think I'll ever get all the smudges off. Look at my walls and doors and mirrors. Good God, you've even ruined my brass lamps."

"Don't worry," said Cursore. "We think the perpetrator was one person. A guy."

"Rave on, Sam Spade," said Mary Lou.

"See those figurines?" said Jasper. "He picked them up by the top or center. A woman who would be much shorter would have grabbed them by the lower portion."

"What if it's a tall woman?" asked Mary Lou.

"She'd have to be about six one or two," said Cursore.

"If you're right, this weirdo could have gotten Dusty's keys. I think I better call the police. And get my locks changed on the door."

An hour later Sergeant Dartwell was seated across from Mary Lou eating chocolate chip cookies and drinking milk. "I've been addicted to chocolate chip cookies all my life. My wife makes a terrific toll house recipe."

Cursore and Jasper sat by the picture window, waiting for the cop to finish eating. He polished off two more cookies, then wiped his large mouth with the tiny doily Mary Lou had provided for his coffee cup. He looked around the room. The place was a confusion of fingerprint smudges.

"I want you to know," he said to Mary Lou, "that we're always grateful for any help we can get from citizens . . . but what you told me over the phone and what I see here makes me think there's . . . a fortune to be made in selling law enforcement paraphernalia to the public. Heh-heh. You people will have to repaint this place."

"I had two friends that were raped by hoodlums. It's too bad that they didn't pack some enforcement paraphernalia, as you call it," snapped Mary Lou.

"I apologize but . . ."

"You've picked the wrong person to patronize, young man. I play bridge with Beatrice Jennson and she happens to be the under-sheriff's aunt. My late husband donated thousands of dollars to your big boss' campaign and there are a great number of the County Hall of Administration officials who will haul your ass over red hot coals if you dare continue to play games with me."

The cop set the last half of an uneaten cookie on his arm rest.

"Mary Lou," said Cursore, "stop being your old sweet self. Show Sergeant Dartwell your sinister side."

Three of the four people laughed. The person who did not laugh was wearing a gun and a crooked grin. "I've issued an All Points Bulletin for this lady from Florida. We've checked the hospitals and teletyped the Miami police. There are several hundred missing people reported each week in this state so I'm sure you can appreciate . . ."

"I can appreciate nothing, young man. There was a criminal in here. Look at the rubber glove marks all over the place. Look at them."

The cop sipped his coffee. "Oh, yes. And the rubber gloves have mysteriously disappeared, right?"

"Correct."

"Whose were they?" Sergeant Dartwell composed himself.

"Mine," said Mary Lou.

"That's just it, ma'am. Maybe you made those marks when you were wearing the gloves. I understand you wore them to protect you from an allergy."

"Similar prints were found in the car," said Mary Lou.

"Yes. A rental car. I've seen a lot of people in car washes using rubber gloves. And may I ask you how you managed to recover the car from impound if Dusty Bleudell is still missing?"

"Pardon?" asked Mary Lou.

The cop stood and walked to the window and looked out. He was annoyed. "I'm sure you thought that by perjuring yourself you hadn't broken any laws." He looked at Jasper. "What you did is punishable by a fine and/or a jail sentence. You are aware of course that Mr. Cursore is on parole from state prison, and if either of you are proven guilty, he might have to serve the remainder of his sentence. Since we can assume he acted as your accomplice. Or vice versa."

"I'm sorry . . . all I was . . ." said Jasper.

The cop held up a ponderous hand. "I don't want to hear it. I know you're concerned about this Dusty Bluedell. We need more concern in our society. But you can't go around breaking laws in order to catch somebody you think might have abducted her. If I were you I'd take the rental car back to the lessee, and I'd wait for Ms. Bleudell to call you."

"Suppose she doesn't?" asked Mary Lou. Her tone was softer.

"Nine out of ten times people who are missing show up. Look, Mr. Cursore, maybe you frightened this girl. You arranged a date with her, didn't you?"

"Yes."

"Did she know about your criminal

record?"

"I don't usually start conversations that way. Mary Lou, did you mention it to her?"

"Of course not."

"OK," said Sergeant Dartwell. "Suppose—and this is only for argument's sake—that Ms. Bleudell meets you and is looking forward to an evening with you and she finds out you're a criminal on parole. You realize it is possible she could find out such a thing. She might have talked to someone around the building. She might have read a news clipping . . ."

"OK," said Cursore.

"All right. If I were an attractive young lady from across the country, out for a good time, and I suddenly discovered I had a date with a criminal, I might split."

"Without a word to me?" asked Mary Lou.

"If you neglected to tell her about his background, Ms. Bleudell might be angry with you. Bent out of shape."

"Sergeant, I think you just took a very cheap shot," said Jasper. "Maybe if I came to a strange town and ended up going out with a 'felon,' I might panic. But I wouldn't leave my suitcase and cosmetics and dump my rental car."

"You're also a streetwise reporter. But let's look at Ms. Bleudell. Into painting and art. Cultured. Out of her element. She's alone in a city with no friends. The only person she really knows is three thousand miles away in Hawaii. She realizes she's involved with a parolee. Now, suppose she's afraid to go back to the apartment for fear she'll get into trouble. Suppose she thinks she's being followed. Maybe she is. Maybe, Mr. Cursore, she spots you and concludes you're following her. You know how easy it is to become paranoid in this city?"

"I never followed her. I was here all day."

"Got an alibi?"

"No."

"There you go."

Silence. Sergeant Dartwell picked up his half-eaten chocolate chip cookie and finished it. *Snap.* He put his hand to his mouth. "Goddamit."

"What?" asked Mary Lou.

"I broke my goddamn tooth." He got up and headed for the door, took a deep angry breath—the air seared his tooth. A shard of enamel and filling fell into his hand. "I try to be nice. I try to indulge you people. Look what happens? Hell. We got an APB out for this Florida woman. Let us handle it! All right? I make myself clear?"

"No need to raise your voice, Sergeant," said Mary Lou.

The Sergeant glowered at her and slammed the door behind him.

The three stared at each other, almost afraid to laugh. Mary Lou started to giggle. Cursore stared at her.

"What's wrong, my dear felon?" asked Mary Lou. "Not funny?"

"Felon?" echoed Jasper. "He's not a felon. He's a masher." She started to laugh.

"He broke his goddamn tooth," Mary Lou screamed. If the two ladies had not been holding onto each other, they would have fallen over.

Cursore, his ears red, lunged for the door. The ladies *grabbed him.* He gave up, started to laugh.

Later, in the garage, Jasper got into her car. "I'll meet you at the rental place, OK?"

"Yeah," said Cursore.

"You mad?"

"I guess not. But if something happened to Dusty . . ."

"No. You're mad we laughed at you."

"No!"

"Liar."

"OK. I'm a little annoyed."

"If we thought you were guilty, we wouldn't have laughed."

"Yeah?"

"Yeah." She squeezed his arm. "Take it easy, OK?"

"I guess I am pretty tense."

"I can get rid of that."

"How?"

"Cold showers. Deep breathing." She kissed him on his nose.

Cursore watched her leave. He wanted to spend the night with her. Wanted more than that. A part of him was glad Dusty was gone—he couldn't handle two relationships at once. The instant the thought occurred he felt guilty. He did not want anything bad to have happened to Dusty. Maybe Sergeant Dartwell was right. Maybe Dusty was frightened off by someone with a criminal record. Someone on parole. He cursed the system for the millionth time for doing something to him that wasn't fair. He thought about Jasper and the anger melted. He slid into the rental car and drove out; the sunlight blazing between the pillars of the parking structure rippled on his face. Ahead, he saw Jasper turn onto Lincoln Boulevard. She twisted around and waved and grinned. He accelerated.

From behind a grey pillar, Jon Andrews watched them. He had planned to wash his Jaguar's trunk earlier that day but he had come upon Jasper and Cursore "dusting" the rental car of the girl from Florida.

The Russian could not understand what was happening. He could feel the vise tightening on him again. He knew that if the two people did not stop, he would have to run sooner than he wanted to. He'd be "caught" between covers. He would be exposed, vulnerable, and he would be hampered from completing his

Master Plan. Before that would happen he would kill them. The kills would be clean and well-planned. Nothing would be left to chance as it had been with the old man. The Russian absently touched his cheek where the old man had clawed him. He had grown careless. No more. He vowed he would be careful, so careful this time.

11

Jon Andrews used his stolen master key to open Jasper's door. He assumed they were returning the rental car. It would take at least half an hour. He set his digital watch alarm to sound in twenty minutes. The Russian was certain he would have to kill Jasper and Cursore, and they would have to die without a link to him or he would be running again. Vulnerable. He slipped on a pair of surgical gloves.

The Russian inspected the kitchen. A good stock of spices. Almond extract from Mexico. A clove of garlic near a garlic press. Dried saffron. Several tins of palm hearts. A dozen kinds of pasta. This Jasper was a good cook, a woman who would look after a man. He forced himself to stop thinking of the possibilities. It was dangerous to feel anything for a person you were going to kill. If you thought of them, you could care for them, and when the time came you might hesitate. Then you could be the one who would die. Jon checked several drawers for knives. He discovered a set of wide-bladed Mac knives—paring knives to butcher knives. There was a glistening trio of cleavers.

Under the sink were half a dozen cleaning fluids and insect bombs.

The Russian walked through the living room. He was amazed that there were so many different kinds of reference books: The Whole Earth Catalog, The Random House Dictionary, The Oxford Dictionary, The Encyclopaedia Britannica, the complete works of Shakespeare, foreign dictionaries, hundreds of additional text books. A dozen folders contained articles in various stages of development, each complete with research material—clippings, hunks of magazines, menus, matchbook covers with scribblings. Organized, but on the surface an impression of total chaos.

In her bedroom Jon found a drawer overflowing with bundle after bundle of letters. They were from all over the world, each was dated with a carbon of Jasper's original. She had written so many letters and notes, seemingly trivial —a letter to a distant niece supplying information on graduate schools, a note to a friend of a friend giving information on a London bookstore, a recipe for vegetarian hamburgers written to an acquaintance in Bombay. The Russian found himself wondering how anyone could be so thoughtful. The next drawer was jammed with more letters. In fact, the entire dresser yielded hundreds of such letters. The top drawer contained a photo album: Jasper in Agra beside the Taj, Jasper with her leg in a cast in a hospital room and five friends clowning in bed with her, Jasper in a football uniform, Jasper with mud on her face after being tackled, Jasper holding a puppy, Jasper in a prom formal, Jasper in a church choir. He closed the white album. He did not want to remember her as someone with a soul or what the Americans called a soul. The soul was simply a device Westerners used to overcome their fear of death. When you were dead, you were dead. That was it. That's why it did not really matter who you killed or why because some day you too would be dead. That would be it. Best to enjoy life while it lasted. When it ended, there would be only blackness. Perhaps not even that. For blackness was something.

He swung open the door to her closet. It ran the length of one wall. Dresses. Slacks, skirts. Several jeans. Five or six pairs of running shoes; perhaps a dozen pumps and sandals. The closet was neat but he was surprised to see so few clothes in it. Obviously, she spent her money on books and stamps. Not as much of a capitalist as most American women—*stop,* he told himself. Don't think of her that way.

Another closet was a tiny office.

Behind sliding doors was a typewriter on a table. Stacks of bond. A jar of sharpened pencils. A bulletin board with various assignments and notes on editors. Who was buying what. Someone from Playboy was looking for an article on ground hogs. William F. Buckley's thoughts on best sellers. An article on computer crime. There was a xerox of a news clipping from the L.A. Times on a computer expert who had illegally penetrated a bank security system and shifted funds to his account. The man had been sentenced to four years in jail. Ah! The man's name was David Cursore. The Russian noted the news clipping's date, then moved into the bathroom. More cleansers and some bug killers under the sink. Several expensive perfumes—Joy, Chanel. Half a tube of toothpaste. Very little makeup. He opened another drawer and found small packages of Kleenex, tweezers. Behind the mirror were more cosmetics and soap.

In the last drawer he found what he had been searching for.

Jasper's front door bell rang. The Russian froze. The door bell rang again.

He considered hiding in the makeshift office. Maybe whoever was ringing the bell so insistently also had a key. He had not set the deadbolt. Moving quickly across the thick carpet, the Russian arrived at the door as the bell howled. He took a breath and then softly, ever so softly clicked the dead lock shut. He brought his eye level with the security peephole in the thick oak door.

Through the tiny hole he saw the distorted image of the woman he had killed! *Donna Grey.*

He jerked his head away and leaned against the door. Impossible! His mind was going. They had tortured him, kept him in a urine-stained tiny cubicle in Hong Kong, and now the flood of memories seared his brain. Silence. The putrid odor of stale rice. His amusement with numbers. Ten times ten . . . the answer was five. It was. Really. Focusing through the tiny peephole was like squinting back through time. Everything was distorted. As a prisoner, his mind had tricked him. Again and again he had seen the images of his dead mother. They had even talked. Looking through the peephole *must* have triggered some switch in his mind. He had killed the black girl. He had taken her in two suitcases and dumped her into a sewer drain and fish were feeding on her now. It was impossible that she could be alive. *Impossible.* But she *was* outside the door.

He wanted to look through the peephole again but he could not. The door bell rang again—a long, unceasing *r-r-ringgg*. He forced himself to look again. Donna was there. Then she was gone and he was staring at a circular sphere of curved carpet, wall and ceiling. The bell rang again—impossible, she was gone. She was a ghost—come to torture. He started to laugh. It was not the door bell. It was the alarm in his watch. He opened the door and stepped into the corridor.

The woman had vanished.

His mind had been playing tricks on him.

The Russian walked briskly to the stairwell and started up. Halfway to the next floor, a landing. On the landing, Donna Grey, the woman he had killed, was standing, calmly looking at him. He was going mad. The Americans would find him now. The game was over. Finished.

"Are you OK?" she said. The voice was different. Yes. A different voice.

"Uh, yes. I've had the flu—I'm a little shaky."

"I didn't mean to startle you."

"Do you live in this apartment?" was all he could think to say. He hoped she could not tell how frightened he was. Now, looking at her clearly, without the distortion of the peephole, he realized she was not Donna. Perhaps a close relative of the murdered woman. A twin?

"I'm trying to find my sister. The manager said I could pass these out." She reached into her wide purse and brought out a photograph of Donna Grey, the woman he had killed.

"Never saw her. She looks like you a lot." So that was the connection.

"You sure you haven't seen her?"

"No. Why do you think she was around here?"

"My brother and I have been looking for her since Saturday night. We spotted her car on the roof of the parking structure beside this building."

He cursed himself in Ukrainian. He'd forgotten about her car completely. He had felt it would be safe on the roof until he moved it. But he had forgotten.

"Hardly anyone goes on the roof."

"That's how we found it. See, my sister has this old rattletrap of an MG and my brother has one of those ultra lights. The things like hang gliders with little motors? He flew over the area around the Parlour—that's where my sister always goes on Saturday morning. You know the place?"

"Uh, yes. It's on Main Street, isn't it?"

"Yes." She pressed the dead girl's photograph on him. "Will you keep this and show it to your friends? My phone number is on the back."

"Sure."

"You always take the stairs?" she asked.

"Exercise," he said. "You get twice as much exercise as jogging by climbing stairs." His mind was racing. Here was the sister of the woman he had murdered. Walking beside him. Asking him about the Omelet Parlour. It would only be a matter of time before someone at the Omelet Parlour remembered that Donna Grey had left in her broken down MG with a man in a jogging suit. Maybe someone would remember him coming into the building with her. Bad luck. He could feel the noose tightening. Who would give him away? Probably one of the regulars who ate breakfast at the Omelet Parlour on the weekend. Someone would remember him. This girl, talking to him, searching for her sister would soon check with the weekend patrons when they returned next Saturday. Five days. He needed more time than that. Had to have more time for the Master Plan.

"Thanks for your help," she said.

"Look, I did see a girl who looked like this come in the building with one of the other tenants. I think it was Saturday."

"Which apartment?"

"Not sure. It was a man; I've seen him around before. I could call the manager and describe him. Would that help you?"

"It sure would."

His penthouse apartment had just been cleaned and the mirrored coffee table shone like the sun itself. The black girl paused in the doorway, uncertain. Not frightened but uncertain. "Miss," he said. "I can understand you being nervous. Look—call your brother or a friend and tell them where you are. I have to go to the bathroom. Excuse me, OK?" He walked through the front room and then down a corridor.

For an instant the girl stood in the doorway, then determinedly walked to the phone and picked it up. She dialed a number. Around the corner, Jon Andrews listened to the black girl. She said, "Hello, this is May. I'm at the Marina. I'll call you later. I'm at 555-2112."

The Russian heard her hang up. He called out: "I'll be there in a minute. Make yourself at home." Then he went into his opulent bathroom and closed the door. He filled the marble sink with cold water and splashed it against his face. He stared at his reflection.

Everything seemed to be spinning out of control. He realized he was spending too much precious time covering his tracks. *Unorganized.* He was puzzled that in a city of millions things were closing in so quickly on him. He had thought it would be so simple to lose himself in a metropolis—now he felt naked, vulnerable—people seemed to discover his mistakes so quickly. Bad luck that some fool computer expert had decided to become a hero by tracking down the woman from Florida. And now the man had a reporter working with him. The two of them were in his very own apartment complex, inexorably closing in on him, trying to piece together an impossible set of clues. On the other hand, he had done something right—leaving no fingerprints. And no one had seen him with the blonde.

As he stood looking at himself he wondered if it were possible that the people who had trained him in Russia had deliberately programmed him for failure.

Did they want to sacrifice him for reasons he did not understand? Doubtful. The Russian thought back over his training lectures. He had learned all the skills of blending in with the local population. Become a chameleon, his teacher had said. First, create a life for yourself—home, job, friends. Then "operate" outside the territory of your "mini" world. That was all well and good as long as one was being supported with intelligence and funding. But how does someone with *no funding, no external support,* survive in a place like America? His teachers had hinted at the solution. *Stay with the familiar.* Do not operate outside of your sphere of understanding. If you do, you will be caught. So when his own people tried to kill him, Jon Andrews had disappeared. He felt comfortable among the wealthy, thus he chose an exclusive ocean apartment—large enough so no one paid him much attention, small enough that he could master its nuances. He knew he would have to steal to maintain his lifestyle. He had reasoned that among the very wealthy, he would only have to steal occasionally —and if he were cautious no one would ever suspect him.

He had found the perfect identity. In New Jersey he had read about a stock consultant who had died in the Bahamas. No family, the obituary had said. Jon had gone to the man's funeral, pleased to see that there were only a dozen people in attendance. His teachers had told him America had no national registry of deaths. Thus it was a simple matter to assume the identity of a deceased individual. The man in the coffin looked like Jon, perhaps ten years older.

The dead man's effects were given to a female cousin. The Russian followed the cousin and when she stopped to have her hair done, the Russian broke into her car and stole a bulging cardboard box of the personal papers that belonged to the deceased, then set the car on fire. An hour later, he became the stock consultant.

When he arrived in California, he immediately opened a bank account. Since he made an initial deposit of several thousand dollars, the manager of the bank welcomed him with the largest grin in Southern California. Jon Andrews substituted his picture in the dead man's passport. With a passport he applied for and received a California driver's license. He took his new "friend," the banker, out for lunch and applied for several credit cards. The banker, checking the references of a dead man, was delighted to discover what a solid citizen had entered his bank.

Jon Andrews applied for Blue Cross and three weeks later received a plastic card in the mail. His banker suggested an American Express Gold Card. Jon declined for he had heard that American Express did an extremely thorough check on applicants.

In order to maintain his lifestyle, money was essential. One thing was in the Russian's favor—plenty of victims. And many with more money than they knew what to do with. The Russian became a masterful hunter. In selecting his victims (or his *safeties,* as he dubbed them) he looked for certain things. First, a victim had to look as though she had money. This was fairly easy to determine, despite the ubiquitous jeans and T-shirts many people wore. A diamond would give a young and restless divorcee away, or perhaps an 18-carat Rolex watch, tucked under a cheap cotton blouse. All of Jon's *safeties* were women. Women controlled surprising wealth in America, especially divorcees who were beguiling enough to talk their husbands out of diamonds and gold watches. Jon's usual approach to the hunt was to find a divorcee, make friends with her, sleep with her, force her to give him her money and then kill her. He dated several flight attendants around the complex. He treated them with total respect and gallantry. They were his cover, lovers of a successful investment banker who drove a Jaguar and owned a yacht and always sent flowers on birthdays.

The Russian was careful to choose stewardesses who flew internationally because they were absent so much, and they did not seem as set on marriage as the working girls in the Marina.

One or two *safeties* a year had seemed like more than enough to supply Jon's financial needs. But it was Southern California. His forty foot yacht had cost him $215,000.00. The Jaguar, which he felt was a necessity, had run over $35,000. So there were more *safeties*. He had no real regrets about his victims. They were Americans and he had been programmed all his life to look at Americans as enemies. Besides, when the KGB finished training Jon, he was a top notch sociopath with only one allegiance —Mother Russia. And when his own people tried to kill him—end of allegiance and loyalty.

Sometimes he wondered if there were other people like him. Fellow Russians. Fellow travelers. He supposed there were, and he wondered how many thousands of Americans who vanished were in fact the work of his comrades or other renegade agents. When he read about the sadistic killers and mass murderers who ranged America, he felt comparatively normal. He killed his victims quickly; when possible, painlessly. He killed only to stay alive. To maintain his life. He was like a country. A country unto himself.

He had thought of several aliases he could use if he was forced to change identities again. The name he had chosen was Jan Country. A country unto himself. He liked that.

He used a thick fluffy towel to blot the cold water from his face. Then he walked back to the living room. The black girl was on his balcony, looking out at the sea. The wind rippled through her hair. She thought she was safe, having given his phone number to the person she had called. The phone number she had read on the Russian's phone was not his. It belonged to a Polish immigrant, a mile away, who spent little time at home.

Jon Andrews poured himself a shot of vodka and sipped it. He was tired. He didn't want to kill her. He considered leaving—withdrawing his money from the bank and leaving—starting someplace else. Maybe Seattle. That would mean abandoning his Master Plan. He did not think of blacks as Americans. He thought of them as slaves, as downtrodden human beings that Americans had enslaved. He had thought about the women he had enjoyed as sexual partners in the last year. They were all black. They had been used. And he had been used—a common heritage.

"The view is beautiful," said the black girl.

"Thanks. Want a drink?"

"OK. Just some wine, please."

He felt warm sleep creeping over him, washing across his mind. His life had become so complicated, so complex. He had to get some rest. Had to plan what he was going to do. Didn't want to kill the black woman on his balcony. Senseless to do that. He thought of her sister. A waste to have killed her, waste to kill this one.

He poured some white wine into a beautiful piece of stemware and took it out to her.

12

Mary Lou, dressed in jeans and a rose and silver Afghan sweater, tottered on one of her captain's chairs and tried to reach a smear of fingerprint powder along the top of an ornate gold-framed mirror.

Cursore and Jasper walked around a locksmith who was on his knees, chiseling a groove in the bedroom doorjamb.

"Did you bring the rubber gloves? This solvent is taking my skin off," said Mary Lou.

"Got 'em right here. Let me help you," said Jasper.

"It's OK."

"It's not OK. It's our fault. We made a terrible mess with that dusting powder," said Jasper. "Do you have a smock or something I can wear?"

"It's OK. I'm just giving the highlights a lick and a promise."

"Why don't you wait for the maid?" asked Cursore.

"Because, Mr. Sherlock Holmes, the maid's daughter is having a baby. I probably won't see her for another month."

"I'm really sorry about this," said Cursore.

Mary Lou polished furiously at the mirror, almost lost her balance, regained it. "I'll bet you're heartbroken. This fingerprint powder is like grease."

"That's because it's got an oil base," said the locksmith, positioning a jig. "Wish I owned the concession on fingerprint powder. Police use it like crazy. Sure made hash out of this place. You ought to send 'em the bill."

"We did this ourselves," said Mary Lou. She opened the rubber glove package and shook them out, slipped them on. "That feels better." She dipped a sponge into a pail of solvent and attacked a series of splotches on the teak mantle over the fireplace.

The locksmith wiped his hands on stained overalls and looked around the room. "Looks like a Tasmanian Devil in heat scampered through a tar pit before he took on this place. You'll never get that powder off them white curtains. Not even if you dry clean 'em."

"Thanks a lot," said Cursore.

The locksmith picked up a power drill and zeroed in on the door frame. Chips and sawdust flew across the room. When he finished with the drilling, the locksmith took out a small vacuum and cleaned up the mess. "Always suck up as you go along. You get satisfied customers that way."

"You think that new deadbolt is really going to do any good?" asked Mary Lou.

"Well, I changed the key for your front door. So if someone could get in, they can't now. And once in here, only one thief in a thousand will try to enter a locked bedroom. You could be sleeping with a scatter gun for a pillow."

"You think so?"

"If thieves want to knock over a place, nothing can stop 'em," said the locksmith, screwing the new lock cover in place. "This'll slow 'em down, that's all. Like I told you, if you want good protection, then you got to put in an alarm system."

"I'm not spending money on alarm systems," said Mary Lou.

The locksmith attached the final hardware in place. "Suit yourself. You vigilantes are all the same."

"I don't think we're vigilantes," said Cursore. He was using a sponge in an attempt to remove white fingerprint powder from a lacquered black vase.

"You're not, huh? Anyone who takes the law into his own hands is a vigilante. Know what I mean?"

"No, we don't know what you mean," said Jasper, scrubbing more blotches from a glass porcelain Madonna figure.

"You're a pretty hostile group, aren't you?" said the locksmith as he closed his tool case.

"We have to be hostile," said Mary

Lou. "It's a hostile, goddamn world out there. And the police aren't going to protect us. We shouldn't have to pay someone to come and turn our homes into prisons."

"Ninety dollars."

"Pardon?"

"You owe me ninety bucks for the deadbolt and a new key," said the locksmith. He looked at his watch. "It's past six. I should by rights charge you double time."

"Someone stole all my cash. Will you take a check?"

"No."

"Why?"

"Because it's a hostile world and I don't trust anyone. I told you on the phone that I wanted ninety dollars."

"Here," said Cursore. He reached into his pocket and fished out his wallet. He found five twenties.

"You want change or two more keys?" asked the locksmith.

"Keys still five dollars each?" asked Mary Lou.

"Like I told you on the phone."

"We'll make our own key" she snapped.

"Just like you do your own detective work. This place is awful. You'll have to repaint it." He gave Cursore ten dollars change, hefted his tool case and left.

They could hear him laughing in the hall.

Mary Lou got off the chair and tried the new lock. "Well, it works OK. I thought it would. Only cocky servicemen do good work."

"Probably right," said Jasper. "This place might have to be repainted."

Mary Lou sat down in an easy chair and lit a cigarette. "So we paint it. What do you think? This eighty year old broad's come a long way?" She exhaled, holding the cigarette in an exaggerated imitation of a young model in a Virginia Slims ad.

"A long way, baby," said Mary Lou.

"So what'd you two find out about the rental car?"

"Brand new—just been checked before Dusty rented it. The service manager swears it had never been near the beach."

"I reported the three hundred dollars to my insurance company. They said they need a crime report so I guess I'll have to call Sergeant Dartwell again. That OK with you, Cursore?"

"Sure."

"You two look pretty glum. I'm the one who's been shunted all over the country all night long. I'm the one who's going to repaint. I'm the one who smokes too much."

"We were talking in the car," said Jasper. "It's so discouraging. The police won't do anything. We try to help them. They get angry with us. And the worst thing is your friend is missing."

Mary Lou took another mighty drag on her Virginia Slim. "I know how you feel. The truth is, I'm getting more worried about Dusty. I've called her place twice in Florida. Got her damn answering service. Her parents are still in Europe. I don't know anyone else in Florida we can call. I suppose I could fly out there."

Cursore looked down at the Marina. "I don't see that it would do any good to go there. She might call here."

"That's right," said Jasper.

Mary Lou reached over and rubbed some fingerprint powder off an ashtray. "Cursore, I don't want you to get upset—promise me, OK?"

"OK."

"Was there any way that you could have frightened her?"

"Are you serious?"

"You know how you are? Full of beans all the time. You love practical jokes."

"And let's not forget I'm a felon on parole."

"Don't take it so personally."

"Listen to yourself, Mary Lou. You're talking just like that police sergeant."

"Well, he came up with a pretty logical reason why Dusty would up and leave. If she got spooked—maybe not by you, for sure not by you—she might have been too frightened to come back here."

"What do you think I did to her?"

"Nothing. I'm just asking."

"I thought you trusted me a little more than that. You really are a disappointment." Cursore stalked out of the apartment, slamming the door behind him.

"He's awfully sensitive—in case you haven't noticed," said Mary Lou. "He doesn't stay mad long."

"You don't think he was guilty, do you?"

"Of that computer scam? No. But he's a hot-blooded American boy and he probably tried to get into Dusty's panties. Maybe she read it wrong."

"You really come out and say what you're thinking," said Jasper.

"When you're my age, you get to say anything you want to. Cursore has an active libido—same as you, I suppose. I hope."

"What was Dusty like?"

"Fun, but she led the boys on. A lot. I'm not saying she had bedroom eyes. She just didn't hand it out in the locker room."

"What do you think I'm like?"

Mary Lou took another long hit of her Virginia Slim and let the smoke trickle through her nostrils. She looked through the smoke at the redhead. "You've worn your heart on your sleeve too much and you've had it pounded into hamburger more times than you want to think about."

"Close."

"You probably like journalism and you're probably very good at it. But what you want is a guy you can depend on.

And someone who wants to depend on you. You're interested in Cursore. And you wish to God he wasn't on parole."

"How'd you get so smart?"

"If I'm so smart, how come I've been smoking these cancer sticks for sixty years?"

"You really think he's innocent, don't you?"

"Bet my life on it, honey."

"He seemed so mad when he left here."

"Frustrated."

"I wish there was something I could do about it."

"There is."

Jasper leaned over and kissed the older lady on her wrinkled cheek, then left for Cursore's apartment.

A few minutes later Jasper knocked on Cursore's door.

"Yeah," he said from the other side.

"You going to let me in?"

"Busy now."

"Look, Cursore—if you're looking for a one-sided relationship we might as well forget this."

He opened the door, considered her, left it open, then turned and walked away. She was on him like Crazy Glue. "Hey, what's wrong with you?"

"Does it matter?"

"It matters. Don't you want to have some kind of relationship with me?"

"You want to get it on with a goddamn felon?"

"You're not a felon."

"I suppose I'm not on parole either?"

"Cursore, I think you could have been set up. And . . ."

"You *think*?!! You don't really *know* though, do you?"

"No, I don't. But I'm willing to give you the benefit of the doubt, and that's a hell of a lot more than I see anyone else doing."

"What about Mary Lou?"

"She doesn't count."

"Why?"

"Because she needs you."

"And you, do you need anyone?" he asked.

"Not that much, sailor."

"I'm glad we got that settled." Cursore slid open his balcony door and walked outside. He leaned his elbows on the railing and looked down at the acres of sails fluttering before him. Jasper stood beside him for a moment. The same breeze that vibrated the sails teased her hair. Her hair changed from coral to ruby to rust as the sun danced against it.

"What now, Mr. Holmes?" she asked.

"At least you're not a quitter," he said.

"Just as long as you aren't."

"I don't know," he said. "We're getting no help from the police. We haven't found any fingerprints. There's no sign of Dusty. I've got Mary Lou upset. Wrecked her apartment, ruined her Hawaiian vacation."

"Let's go out to Malibu."

"And what will we do there?"

"I don't know, Cursore. But according to our calculations, Dusty's car was driven a distance that is appoximately from here to Malibu. There was sand on the floor mats . . ."

Twenty minutes later they were in his 1947 restored Bentley, tooling toward Malibu. They stopped at The Sandcastle Restaurant. Their waitress was Judy, tall and friendly but possessing the kind of angular face that could turn mean suddenly.

"Thank you for the wine, Judy," said Cursore. The bill came to $4.50. Cursore laid a twenty on the tray. "Please keep the change."

Judy picked up the twenty dollars. "I'm good, but sixteen dollars good?"

"I need some information."

"In the movies the detective always asks the bartender where the Maltese Falcon is hidden," said Judy.

"Have you seen this lady?" He showed Judy a picture of Dusty that Mary Lou had given them.

"Don't know her. She's pretty."

"We think she disappeared around here. It's really important we find her."

"I haven't seen her. Have you tried the hospital?"

"We called," said Jasper. "No luck."

"What are her hobbies?" asked Judy.

"Painting and art, I think," said Cursore. "Why?"

"I read a lot of mysteries. Spy thrillers. You can always find somebody by his hobbies. I read where they caught one spy because he liked model trains. The CIA found out where the spy had been but they didn't know his name. So what they did is get the mailing lists of all the model train magazines and ran 'em through a computer. They found one guy who kept changing his mailing address —and that guy had lived at all the places the spy had been. They almost got him, except he was run over by a real train. Funny, huh?"

"Are there a lot of galleries around here?" asked Jasper.

"About a dozen."

"Thanks," said Cursore. He and Jasper spent the rest of the day checking galleries. No one had heard of Dusty or recognized her picture.

"Maybe she didn't come here," said Cursore.

"Maybe. But then where'd the sand come from on the floor mat?"

"They could have driven to Santa Monica and gone down by the pier. Then driven to another part of the city. Or gone to Venice—that's only a couple of miles. Lot of real strange people in Venice."

"Maybe he broke an hourglass in the car."

"Or had a cat and took a sandbox

along." Cursore rubbed his temple. "I can't believe we're joking about this."

"People always joke when they're worried. 'Least I do. The funniest time of the month is when I don't have my rent," said Jasper. "Speaking of making the rent money—how come you don't have to go to work? I've got an excuse—I'm freelance."

"I can pretty much set my own hours."

"Then you have the best of both worlds. All this walking around has art-galleried me out and made me very thirsty..."

"What do you want to drink?"

"Champagne."

"OK. We'll drive back to that restaurant we saw down the road. What was it called? Moonrakers, and I'll..."

Her red hair quivered in the sunset. She smiled a delicious smile. "What would you say if we went across the street and bought a magnum of French champagne and then we checked into that hotel and got a room with a view of the crashing surf and then I seduced you several times?"

He thought about a witty response, then decided the best thing he could do was to take her by the hand and walk across the highway and buy the champagne and let her do exactly what she wanted to do. Turn her loose like a fine thoroughbred. Really give her her head.

And that was exactly what they did.

13

The Russian was dreaming about his mother. He was ten years old and his mother was making potato soup and he had a fever. She brought the soup into his tiny room, a section of a larger room, separated by a blue drape. She held a wooden spoon containing the delicious broth under his nose.

"It has chicken in it, Mother. Where did you get the chicken?"

"Don't I always take care of you?"

"Yes, Mother. We'll always take care of each other, won't we? Promise?"

"Until you find a nice girl of your own."

"But you'll be with me, won't you?"

"Yes." His mother smiled, but seven years later they were on an exchange program in France and she was killed by a drunken American outside a tiny bar that sold wine in silver carafes.

The Russian opened his eyes. He thought he might still be in the cubicle that the Chinese had tortured him in; then he realized from moonlight fluttering across the room, he was in his

Marina penthouse. He was Jon Andrews, safe for the moment.

The black girl watched him. Moonlight spilled across her oval face, endowing it with an iridescent glow. She had finished her drink and was sitting in the semi-darkness, watching him.

An ornate grandfather clock ticked away the seconds. A little past nine.

"I must have dozed off," he said.

"You must be tired," she said.

"I haven't been getting much sleep. I'm sorry." He considered her—she was half his weight and a quarter of his strength. Perhaps not that strong. He got up and locked the patio glass door and snapped the safety bolt shut. The bolt lock was at the top of the window sash, seven feet above the floor. The Russian pulled the curtains shut, blotting out the twinkling portholes of the yachts in the harbor. He turned on a light, then crossed to the main door and made certain it was secured, then took the key from the deadbolt and put in into his pocket.

"You're very security conscious," she said.

"It's a habit. I was robbed a year ago."

"Can I use your bathroom?"

"OK." He did not let her use the master bath; instead he opened the door to the guest bathroom. It had no windows and contained a black toilet and wash basin. Its door was made of something that appeared to be solid oak. A trick of technology. The door was compressed sawdust that would easily crumble under Jon's shoulder.

While the woman used the bathroom, the Russian collected a heavy paper weight, a letter opener and a thick ashtray from one corner of the living room. Jon Andrews quickly checked the woman's purse. Several dozen pictures of Donna Grey—they looked like they had all been cut from dancing or acting composites. Assorted cosmetics. Driver's license. He name was May Grey. She was in a nursing program at UCLA. Some breath mints. Theatre ticket stubs. Some change. When May Grey came out of the guest bathroom, he told her to sit on the overstuffed sofa. (She would be unable to reach any kind of weapon from that position.)

She had the same kind of supple motion as her sister. He imagined that if she had chosen dancing instead of nursing, she would have done rather well.

On the mirrored coffee table before her were a dozen children's story books, filled with contemporary nursery rhymes. May glanced at these. "You must like children."

"Yes." He did not tell her he had just bought them. He had to find out about American nursery rhymes.

"Do you have any children?" she

asked.

"No. I've never married." He had a feeling he could trust her. Of course he couldn't be certain, yet he had a feeling. If she ever suspected he had killed her sister, she would instantly call the police; she might even kill him herself. He could not blame her for this. When he had heard a drunken American had killed his mother, he had wanted to kill the man. Natural reaction.

"Did I tell you my name was May?" she asked.

"You can call me Russ," said Jon.

"Are you hungry, Russ?"

"Come to think of it, yes."

"Do you want me to make you something to eat?" she asked.

"I'll do it." He did not trust her with the kitchen knives. There was a passway from the kitchen counter to the living room, and while he made sandwiches, he watched her. She picked up one of the children's nursery rhymes and read it. Occasionally she looked at him and smiled. He brewed coffee and made turkey sandwiches. He heated them in the microwave.

She ate her turkey sandwich, washing it down with the hot coffee. She did not seem to taste the food. "Can I have some milk, please?"

"Yes. It's in the fridge." A test. He wanted to see if she could be trusted.

She went to the kitchen and poured

some milk in a sparkling long stemmed glass. She walked back to where he had told her to sit down and slowly drank the milk. She made no attempt to bolt from the penthouse.

"What's wrong?" she asked.

"Why?"

"I'm a nurse. I work with emotionally dis— . . . I work with people who are going through problems."

"I probably have a lot of problems. I guess it shows."

"Tell me about them." She set her empty glass down.

Maybe she was smarter than her sister. Didn't matter now. He could not remember talking with anyone about how he really felt in such a long time. He had thought several times of going to a Catholic priest. Just to talk. But he was not a Catholic and he did not believe that a priest, a stranger, could be trusted.

"I bet you have led a very interesting life."

"Why?"

"Look at you. You live in a fantastic penthouse. You dress great. You're good looking. I think you're very intelligent." She glanced at one of the books of nursery rhymes on the mirrored coffee table. "You like children."

He thought he would tell her something about himself. He needed to talk to someone; it had been so many years. So many years of mistrust. "I don't like children that much."

"Why all these books?"

"I'm trying to learn American nursery rhymes."

"Why?" She leaned forward, unaware of any danger, seemingly fascinated by him.

"I was born in the Ukraine. My nursery rhymes are about cathedrals and ballet dancers and cossacks and violinists. I don't care about the Pacific Ocean out there. I care about the Volga and the Ural and the Lena." He was growing passionate for things he had not allowed himself to think about for years.

"That's OK. That's nice."

"But don't you see? I'm a Russian. I do not belong in this country."

"Russ for Russian? How did you get here?"

"I worked for the Russian embassy. I ran away."

She did not understand. Who could understand him? His mother had promised him that someday there would be such a woman. Could this black girl be the one?

"Can't you go back to your country then?" she asked.

"No. My people would kill me. They already tried to kill me because I disobeyed an order. I refused to kill an American." That was his first lie. He wondered if she could see through him.

She couldn't. She seemed swept away by his passion, passion infused with lies. "Russ, you could go to the authorities. Get political asylum."

"I have thought about it. But it must be done the right way. My own people have already branded me a murderer. When I failed to carry through with an assassination, other Russian agents did it and made it look as though I had. But I cannot kill anyone."

"My God!"

Now for the next lie. "Several weeks ago I was at the Omelet Parlour and I recognized a Russian agent . . . I was terrified." He held his hand to his eyes and was surprised to feel his warm tears. He wondered what the black woman would do. He was pleased by his ability to act. He thought of the lies he had just told her; he was overjoyed at how well he was doing.

The woman moved to him and put her arms around his shoulder. She was wearing perfume, lilac, and her soft breasts gave slightly as he wept. "It's all right, it's all right. I'm not going to hurt you. You can trust me."

"I'm ashamed to cry," he said. He was embarrassed but there was no way to stay the tears. He had never wept like this. He tried to determine why—maybe it was his sorrow over killing the black girl. Maybe it was the confusion that seemed to have attended his life in the last week. Everything had happened so fast: no control of his future, running out of money, keeping everything inside him. Never being able to talk to anyone, always living in the shadows, always looking in the shadows. The computer expert and the reporter moving toward him, relentlessly. And of course there was the dream of his mother.

"There's nothing wrong with crying. A man who cannot cry cannot be a man."

"Do you believe that?"

"Part of being a human is crying, feeling emotion. Let it happen."

He cried a little longer and he was delighted the way his tears affected her. Her fear was gone, replaced by concern that almost approached adoration. Maybe she had spent her life searching for a cause. And maybe he was it. If that was true, he told himself, then I am indeed a fortunate man.

"Do you want me to stay?" she asked.

"What about your sister?"

"I'll keep looking for her tomorrow. I could sleep in your guest bedroom."

"I would like that. Would you?"

"Yes. I better call my brother again and tell him what's happening. OK?"

This was the moment of truth, he realized. Either she would agree to play by his rules or he would have to silence her. A quick blow to her temple—she would never wake up. "Go ahead," he said. "Just leave a phone number, OK?"

"Sure. I understand."

He watched her dial the phone. She still did not know the number on his receiver was incorrect. Don't advertise—the key to survival. And maybe a second key was get a little help, a little support, where you could find it.

He watched her lips moving. "Ken, me again. I'll be in the Marina tonight. Still at 555-2112 if you need me. But don't phone unless you have to. I'm fine. Call you tomorrow." She hung up and smiled at him. May had beautiful, warm succulent lips. "Ken's like all big brothers—big worry wart. I've got some things in my car. I'll get them, OK?"

"OK," he heard himself saying. "Want me to go down with you?"

"I can manage."

He took the key out of his pocket, tossed it to her. "If you tell anyone about me, I'm dead. OK?"

"You can trust me. I know what it's like when the world's against you. I've been there."

She left and he waited. He waited for twelve minutes. He estimated it would take her fifteen minutes to go downstairs, get her things and come back. If she did not return, he knew what he would do. He would take his available cash. He would go downstairs and drive to her address that he had found in her purse. He would take the route past the Marina del Rey Sheriff's office, and he would kill her there if he could. That would be the logical place for her to go. If she thought he had lied to her or she was lying to him, she would not remain around his building.

If he couldn't kill her or he couldn't find her, he would drive to the airport and he would fly to Las Vegas, then to Seattle, and he would start over again. He would have to abandon his Master Plan. But she came back.

"Hi. Sorry I took so long. Will my car be OK in the visitors' parking?"

She had been gone thirteen minutes. Why did Americans think thirteen was unlucky? It was a lucky number for him. Six and twelve made thirteen. Or did it?

"Can I use your bathroom again?" she asked.

This time he took her into the master bath. It was the size of a small bedroom, complete with sunken jacuzzi tub, a skylight, a bidet, and a twenty foot dressing mirror with a perimeter of clear "stage" makeup lights.

"Are those taps gold?"

"Gold-plated, I guess."

"Do all spies live like this?"

"Only the lucky ones." He realized she had returned for the adventure, for the romance. Since she thought her brother had her number she felt safe. Besides, she had let slip she was a nurse for "disturbed patients." A psychiatric nurse. One had only to note the number of psychopaths, ax murderers and rapists running loose on the streets with "weekend passes" to attest to the complete stupidity of most American psychiatric professionals.

She looked up at the skylight. "Can you see stars through there?"

"If it's dark."

She turned off the lights and the stars shone faintly through the skylight.

"Will you turn on the bath, Comrade?"

He turned on the bath. "You like the water warm or hot?" He could not believe how clever it had been to cry. His tears had always affected his mother. But other women?

"Warm to begin with," she said, and when he stood she had taken off her clothes and the moonlight seemed to have transformed her into an ebony sculpture. "That's an awfully big tub, isn't it?"

"Yes."

She unbuckled his belt, gently tugged the corners of his shirt out, gently pulled the shirt from his arms, gently kissed his chest, gently worked her way downward. He felt her moist tongue against his body, felt it pressing warmly against his chest, felt it probing his navel, teasing him. She undid his zipper with her teeth.

They held each other in the oversized tub in the moonlight, their lips together.

He felt like crying again. Felt so happy. He had made a mistake killing her sister;

he prayed he would not have to kill this one. She moved a soapy arm around him. He remembered that he didn't believe in prayer. Didn't matter. He still prayed to the stars glistening above that he would not have to kill her. She was so young. The Russian thought about death and dying. Each time he had celebrated a birthday he had thought to himself that his life was just half over. He kissed her slippery shoulder. He wondered how he would feel when he was fifty. Would he still think he would live to be twice as old as that? What was two times fifty? One hundred twenty-five? Or was it sixty?

Didn't matter. He pulled the black woman closer to his wet skin.

14

"Magic" MacDonal was a Wunderkind. Only thirty-four, he was already vice president in charge of creative affairs for Taggart Advertising. TA didn't do near the billing of say, the top five ad agencies, but TA was a comer. A real comer in the city that never slept. And the reason TA was flying high was that Magic MacDonal hardly ever slept himself. Go. Go. Go. Take a letter, Miss Smith; take a meeting, Mr. Brown; take the red-eye to L.A.; take a snort...

Magic came out of the midwest when he was twenty-two. Started in the mail room of J. Walter Thompson. Was writing copy at twenty-six, was designing campaigns at thirty, was on his way to the *freakin'* moon, and not yet thirty-five. God, what an accomplishment—thirty-four going on twenty-one, and VP in charge of friggin' creative affairs for the hottest new agency in New York, New York. The lad had the touch for copy, clients and cookies. Cookies... pussy. Magic had a name for everything, God love him!

Nobody could touch him since the "Kaam Campaign." A month after he came up with that one he was kicked upstairs to VP. And now in his fifty-sixth floor office in Rockefeller Plaza, behind his black teak desk, sitting in his black leather panther chair, Magic was handling a cookie. The cookie's name was Ms. Bags, a freelance reporter from New Woman. Vassar grad, silk dress, freakin' IBM computer for a mind, and a cookie fabricated out of a high speed electric pencil sharpener. Don't let those hazy brown eyes and blow-dried blonde hair off a Farah Fawcett mannequin fool you. Ms. Bags thought of her typewriter as a battering ram and the truth was an occupational hazard. Had lotta readers, that Ms. Bags. Gave great interviews. But when she found your weak spot, she tore out yer old jugular—just to get acquainted.

Ms. Bags adjusted her Gold Targa pen, considered her no-nonsense legal pad on her lucite clipboard. (The clipboard was engraved with: "Ms. Bags/Project 7" —kinda gave people perspective as to where they fit in with Ms. Bags' universe.) Ms. Bags pouted, perhaps overdoing her well-cultivated image as thoughtful interviewer and said: "Mr. MacDonal, what I'd like to know is . . ."

"Please call me 'Magic.' All my friends do."

"Gosh, I'd love to be your friend."

"Done."

"OK, Magic, if I can be straightforward with you . . ."

"Always . . ."

"Yes. If I can be straightforward with you—what do you know about women's vaginas?"

"A lot more than I know about men's."

She laughed. He laughed. Nice to be adults. Ms. Bags' soft brown eyes flickered and became lasers. "What do you know about vaginas?"

Maintaining constant eye contact, Magic reached below his spotless desk and brought out a five inch thick leather binder. The title was "A Comprehensive Study of Birth Contraception in America. Abridged." His eyes did not melt under the lasers. "Before we started the Kaam project, I commissioned twelve of this nation's leading Ob-Gyn's to compile a review of all the existing forms of birth control practiced by Americans. In doing so I spent four months at Harvard Medical School working with Dr. Margaret Fieldstein and Dr. Catherine Rogers, both of whom are recognized as international authorities on the male and female reproductive organs. About five percent of our work is summarized in this volume, so I would say quite candidly that I probably know as much about the vagina as any lay person and possibly as much as most general practitioners."

"May I look at that report?"

"This is your copy." Magic moved his hand away to reveal her name, stenciled in gold on the bottom of it. He pushed it across his desk and smiled slightly, warmly.

"I'm impressed."

"And I'm impressed with your reputation for thoroughness, Ms. Bags . . ." (Goddamn, he was thinking, I nail her I got twenty million cookies reading about Kaam.)

"My friends call me Irene."

"Thank you. Anyway, between you and me, Irene, I really feel I did my homework on vaginas."

They laughed.

"How does it feel to have changed the contraceptive habits of twenty-five million women, Magic?"

He looked down at the desk, then he considered his right thumb nail. Time to go to the manicurist. "Truth? Humble and good. It's a satisfying feeling to do something that you know is right. Just consider the various forms of birth control—vasectomies and tubal ligations, people don't want surgery, far too risky; IUD, dangerous; the pill, dangerous, unknown side effects, really throws a woman's hormonal balance out of whack; condom, you know the old saying, 'washing your feet with your shoes on;' diaphragm, problems fitting it correctly; rhythm system, you know what you call people who rely on it?

Parents. And then there's celibacy but..."

"It takes too much cold water. All those showers?" quipped Ms. Bags.

"Right. And except for the condom, the other methods all require a visit to a physician..." He was perking.

"And your market research indicated that most women in America are distrustful of doctors?" She was picking up his energy, his enthusiasm.

"Right on. What we wanted to discover was the best and safest way for a woman to plan her life. We considered the sex practices of Americans, and we developed a foolproof method of birth control which would be satisfying for the woman and the man—with no harmful side effects."

"Eureka. You developed Kaam." She opened her purse and took out a small green package and read the following: "... the modern woman's answer to controlling her life."

"There's nothing as safe as it is."

"Let's talk about a vasectomy. We kind of skimmed over that..."

"Sure, Irene. A vasectomy is usually irreversible. Like a tubal ligation. Requires risky medical procedures. I happen to believe in marriage, and most people in America do. I know from your columns that you do. With that kind of radical surgery you can't change your plans very easily. And if a woman who wants to remain fertile chooses to have a variety of sexual partners, she'd limit herself dramatically if each of those partners had to have a vasectomy. Besides, all of the information on long term effects of vasectomies is not in. The purpose of Kaam is to allow a woman and a man to plan their lives in a safe way. As a foam, Kaam has no adverse effects to any of the delicate tissues. The only thing Kaam harms is sperm. Totally safe in both the male and female reproductive and urinary membranes."

"And according to all the medical information available, you're correct. But the sponteneity of lovemaking is diminished, isn't it?"

"No. Actually lovemaking, I believe, is enhanced since Kaam contains several pheromones that act on the olfactory centers."

"So it's an aphrodisiac?"

"We don't make that claim. But the pheromones, which are harmless, have been proven to increase arousal in both male and females. Maybe part of it is psychosomatic, but I have to admit I'm more turned on when my sex partner uses Kaam."

"And what about the charges by certain religious groups that your television ads are pornographic?"

"We maintain the highest broadcast standards in America, and we are subject to constant scrutiny by the FCC."

"Didn't several groups accuse you of having your model pronounce Kaam so it sounded like *cum*?"

"I believe there was some such allegation which Broadcast Standards found no truth in."

"Is it true that Kaam has made you a millionaire?"

"I make a good living but I'm far from a millionaire. The reason I make a good living is because I like my work. If I had to I'd do what I do for much less than I make." Wasn't that the truth? He'd only earned a quarter of his present salary a year ago.

"It's nice to meet a man who loves his work."

"It's nice to be that man. I'm lucky."

"Do you plan on bringing out other products with the Kaam logo? Such as perfumes, toothpaste, headache remedies—that kind of thing?"

"If the American public continues to support Kaam then we may do it. The final decision is of course in the hands of the manufacturer. We discover ways of marketing their products. And in order for any agency to do that job competently, that agency must have faith in the product. We have faith in Kaam."

"Have you ever thought of starting your own agency?"

"Very happy here."

"But have you thought of starting your own?"

"This is America. And America is made of dreams. And, Irene, like any other American, I dream." He was looking at her breasts.

"Would you like to have dinner and continue the interview then?"

"No."

"You are not intimidated by a woman who comes on to you?"

"I want to have dinner with you. But I don't want to talk shop."

"Seven?"

"Great. Done."

After she left, Magic propped his feet up on his desk and tilted his chair back and looked at the Hudson River. He felt like he owned the whole bloody world. He felt alive and good. Not great. Good. He did a line of coke at 11:30. He thought of the West Coast. People would be waking up there now. Magic had designed a special "California" commercial for Kaam. He knew it was going to blow everyone away. Everyone. He was the best. There was something cosmic in the fact that clients, cookies and campaigns all started with "C." Uh, so did coke. He felt great. Strike great. Consummate. Consummate for "C." See? Goddamn, that coke could get behind a guy, really sneak up on him if he were only mortal.

15

The sunlight sifted through gauze curtains and warmed Cursore's face. The light endowed his rawboned face with gentleness. Without opening his eyes, he knew he was in the hotel room, overlooking the Pacific Ocean. Totally relaxed, every fiber in his body had been taxed to the limit during the night and he smiled, still keeping his eyes closed. He was aware of someone tapping at the door. He felt Jasper swing out of bed, heard her pad across the room, heard her say something, heard the sound of a purse being opened, heard the door close softly, smelled that scent of fresh croissants and hot chocolate, felt soft pressure on his tummy.

He opened his eyes, and Jasper was looking over a wicker breakfast tray that she brought to him. Tiny globules of hot chocolate clung to a thick hotel cup. Two droplets of hot chocolate glided down the smooth porcelain where they melted together in the saucer.

Jasper twisted her head around to

watch the descent of the chocolate. "That's just like us."

"How do you mean?"

"Sliding off the edge of the earth. All wet."

"You're a real cynic."

"You didn't say that last night."

Before he could reply, Jasper stuffed a strawberry croissant into his open mouth. He munched it thoughtfully. Jane Pauley was talking on the Today Show. She smiled and her image changed to a commercial for Kaam. Jasper turned the volume down.

The ad showed a man and a woman in their late twenties establishing eye contact across a crowded room. Then a montage of the pair: scuba diving, hot air ballooning, and finally walking hand in hand across a Malibu beach. As an orchestra played Tchaikovsky's First Piano Concerto, an authoritative female voice said: ". . . for the woman who wants to take control of her life, safely."

Jasper pressed the remote channel changer, built into the nightstand. Four other stations were running the identical Kaam ad. One of the local stations was telecasting The Flintstones. She laughed at their antics, got back into bed, and together they finished off six croissants and four cups of hot chocolate.

"You use Kaam?" he asked as they drove back to Marina Towers.

"Yes."

"Heard it was an aphrodisiac."

"You think it is?"

"I don't know what was going on last night but I've never had an experience like that."

"Neither have I." As they kissed each other again, she giggled.

"What's funny?"

"Last night. I didn't use anything."

"Thanks a lot," he said.

"It's OK. Nothing's going to happen." A strange expression crossed her face. She placed her hand on her tummy. "I felt something move. Think it's a boy?"

"Very funny."

He smiled. "I don't understand how I could have spent such a long time at Marina Towers and never met you."

"You always leave early and come home late. Buff Tallons says you're obsessive."

"I become obsessive with everything I like." He caressed her cheek with the knuckle of his forefinger.

Later, as they drove into the underground garage she said: "What happened last night... It was really nice but I don't want you to think you're getting cornered."

"Am I getting cornered?"

"Of course. But I don't want you to think you are."

"Fair enough." They walked to the elevator and he rubbed his whiskers. "Got to shave. I don't want to take all your time but I have to go to work. If you want to come over to Integrated Electronics, you might be able to do your story and then afterwards we could have some lunch and then come back here and make love."

"You putting pressure on me?"

"Yes. I just don't want you to feel like I am."

He rubbed his chin thoughtfully. She rubbed hers. "Think we both need a shave?" she asked.

"Huh?"

"Oh, I didn't tell you I shaved. Do it every morning. See what you find out when you really get to know a person?"

He brushed her cheek with his lips as she got off the elevator. "Soft as a baby's backside."

"How many babies tushes have you kissed?"

"Like you said, we're discovering a world of information about each other. See you at the Bentley in half an hour."

"Just call it a car, OK?"

"OK."

"Make it thirty minutes."

Before he could reply, the elevator door opened and she hurried away.

An hour later, she was squinting through a microscope in his lab at Integrated. She frowned. "OK. Explain it to me again."

"Sure. You understand what a

computer is. Well, this system . . ."

"No."

"No what?"

"I don't understand what a computer is."

"OK. In its simplest form, it's a device that says 'yes' or 'no' very quickly. Suppose, for example, you wanted to go from Los Angeles to Montreal by car. You'd get your car and drive. On the way you'd have maybe one hundred intersections. You could go to the right or left. Each time you make a turn you're saying 'yes' or 'no' to a choice. Our mind therefore is simply a complex computer . . ."

"OK . . ."

"Suppose, I decided that I wanted to go to New Orleans instead of Montreal. More choices and intersections. More decisions."

"Got it."

"Suppose I don't take the trips. Suppose I ask the computer which city of all the cities in the world has the fewest number of intersections. Bingo. The computer tells me. Almost instantly, because it's capable of making all those no-yes choices so fast. A human being can do the same thing. But because of the computer's ability to calculate so quickly it's much faster."

"You make it sound very simple."

"It is simple. In the old days the switches that said 'yes' or 'no' were called vacuum tube triodes. They were large; they used a lot of energy and they burnt out."

"Then came the transistor?"

"Correct. Smaller, more efficient, used less energy. But still problems. You had to paste a bunch of transistors on a circuit board. Then you had to connect all the transistors together. Things kept breaking or overheating. A guy from Texas Instruments, Jack Kilby, came up with a crazy idea."

"An abacus?"

"Not quite. The transistors were made of crystals of silicon. Kilby hit upon a brilliant concept—use the crystal itself as its own circuit board. It was called an integrated circuit."

"Or a chip."

"Right."

"And that's what you're working on?"

"Yes. Except that I don't use silicon to make the chip. I'm trying to find out a way to use molecules."

"What kind of molecules?"

"I'm thinking of DNA. That way they could duplicate themselves."

"Is it possible?"

"Well, I think so."

"How would you hook the molecule up to the rest of the computer?"

"I don't know. But the DNA in our body certainly interacts with our brain."

She returned to the microscope. "Why am I looking at hemoglobin?"

"Because it is always in one of two

states. 'A'—it binds with oxygen atoms. 'B'—it does not bind with oxygen."

"An on-off switch."

"Yep, and we've got millions of 'em in our bloodstream . . ."

"Sure, sure, sure," rasped a voice. "Off the shelf molecules. Sounds pretty off the wall to me." Dr. Donald Beechman stood in the doorway. He was a beanstalk of a man whose thick metal glasses looked heavy enough to mess up his center of gravity. He was bald and attired in western jeans and shirt. He wore a braided rope tie held in place with a magnificent silver eagle. His hands seemed too large for his body; his feet, stuffed in lizard skin boots, too small. He had the look of a pogo stick that had been inverted.

"You got my message," said Cursore.

"I did indeed. Indeed I did." He smiled at the woman. "And you must be Jasper, the reporter. I say, you are an exceptionally beautiful woman. You don't mind me saying that, do you?"

"I don't mind. Cursore said to watch out for you, said you were full of it. Also said you could grow a garden on a ball bearing."

"He's wrong. I don't need a ball bearing. Just a picture of one. Now I'm taking the pair of you out for some decent grub. Right across the street . . ."

By one p.m., seated in an open patio, they had finished off their burritos and tacos and chile rellenos. Donald Beechman had regaled them with his reports on hydroponics and intensive gardening methods that he was conducting for the UCLA agricultural department.

"You really like your work, don't you?" asked Jasper.

"I do. You don't have any friends that look like you who want to interview me, do you?"

"Sure."

"Told you to watch old Beechman. He moves pretty fast."

"Cursore, I've lots of friends that would love to meet a man who's going to solve the world's food shortages," said Jasper.

"Speaking about solving things." Beechman tossed a three-by-five card on the wooden table as the waitress cleared their dishes. Taped to the card was the wheat-colored pieces of grass that Jasper had found on the rug of the rented Mustang.

"What kind of plant is it?" asked Cursore.

"What color is it?" replied Beechman. He turned his attention on Jasper. "You really have some friends who look like you?"

"Yes. It's yellow."

"Or?"

"Gold," said Cursore.

"Trouble with you computer guys is you get all the good looking women and you don't deserve it. You're not going to be happy until you blow up the world with your trajectory systems and fail-safe systems. What's another color?"

"Wheat," said Jasper.

"At last. Not only good looking but I bet you're a tiger at Scrabble."

"I don't get it," said Cursore. "What has the color shade got to . . ."

"It's a *stalk of wheat*. A grain?" Jasper's eyes sparkled in the sunlight. "That right?"

"Yep," said Beechman. "Except this is a very special wheat. I don't know where you got it from but I'd say either the desert or the beach—this stuff is a hybrid. It's actual name is Sea-Wheat. It'll grow in sandy soil that's been irrigated with salt water. Interesting, huh? Almost nothing will grow in salt water in the grain family. This Sea-Wheat is high in proteins, high in carbohydrates."

"I'm going to get you a date with the entire Radio City Music Hall chorus line," said Jasper. "How do you know so much about this stuff?"

"Because one of my students has been experimenting with it. Has a whole backyard planted with the stuff."

"Does he live at Malibu?" asked Cursore.

"Did I tell you about him?"

"No."

"How'd you know then?"

"Good guess. Is there any more of this kind of wheat planted anywhere that you know of?"

"No, don't think so . . . Leifur would know. He keeps track of it. I would have brought him with me today but unfortunately he had to attend his grandfather's funeral. Leifur's only twenty four—lost his parents six years ago. Now his grandfather. Doesn't have anyone . . ."

"I'm sorry," said Jasper.

"His grandfather wasn't much older than me. Apparently he took his life. Jumped in front of a bus or something on Pacific Coast Highway. Why are you so interested in this Sea-Wheat?"

"I don't know if any of it will make sense . . . I'll tell you after we talk to this Leifur. Can you give us his address?"

"One step ahead of you. Here." Beechman picked a folded sheet out of his pocket and gave it to Cursore. "Full name, address, and phone number both at home and at UCLA. Your turn to pay."

"Pleasure," said Cursore, grabbing the bill and taking Jasper by the hand.

Beechman finished his coffee. "Hey," he yelled after them, "don't forget my Radio City Music Hall date."

After they had gone, Donald ordered another cup of coffee. The waitress was pleasant, plump and attentive. "Say," said Beechman, "you don't know me but I'm working on solving the world's hunger problems. Would you be interested in trying a new variety of grapefruit with me?"

"Maybe. How's it new?"

"New kind of fertilizer."

"Oh. What kind?"

"Human."

"I think I'll pass," she said. She finished clearing the dishes from the next table and carried them through the main part of the indoor dining room.

At the back of the room, the Russian sat. He had been watching Cursore, Jasper and Beechman. He had heard snatches of their conversation—something about Malibu and an old man's death. How, wondered the Russian, did the computer expert and the reporter discover a link to the Malibu death so quickly? He could not recall leaving anything in the rented car that would connect him to Malibu. A parking ticket perhaps? No. Why then had the three been talking about the old man's death?

For amatuers they were getting close and they were very lucky. The Russian knew he had covered his tracks carefully—no way to associate him with the rental car. Unless someone had seen him in it. That was paranoid. No one had seen him in it. No one.

The Russian was about to bite into his taco when his hand stopped in midair. A man was walking across the street. He was about sixty, in good shape, well dressed. The man moved with a casual but confident demeanor.

The waitress freshened the Russian's coffee. "Who's that man in the pin stripe suit, out on the patio?" he asked.

"Him. Oh, that's Mr. Tallons. Runs Integrated Electronics. A lot of their executives eat over here at lunch. We've got a real great patio, the best around here. That enough coffee?"

"Yes."

"You a friend of Mr. Tallons?"

"No. I thought he was someone else. I don't have my glasses with me but I can see he's not the person I thought he was."

"OK. There's space to sit out on the patio if you want."

"I'm fine here," said the Russian.

"OK. Whistle if you want anything else. Got great pie for dessert." She returned to the kitchen.

The Russian was aware that his hand was shaking. There was a glass partition between the main dining room and the patio. The sun sparkled against the glass and the Russian was certain that no one outside could see into the main dining room, certainly not in the darker section where he sat. His hand stopped trembling and he set the cup down on its saucer.

16

Five miles north of Pepperdine College, Pacific Coast Highway juts into the Pacific. Point Dume. Thirty people in the funeral party stood on the most northern bluff, watching a single-engine Piper Cub drone across the perse sky, about a mile offshore. The plane slowly dipped toward the ocean, then banked and headed back to the Santa Monica Airport.

Leifur Thaker stared at the spot the plane had turned. He imagined the ashes of his grandfather settling upon the waves. He imagined the waves folding over them. He imagined the ashes sinking, tumbling to the ocean bed. *Go in Peace, Grandfather. Love you.* The ashes would mix with sand; something would grow from the sand. The process of life would begin anew. *At least I sure hope so.*

Everyone walked back to the black limos waiting along the highway. "Excuse me."

"Yes," Leifur said to the redhead.

"I'm Jasper Garner and this is David

Cursore. May we talk to you about your grandfather?"

"Were you a friend of his?"

"Professor Beechman sent us."

"Oh."

"Donald has been one of my best friends for twenty years," Cursore said. "We didn't know your grandfather but we really need to talk with you."

"You know where our place is?"

"Yes."

"I could meet you back there."

Leifur had lived in the beach house with his grandfather, and judging by the terraced gardens and hundreds of neatly arranged potted plants in the back yard, the pair had devoted incredible time to looking after the place. Cursore and Jasper sat beside a potted palm tree while Leifur brought a pitcher of cold lemonade out through the back door.

"We more or less lived here. Just the two of us over the last six years."

"Donald said your grandfather cared deeply about the ocean," said Jasper.

"Taught me everything about it. I suppose that's why I got into marine biology."

"It's a fascinating field. I think the solution to the world's hunger problems is the sea." Cursore sipped his lemonade and watched the breeze ruffle a small patch of yellow-colored grain. It was the kind of wheat that Jasper had found on the floor mat of the Mustang.

"Gramps always said that it took about the same time to do something the right way as it did the wrong way. That's the way he lived. And if he had chosen to kill himself, he never would have made such a mess of himself. Never."

"We don't think he killed himself, either," said Jasper.

"Why do you say that?" asked the young man. He leaned forward.

"According to your neighbors, your grandfather was a feisty old codger, got a bang out of life. People like that don't take their lives—unless of course they have some kind of terrible illness or financial problem . . ." said Cursore.

"Gramps had nothing wrong with him. We had enough money to get by, as much as we've ever had."

"We thought so," Cursore picked one of the stalks of sea wheat and smelled it. "So if your grandfather didn't take his life—there's a couple of obvious possibilities. The first is—he tripped accidentally and fell into the path of traffic. Second—he was killed."

"I've told the police someone must have killed him. They said they're investigating . . ."

"Cursore," interrupted Jasper. "Leifur has gone through so much . . ."

"It's OK. I want to talk about it. I'll tell you why Gramps didn't accidentally fall into traffic. He hated that Highway. Despised cars. He told me he was going to bed early the night he got killed. Had a touch of the flu. Said he was getting it from the fumes from the highway. No way Gramps would have walked over that knoll in the middle of the night. No way. Do you know something about his death? Because if you do, I want to know."

"It's only a theory." Cursore took the three-by-five card with the wheat taped to it and handed it to the young botanist.

"This is sea wheat. Where'd you get it?"

"A friend of ours disappeared. We think she was kidnapped, or something worse. Her car had about sixty miles on it that we can't account for. That's the distance between our place and here. We found that new strain of wheat on the floor mat of her car."

"Really?"

Cursore nodded.

"The only place that has this wheat is right here," said Leifur. "Oh, there's a couple of pots of the stuff over by UCLA. But it's not as mature as the sample on this card."

"Then the kidnapper must have come here," said Cursore.

"Gramps would not have let him in. We get a lot of crazies around the beach. Especially after dark. He doesn't open up for anyone he doesn't know."

"Maybe your grandfather knew him," said Jasper.

"Maybe."

"Maybe," she said, "some of that wheat could have blown over the fence and it's growing wild."

"I don't think so," said Leifur. "This is a controlled study."

"You're reaching," said Cursore.

"I saw something that looked like it in the alley when we drove up."

A few minutes later, the three were kneeling in the alleyway behind the beach house.

"You're right," said Leifur. "So much for the controlled experiment."

"Do you think there could be any more of this wheat around?" asked Cursore.

"No. At least not more than a few hundred yards from our beach house. I'm going to call the police back."

"We can't get them to take our friend's disappearance seriously at all . . ." said Cursore.

"I've got a couple of friends in the Malibu Sheriff's station—I'll tell 'em. Can I keep that card with this sea wheat on it?"

"Sure."

"Maybe we should ask the neighbors along here if they saw anything Sunday night," said Jasper.

"I've already done it. No one knows anything," said the young man.

"Maybe someone was parking. Maybe there was a hitchhiker. Maybe a delivery."

"I'll keep asking. I've known all along that someone killed my grandfather."

"But there's something else," said Jasper.

"What?"

"Dusty—that's our friend—disappeared Saturday. They found her car Sunday afternoon. As Cursore said it had gone about sixty miles."

"So, why then would her kidnapper return here Sunday night and kill my grandfather?"

"Maybe she's being held in this area and the kidnapper came back to see her," said Cursore.

"No, there's only four other beach houses along this road. I've known the people who live in them for fifteen years. There is absolutely no way that any of those people would let their houses be used to kidnap anyone."

"Maybe we should check them anyway," said Jasper.

"I'll do it."

"This is becoming more confusing by the minute," said Cursore.

"Maybe your grandfather saw something," said Jasper.

"If Gramps had, he would have told me and called the police. We wouldn't have kept quiet. I know he would have told me —and we had plenty of time to talk. We spent all Sunday afternoon together, and he didn't mention a thing about anybody bringing a woman around here. Or around anywhere."

"It could be more than one kidnapper," said Jasper.

"Unrelated," said Cursore. "Somebody kidnaps Dusty and then someone totally different does that to your grandfather."

"Yes. Over the weekend a dozen people lose their lives unexpectedly in Los Angeles. Nothing says any of those deaths are connected." Jasper held her drink in her hand, swirling the liquid around in it.

"She's right," said Leifur.

"But the wheat . . ." said Cursore. "I guess all that could mean was a kidnapper happened to be in the vicinity where someone was murdered. Nothing says they have to be connected."

"Since they happened out of sequence, maybe they're not. On the other hand, I have this feeling—and I don't know why—that they are connected," said Jasper.

"Leifur, I'm sorry that we have to lay this trip on you in the middle of everything," said Cursore. "What you're going through is awfully painful. I was very close to my grandfather and when he passed away, well . . . I still think of him every day and that was four years ago."

"It's OK. Look, I'll keep asking around. I appreciate your coming out here. We'll keep in touch. OK? I'd like to be alone now. OK?"

As Cursore and Jasper drove back to the city, a light rain began to fall. The evening was going to be dismal. The ocean was turning a sad dull pearl hue. Gulls skimmed the water, squawking in annoyance.

"For the record I think you're terrific. You really care about people," said Jasper.

"Thanks. I wish we'd come up with something solid."

"If anyone can find her, you can."

"You're not such a bad detective yourself. Guess you pick that up from being a reporter."

"I work mostly on intuition."

"Really?"

"Sure. For example, you know more than you're letting on."

"I do?"

"Yes. I think you've discovered something about Dusty that you haven't told me about."

"Maybe."

"Tell me. Please."

"The day she disappeared she took over $5,000.00 out of her checking account in cash."

"Oh. You been peeking in computer networks?"

"Yes."

"Thanks for tellilng me." Jasper

leaned across the seat and kissed him softly, the tips of her fingers touched the inside of his thigh.

"You keeping any secrets from me?" he asked.

"One."

"What?"

"I work for the parole board."

"Can we make love once more before you toss me back in the slammer?"

"I'll make you a deal. If your performance is up to last night, your secret's safe."

"OK."

She cuddled up beside him as the rain increased in tempo. Westward, near Point Dume, an icy flash of lightning sliced the dark sky in jagged halves but they were too far away to hear any thunder.

"It's horrible of me to say this," she said, "but I'm jealous of Dusty. I don't know if I want you to find her. Isn't that horrible?"

"No."

17

The Russian parked near a playground in Pacific Palisades. His cassette was playing tape recordings of children's nursery rhymes. When Little Bo Peep ended, he killed the ignition and stepped out of his car, slipping on a light trench coat. He could see the rain slashing around the street lights that glowed in the hazy night air, heavy with moisture.

He walked into a drugstore and made several purchases of the same item. He repeated this same transaction at five other drugstores in various sections of the West Los Angeles area.

It was 10:30 when Jon Andrews arrived at the Brentwood Bar. He wanted to order a shot of vodka but settled for a glass of soda water and wine. He was aware of the sounds of the bar—talking, laughing, giggling, rain falling against the stained glass window, the bartender hustling about checking drinks, trading quips with the regulars.

At the back of the bar was a lady in a red skirt and white blouse, late forties. She set her drink down, careful not to spill it, and tossed a dart. She missed the dartboard by several feet. Jon saw that she was wearing an expensive pearl necklace and matching earrings. He needed a final *safety*—not so much for money. For a final test. His Master Plan. Master Project.

A few minutes later they were playing darts with each other.

"How long you going to stay in L.A.?" he asked.

"Until the tour ship leaves. You ever been to Greece?"

"It's wonderful. Nothing like the Adriatic Sea. I'll give you some names of my cousins there. They'll love you."

"Why?"

"You have that fierce independent look, but also the soul of a woman who likes to treat a man like a man."

"Why don't you take the tour with me?"

"Give anything to leave this smoggy city. But my clients would have my head on a stick," he said, pleased with the way he was incorporating American idioms into his speech.

"Why?" she asked *why* a lot. Booze was transforming her into a boring conversationalist of monosyllables.

"Because they have too much money to invest and people with too much money are only happy when you make too much money for them—and you can never do that."

"You're a counselor?"

"Investment banker, and if I were good at it, I would be retired."

"Saw your Jaguar. You can't be doing that badly."

"Not that badly," he agreed. "May I get you another drink?"

"Yeah."

After three more drinks they headed for her hotel. The rain had stopped, leaving the sidewalks shimmering beneath mercury vapor lights. They laughed at their glistening reflections in the wet plate glass windows. When they went through the lobby he was careful to turn his head away from the desk clerk. It didn't take long to discover the woman's background. Her name was Andria Bevan and she had just divorced her husband in Idaho. He had owned two potato ranches; after the divorce they each were awarded one. Andria was ready for adventure and romance as she collapsed on her queen-sized bed, fumbling open the buttons on her blouse. Five minutes later she was naked, securely bound and gagged with one-inch surgical tape. Andria had dull black eyes under smudged black slashes of eyebrow pencil. The black eyes, puffy with fear, followed Jon's every motion.

Jon removed rubber gloves from the man's purse she had teased him about earlier. He moved about the hotel room with an economy of motion, quickly ransacking the dresser, her two purses and three cases. He discovered a passport, bank books, and several pamphlets on the cruise ship. There were three books on how to win at blackjack.

He went into the bathroom and ripped her cosmetic bag apart, quickly sorted through tubes of lipstick and bottles of exotic creams. He turned the cold water on full blast.

"I'm going to take the tape off your mouth. No one can hear you with the water running. If you yell or scream, I'll knock you out. Understand?"

She urgently nodded her head.

He jerked the tape from her mouth. "Please don't hurt me," she whispered. "You can take anything you want. Don't hurt me." The earlier slur in her voice was gone.

"Where's the rest of your money?"

Her eyes flickered to the dresser where he had assembled the cash from her purse and suitcase. "You've got over five hundred dollars—take it. All there is."

"Look, you just got divorced. You're going on a cruise. You circled the information about casinos on the travel brochure. You don't have any travelers' checks with you. You've got three books on outsmarting blackjack dealers. You need a lot more than five hundred bucks to do that. Where is it?"

"If I tell you will you let me go?"

"Yes."

"It's in that wide black belt around my blue dress in the closet."

Jon unbuckled the belt and turned it over. He unzipped a hidden pocket that ran the length of the belt. It was filled with closely packed hundred dollar bills. There was seventy of them. Seventy times a hundred, thought Jon, that would be a thousand dollars, no—twelve hundred dollars. No, two hundred thousand. He cursed in Ukrainian. The months he had spent in the Chinese pit had done that to him. He laughed. He had confused himself so well when he had been captive that he was now unable to figure out a grade school mathematical problem. "How much money is here?"

"Seven thousand dollars. It's all yours. Just let me go."

He took the money into the bathroom and folded it into a neat bundle and stuffed it into his brown purse. The bag contained a "travel" canister of Kaam along with it applicator. The applicator was made of transparent plastic four inches long, half an inch in diameter. It was hollow with a small hole in its end. Jon checked to make certain that his rubber gloves were secure, then pressed the tip of the applicator against the canister's top. The downward force on the canister opened a small valve, and birth control foam began to fill the applicator. When it was half filled, Jon stopped and took a small blue bottle from his purse. He unscrewed an eyedropper from it and squirted three drops of white liquid into the applicator. He screwed the eyedropper back into the blue bottle and finished filling the applicator with foam. He held his thumb, covered with a rubber glove, over the hole in the curved tip of the applicator. If he had not done this, the foam, under pressure, would have flowed out. At the other end of the applicator was a plunger. By pressing it, it was possible to evacuate the foam from the applicator in a few seconds.

He walked back to the bedroom.

"What are you going to do?" Then she recognized the familiar applicator with its transparent green plunger.

Although she was a *safety* he did not want to kill her because he was thinking of the black nurse he had met.

"Look," she said. "If you want me, you don't have to go through all that."

He said nothing. He kept thinking of the black nurse from UCLA.

"My husband divorced me because I couldn't have children. Took up with some goddamn waitress from Pocatello because she was fertile..."

"I'm sorry that I have to do this."

"What? Give me a shot of Kaam? You believe those stories about some kind of

Spanish fly in it? Shit. Just do what you have to do."

She did not understand.

The next morning, the housekeeper discovered the body. She followed procedure and called the house detective. His name was Jorge Gondel, a retired L.A. homicide cop who had experienced nearly all the gore that life held—but when he pulled the sheet back from the corpse in room 924, he ran into the bathroom to throw up. The central area of the body was crimson with blood, and every orifice of the corpse was caked with dried blood.

An hour later four L.A. policemen and an assistant medical examiner, Dr. Jane Florence, crowded into room 924. Dr. Florence was a pathologist who had devoted her life to medicine, loved wok cooking, and was helplessly addicted to The New York Times daily crossword puzzles. She was not beautiful, but because of her charm and compassion, most people were unaware of her elongated face with its crooked teeth and her broken nose that had never been set properly. "How long since anyone saw her alive?" asked Dr. Florence.

"Night clerk saw her come in around ten or ten-thirty last night. She was with a guy—no one paid any attention to him," said Gondel. "I've never seen so much blood. He must have ripped her up bad."

"We'll see," said Dr. Florence. After the I-dent squad finished, the doctor completed her primary examination. "No abrasions of any kind. No sign of any entrance wound. Hmm, what's this? See white flecks on the wrists? Looks like they may have been bound with adhesive tape. Ankles are the same. Look—black and blue. Yeah . . . I'd say someone tied this lady up. New kind of room service, Jorge?"

"I don't know how you can ignore all that blood."

"I'm not ignoring it. But she's dead—and the only way we're going to help her now is to find out what happened. Let's get her back to the office."

"How come she bled so much?"

"We'll find out."

Jorge Gondel nodded, then dropped to one knee and looked under the bed. He reached under the faded hem of the bedspread and picked up a plastic Visa charge card. He was careful to hold the charge card by the edges.

"You might make a detective someday," said Dr. Florence. "What have you got there?"

"Charge card. Belongs to someone named David Cursore."

18

Jasper kept her eyes closed. She could feel the bed jiggle as Cursore got up, she heard him open the door, heard him talking softly, felt Cursore sit on the bed, was aware of the breakfast tray he placed across her tummy. She smelled the marvelous aroma of lemon-filled croissants and hot chocolate. "Hi," she said and opened her eyes.

Cursore kissed her softly on her nose. "Hi, yourself."

They were back in the same hotel room that they had spent the previous night in. "We're kind of becoming regulars around here, aren't we?"

"Yeah, they'll be calling us the croissant sinners." He offered her a bite, but an instant before she bit down, he pulled the croissant away.

She realized how happy she felt. "Don't be so naughty."

"That's not what you said last night."

Outside the day was picture postcard perfect. Already glistening surfers in wet suits were bobbing past the breakers. A pair of windsurfers skimmed across the sea.

Cursore and Jasper took their breakfast out on the balcony. She thought everything tasted better than the previous day. "I'm frightened."

"Of what?"

"This relationship is getting better."

"Wait until tomorrow—today'll look like a downer."

"Promise?"

He reached across the small table and held her hand softly.

She considered his hand—for a man who worked indoors, his hand was muscular and calloused. It was wrong and unfair that he was on parole. The system stank. Mary Lou was right. Cursore might know how to penetrate a computer network but there was no way he was going to defraud anyone. A small red warning light flashed in the back of Jasper's mind—*where there's smoke, there's fire.* Cursore certainly knew his way around computers, and a lot of money had disappeared, and supposedly some of it, according to the newspaper reports she had read, had turned up in his account. Tough to explain. Tougher still to justify. Why the hell did she have to fall for a guy who was a felon? Fall? Am I falling for him? I better get out of this before . . . .

"What are you daydreaming about?" he asked, shattering her thoughts.

"Since we've come to a blind alley and since the police are going to be of very little value at this point, maybe you could trace Dusty by her credit cards." Why am I testing him, she asked herself.

"I was thinking the same thing," he said.

"But on the other hand, it's pretty risky, isn't it?" Is he going to break the law again? But it's OK—he's helping someone. I'm sure it's OK.

"That ocean is beautiful, isn't it? Someday I'd like to build an ocean-going sailboat and head for the South Seas."

"You need a crew, Captain?" Why couldn't we run away? God . . . I wish we could.

"Captain. That's a step up from sailor."

"You get an ocean-going sailboat— I'll call you Captain all the time, sailor." I want to run away with you, she thought. Damn. Why can't we?

When they arrived at Mary Lou's she was pruning her bonsai elm. "I see you two have fallen in love or lust or something," she said, lighting up a Virginia Slim. "I waited for you to call from Malibu."

"Dead end. You heard anything?" asked Cursore.

"No. There's some cold chicken in the fridge if you want it."

"We had a late breakfast. You mind if

we look through Dusty's luggage again?"

"Here's what you came for," said Mary Lou. She got up from her knees beside her plant and walked across the room, favoring her right leg. "Damn rheumatism—let me give you both some advice—never get old. Pain in the neck. And other places." She opened a drawer and took out a small candy box.

Cursore opened the box that contained half a dozen sales slips, and receipts from Visa, Master Charge and American Express. "How'd you know?" he asked.

Mary Lou rolled her eyes. "I know you better than anyone in the world, don't I?"

"Yeah, you do. Sorry we didn't call last night . . ."

"I know how it is when you're in heat."

"Don't be so crude," said Cursore.

"Gimme a break. At my age crudeness is the only vice I have left. Except these goddamn cigarettes. I'm glad neither one of you smoke."

"Is there anything we can pick up for you, Mary Lou?" asked Jasper.

"Yeah. A clean old man. And if you can't find one of them, how about a dirty old man?"

"Are there any other kind?" asked Jasper.

An hour later, she and Cursore were seated behind a computer console at

Integrated Electronics. Cursore concentrated on figures and numbers flashing across the video screen in front of them. She watched him. "Aren't you afraid that you're going to alert Tallons again?"

He stared at a small rectangle of light as it skipped across the video screen. "You see that?" he asked.

"The little rectangle of light?"

"Yes."

"Know what it is?"

"A cursor—comes from the Latin word for runner."

"You're pretty smart."

"I'm a journalist, dumb-dumb. Words are my hobby."

"I'll remember that next time I'm doing a crossword puzzle." He tapped various letters and numbers on the keyboard and the cursor skipped around the screen. Suddenly a series of words disappeared and he quickly tapped in new instructions. "You see, Tallons has given our computer an instruction to report any unauthorized use of the Alpha codes. I just slipped in an extra command so that I can use the codes without setting off warning lights."

"And what are Alpha codes?"

"You're the wordsmith."

"Don't be a smart ass, sailor."

"The Alpha codes are keys to access a variety of bank computer networks. Now let's check her Visa number." Cursore quickly entered her Visa card number into the computer and an instant later the video screen displayed the following:

FLORIDA STATE BANK VISA PAYMENT

Sept. 11 Coral Gbls Mobil..................................23.29

Sept. 11 Coral Gbls Leather Goods of Fla.......78.00

Sept. 11 Coral Gbls Palm Drugs.......................43.12

Sept. 11 Coral Gbls Palm Drugs..........................4.99

Sept. 11 Coral Gbls Florida Travel..................345.99

Sept. 11 Coral Gbls Flowers By Mail................45.99

Sept. 11 Coral Gbls Beach Restaurant..............9.56

Sept. 11 Coral Gbls The Keys Bookstore.........46.32

"She bought a lot of stuff before she flew here," said Cursore.

"I wonder why she'd buy flowers. Almost fifty dollars worth?" asked Jasper.

"Wedding? Funeral? Look, it's by telex. We can pull that," said Cursore. A moment later he had the Flowers By Mail account. He tapped several more keys and the following appeared on the display screen:

Sept. 12 Acct. 4412 546 888 000

Flowers By Mail/Telex Ft. Worth Flowers Inc. Delivery to Debbie Bleudell

Sept. 12/82 Ft. Worth, TX ph 817 555 2435
Send one dozen red roses, card to read
Welcome to grad school/love D.

Cursore pressed a button and the information on the screen was transferred to a typewriter that suddenly came alive, banging out the information at five hundred words per minute on an Olivetti hard printer.

"I'll be damned," said Jasper. "Let's call her up . . ."

"Hold on. Let's see what else I can pull up for us."

Methodically Cursore hunted through various computer networks and within an hour had assembled a dozen pages of background on Dusty. Where she shopped. What kind of restaurants she ate in. Theatre tickerts she had purchased with the name of the plays. She'd seen "Mornings at Eight" in a dinner theatre in Fort Lauderdale. She'd bought a sweater there, too.

Jasper was fascinated by the process. "There's no privacy anymore is there?"

In answer, Cursore pulled his Visa card charges from the computer. A moment later the display showed his debit for one night at the hotel where they had made love.

"What happened to last night? We fool the computer?" asked Jasper.

"Unless you have the new instant touch tone entry system, it takes about thirty-six hours to post anything. Either way it's bad news for Dusty."

"Why?"

"Because she hasn't charged anything since she went AWOL Saturday night. She's made no deposits to her bank accounts. According to her charge cards she's ceased to exist."

"Let's call her relative in Texas."

"There's a WATTS line," said Cursore, indicating a blue phone.

A few moments later, Jasper got through. A female voice said "Hi."

"Hi," said Jasper, "this is a friend of Dusty's in California."

"Oh, Mary Lou?" asked Debbie.

"No. I'm a friend of Mary Lou's . . . she's kind of worried about Dusty."

"What happened?"

"We don't know. She was here until the weekend and then she just left. We thought you might have heard from her."

"What'd you say your name was? Jasper?"

"Yes." Jasper sensed the fear in Debbie's voice.

"I don't want to upset you but . . ."

"I'm concerned. See, Dusty wired me a dozen flowers when I was accepted to grad school. I tried to call her but we've ended up talking to each other's answering service."

"When did she call last?"

"Let's see. Today is Tuesday, isn't it? I guess she called Friday night. She left a message that she'd call back Saturday or Sunday."

"Has she ever just taken off?"

"No," said Debbie. "What do you mean she just left? She was planning on staying with Mary Lou for at least a week."

"We thought so, too. Before Mary Lou could return from Hawaii, your sister just left. She had a date with a friend of Mary Lou's named Cursore . . ."

"The ex-con?"

"Uh, yes. Your sister knew about that?"

"Sure. She said if Mary Lou recommended the guy, she'd give it a try. My God, he didn't do anything with her, did he? I'm not prejudiced, but I wouldn't go out with someone on parole."

"They never went out together . . ."

"Oh. Dusty was pretty excited about buying some California art. Maybe she discovered some new artist. She's a bit impetuous."

"Do you think she would have abandoned her car?"

"She did *that*?"

"Yes."

"There's something going on. I'm going to try and reach her at a couple of numbers I have, then I'll call you back. OK?"

Jasper gave Debbie her and Mary Lou's numbers.

"When will Mary Lou be back from

Hawaii?"

"She's back. She was a little concerned..."

"I'm more than a little concerned."

"We're hoping it's nothing serious. But I'll be at Mary Lou's for dinner tonight if you want to call there."

"Thanks, I really appreciate what you're doing."

They said goodbye and hung up. Cursore, who had been listening on an extension, set his receiver back on its cradle.

"I didn't think Mary Lou would tell a stranger I was a con."

"Don't be so sensitive. Besides, what's the point in lining you up with a woman if she turns out to be queasy about your background?"

"I really feel that Mary Lou talks too much, you know."

"Stop it! If I know Mary Lou she raved about what a great guy you were and probably insisted you'd been framed. And Dusty probably thought you were great when she met you and didn't care you had a record."

"I don't know."

"Did she act uptight?"

"No."

"See? That means there was no reason for her to run because she found out about you. I'm beginning to think you're right. Something happened to her."

They continued to hunt through Visa, Master Charge and American Express charge records until almost five, then they went to Mary Lou's for dinner.

Mary Lou had prepared her specialty —Yorkshire pudding and roast beef. This was followed by steaming apple pie with mounds of vanilla Haagen-Dazs ice cream and freshly ground mocha coffee.

"You want some more apple pie?" she asked, clearing the salad plates.

"Couldn't eat another bite. That was the best meal I've had in my life," said Cursore.

"Me, too," said Jasper.

Mary Lou took a long drag of her cigarette, coughed nonstop for thirty seconds and said, "Cursore . . . you forgive me?"

"For what?"

"For telling Dusty you were in jail?"

Cursore glanced questioningly toward Jasper.

Mary Lou grabbed some water and quenched her cough. "Jasper didn't tell me anything. While I was making dinner for you, Dusty's sister called me a couple of times. She told me about your phone call. You get her name out of the computer?"

"Yes," said Cursore.

"You didn't answer the question . . . mad at me?"

"No, it doesn't matter."

"That's good because I don't want you starting to pout." Mary Lou took another drag, then grabbed some water and washed down the smoke before she could begin to cough.

"I don't pout all that much." He seemed rather sheepish. "I'm sorry I left here a bit annoyed the other day."

"A bit annoyed? Jasper, would you say he was a bit more than a bit annoyed?"

Jasper nodded.

"Will you two females stop trying to make me feel guilty? What'd you tell Dusty's sister?"

"That we were concerned. That Dusty even left her suitcases and clothing here."

"From the way Debbie talked I got the impression Dusty is pretty dependable," said Jasper.

Outside, another crystal clear night folded over the harbor. Mary Lou glanced out through her patio door. "The world seems so calm, just like the harbor out there. Warm and loving and happy. But it's not that way. There's some very sick people out there. Remember that Tylenol thing. My God, how could any human being pull off something like that? And that crazy they caught putting acid in eyedrops? We have to face it—there's a lot of kooks out there. I'm lucky—I've made it way past my three score and ten, but I feel sorry for you kids—and your children. I really do."

"How come you're so optimistic?" asked Cursore.

"I don't know. Look at what's happened to you? I bet there's not a dozen people in the world that would give you the benefit of the doubt as far as your so-called criminal record is concerned."

"At least I was never bitter about it," said Cursore.

"You weren't, huh?" Mary Lou started to laugh. "You tramped around this apartment like a jackass with a toothache until Tallons gave you a job."

"I was that bad? Really?"

"Yeah. Worse," said Mary Lou. "What are we going to do about Dusty?"

"We could put up posters," said Jasper. "I could get some radio and tv time."

"I don't want to be grim," said Mary Lou, "but I hope that girl is staggering around the city with amnesia. Problem is —amnesia only happens in the movies. If she doesn't have amnesia . . . I'd hate to think what's happened to her."

"It may not be that serious," said Jasper.

"Really?" asked the older woman. "She used any of her credit cards?"

Cursore shook his head.

"I didn't figure so, or you would have told me."

"So there's a crazy running around," said Jasper. My God, she thought, this could be one helluva story. Then she felt terrible for thinking so negatively.

"I can't think of any other explanation," said the older lady, lighting a fresh Virginia Slim from a glowing butt. "I sensed there was some kind of a crazy in here—he stole my rubber gloves. That's why I changed my lock. You two ought to do the same thing."

"You're right," said Jasper. "The reason I suggested we put up posters is that I saw several around the neighborhood. A black girl disappeared a couple of nights ago. Did you see that poster?"

"While I was shopping for this grub, I think I did," replied Mary Lou. "A girl about twenty from Westwood?"

"That's it."

Mary Lou stubbed out her cigarette. "I'd call the police again but I've already pestered them twice. And you know what some clown in Missing Persons said— said they couldn't do anything until there's something substantial to go on or the victim was gone for at least a week. Do you realize what can happen to a person in a week? Hell—in half an hour? When I think of poor Dusty . . ."

"Maybe we're overreacting," said Cursore.

"We're not overreacting. We live like a bunch of goddamn criminals. You know how long it takes me to bar and lock this place up every night? Half the night. Do you know that every day nearly nineteen hundred children are reported missing in this country? There's nearly two million kids that no one can find. Every year two thousand children are buried without names in this so-called Land of the Free. My God—we live in total fear for our lives!"

"Easy, Mary Lou . . ."

"Cursore, something awful has happened. And there doesn't seem to be anything any of us can do." Mary Lou fought back the tears, then got to her feet and headed for her bedroom. "I'm going to sleep—will you two excuse me? Lock the door when you leave. I'm in overwhelm. I hate to be old and afraid." She left the room.

"Should I see if she's OK?" asked Jasper.

"No. I've seen her like this before. Like she says—she's old and frightened. She's terrified and the only way we're going to help her is to find out what's going on."

"I guess so . . ."

"Come on. Let's go to my place," said Cursore.

"OK. Should we do the dishes first?"

"Sure."

When they finished the dishes and put away the stemware, Jasper said, "But maybe we should stay here."

"She was pretty scared, wasn't she?"

"You don't mind?"

"It's OK. You want to get your nightgown?"

"Do you mind getting it?"

"Nope."

When he left Jasper knocked gently on Mary Lou's door. "Yes."

"It's Jasper. Can I come in?"

"If you want." Mary Lou unlocked her deadbolt.

Jasper opened the door. She found Mary Lou in bed. She was wearing red satin pajamas. There was a .38 caliber pistol on her bedside.

"We're going to sleep with you tonight."

"I guess there's room for all three of us in this bed," said Mary Lou.

"We'll be in the guest bedroom. That OK?"

"If you want to." Then she smiled. "That would be nice."

"We felt that if someone is running around . . . well . . . there was no sense leaving you alone."

"Thank you. You're a very thoughtful person."

Five minutes later, Cursore returned with Jasper's nightgown and her overnight case. He was also carrying an athletic case with a robe and toilet articles. They said goodnight to Mary Lou, then Cursore made certain that the door was bolted correctly and that all the windows were locked, including the patio door. He found a length of broom and jammed it between the patio door and the wall so it could not be forced open if someone somehow managed to gain access to the eighth story patio. Then he went into the guest bedroom.

Jasper was under the covers. Her nightgown was not.

He showered, then turned off the light and slipped into bed with her.

"Do you mind holding me tonight?" she asked.

"I don't mind."

"Is it OK if we make love twice tomorrow and kind of skip tonight?" she asked as he cradled her head in his arms and nuzzled her neck.

"Sure. Why?"

"You forgot to bring the magic foam."

"I thought you had some in your purse."

"I left my purse in your car."

"Thanks a lot." He kissed her neck gently, her body quivered and she could feel the energy pulse within her.

"Maybe it's still safe to make love. A woman is only really fertile about forty hours a month."

"Let's not risk it," he said. "I don't mind just holding you."

"Liar," she kissed him back.

And suddenly they were kissing each other hard.

Behind the fire door of the corridor on Jasper's level the Russian was watching her apartment. He had opened the door a quarter of an inch so that he had a clear view of her place. Because the staircase was concrete and filled with dead air and the Russian could easily hear the footsteps of anyone approaching, he felt reasonably safe. Jon Andrews had set a trap for the woman and the man who were hunting him. For the trap to work, the woman would have to return to her apartment to pick up something from her bedside table. It would only be a matter of time. And then she would be dead. At one a.m. the Russian decided that she was sleeping in the computer expert's penthouse. That would make more sense....

At 1:30, after ringing Cursore's buzzer and getting no answer, the Russian let himself into the penthouse. He was carrying a Luger with a silencer on it. The Russian moved stealthily to the master bedroom. He pointed his weapon at the bed but it didn't matter. No one was there.

Strange—they were out again. And then Jon Andrews realized that perhaps the computer expert and the reporter had slept together in her place—perhaps they had somehow entered her apartment without being seen. If that was the case, they would be dead.

Using his passkey the Russian checked Jasper's apartment. Empty.

Perhaps, thought the Russian, they are staying with the old woman. Why? For protection? Out of fear? The Russian took the elevator to Mary Lou's floor and walked to her door. He slipped his key into her lock. It had been changed. He cursed in Ukrainian. For the moment they were safe.

But when they slept in the reporter's apartment they would be dead.

And even if they slept someplace else, they would be dead soon. The Russian had planned the perfect murder—one that would leave no link to him. His teachers in Moscow would be proud of him.

19

Earlier Tuesday evening Dr. Jane Florence adjusted her designer glasses and leaned back in her chair and rubbed the high bridge of her nose. It had been one of those days that never seemed to end at the L.A. Coroner's Office. Two drownings, three suicides, assorted mayhem on the freeway. No homicides yet. At least not the ones that were obvious—the kind with blunt instruments, knives and assorted handguns.

Dr. Florence scanned the medical report in the brown folder for the second time. The victim was Andria Bevan. Nothing made sense with her death.

Dr. Florence's phone rang. She picked it up, slipped off her right brown pump and wiggled her toes. "Hello. This is Dr. Florence."

"This is Patrick Bevan. I got a call to call you. Is this a coroner's office?"

"Yes. Thank you for calling, Mr. Bevan. I'm afraid I have some bad news for you." She listened for the reaction—no gasp, no anger, just the static hum of the long distance connection to Idaho. "Do you have a wife in Los Angeles. Andria?"

"I guess she's there."

"Is she about forty seven years old?"

"Yeah, yeah. She dead?"

"I'm afraid so."

"We were divorced. I can't say that I'm sorry. You want me to arrange for a funeral? That why you're calling me?"

Dr. Jane Florence took her other shoe off, inspected the run in her nylon over her large toe. If the Bevans weren't divorced, they should have been, she thought. "Mr. Bevan, after the autopsy, we'll notify you."

"I'm not paying for no autopsy."

"You won't be required to. Could you tell me if your wife . . ."

"Ex-wife."

"Could you tell me if your ex-wife was taking any medication?"

"I don't know anything about it if she was. But she never did that I know of. She didn't even have periods so she never even took that Pamprin stuff anymore."

"Did she use drugs?"

"Wouldn't even take aspirins when she got headaches. Never really got 'em —gave 'em. Wouldn't drink hardly at all either."

They talked for a few more minutes then Dr. Florence called a colleague at the twenty-four-hour Rocky Mountain Poison Control Center, an advisory agency in Denver.

"This is Dr. Wainright," said a harried male.

"Hi. It's Jane in L.A."

"Florence Nightingale. Angel of Mercy. God bless you. When are we going to another seminar in Hawaii?"

"Soon I hope. Look, Zale, I've got a problem . . ."

"All ears. Hit me with it. I'm turning on the tape, so watch your language, kid."

She read the highlights of her preliminary report on Andria Bevan to Dr. Zale Wainright.

"Lot of hemorrhaging, huh?"

"Massive. From everywhere. Eyes, nose, ears, mouth, rectum, vagina."

"Anybody else succumb?"

"No."

"Anyone in the victim's vicinity?"

"She was in a hotel room—people on both sides, people probably walking in the corridor. She was with a man, according to the hotel detective."

"How long had she been dead when you discovered her?"

"Ten hours, give or take."

At that moment a lab technician knocked on her door and entered. The young man held a folder open and pointed to a readout of results from a series of tests.

"Christ," said Dr. Florence.

"What'd you say?" asked Dr. Wainright.

"Just got the lab results. You're not

going to like this, but one of the compounds we found in her bloodstream looks like Sarin."

"Sarin. As in nerve gas?"

"That's right. Same stuff the Germans concocted just before World War II."

"I thought it was a gas." She heard him thumbing through papers. "Yes," he said. "It's a gas and it's only a liquid below seventy degrass Fahrenheit."

"I know. But there's some other compound with it that maintains its liquid integrity. Haven't isolated it yet, but there is something in her bloodstream that has got to be one of the most effective anticoagulants I've ever seen."

"I know the military was unhappy with the toxicity of both Sarin and Tabun . . ."

"What do you mean? They kill you deader than a doornail in fifteen minutes."

"I know, Florence. But I've heard they've got some kind of super nerve gas, an offshoot of Sarin as the base, that'll finish anyone off in ninety seconds."

"God!"

"How was the substance introduced into her body?"

"Since it's stable as a liquid . . ."

"Lucky for you or you'd be dead," said Zale.

"Right. It was either injected or applied topically."

"Needle marks?"

"No, but we're still looking."

"Well, something that toxic would go through the skin, especially any of the mucous membrances, like you-know-what through a goose."

"Yeah." She slipped her shoes back on, stood up and rubbed her neck.

"Did you find any containers nearby? Had the victim been drinking, eating . . ."

"Drinking. But there's no trace of this compound in her stomach or intestines. Mostly it's in her bloodstream. A bit in her lungs . . ."

"I'll check with the armed services to see if they're missing any kind of nerve gas. I think you better alert the local police and FBI."

"OK. Thanks, Zale."

"Look, you want to fly to Vegas for the weekend?"

"Maybe. Gotta go." She hung up and thought she would like to see Zale again. Hawaii had been incredible. She loved to combine sex and pathology. I'm getting cynical, thinking like that, she said to herself.

Dr. Florence called downstairs and requested the assistant pathologist recheck for any puncture wounds. He said he already had. She said to look again—in spite of the fact she trusted the pathologist. If he said there were no needle marks, then there were none. So how was the poison introduced into the body? Not through the gut since the stomach was relatively free of the poison. Something injected in the ears? The nose? Eyes? Maybe Andria was a speed freak who shut up by using a needle in her vagina or rectum. The phone rang.

"The victim," said the assistant pathologist, "had some kind of birth control foam in her vagina. We thought there was some semen present but there's not. The poison is concentrated in the vagina."

"Do you think the poison could have been introduced with the birth control foam?"

"You're getting cynical, Dr. Florence."

"I know. What do you think?"

"You might be right. One of the orderlies down here says the foam is Kaam."

"How does he know?"

"Says the strawberry scent is a dead giveaway."

"OK. I'll stay until you run the results. You better tell that orderly to be careful of what he sniffs. If that poison decomposes back to gas . . ."

"Three steps ahead of you. The corpse is in the aerobic tent."

It was after seven, and Dr. Florence poured herself a gin and drank it slowly. It burned all the way down. She was thinking about the Tylenol scare. Pretty sick to lace an aspirin substitute with cyanide. You think that's sick? Try nerve gas in birth control foam? The world was going to hell in a handcart. That's what her father had said. He'd been right. He had also told her to get married instead of going to medical school. At times like this, she had to admit, her old Dad knew what he'd been talking about.

20

Jon Andrews squinted at the clock on his apartment wall: 1:55 a.m. The intercom buzzer rang. "Yes," he said, depressing the talk button.

"It's me," said May. "I tried your phone but got a disconnect. You all right?"

"Yes. Want to come up?"

Five minutes later she was standing in his doorway. "Where have you been?"

"I had so much to do today. I'm sorry." He had forgotten about her, about their date that night. He had been totally unnerved by what he had seen in the Mexican restaurant across from Integrated Electronics.

"I was going out of my gourd worrying about you. I had all these thoughts about someone finding you, harming you. First my sister disappears . . . then . . ."

"It's OK." He sat down and tried to organize his thoughts. He realized that despite his redoubled efforts to be careful he was making terrible mistakes, mistakes that could be fatal. "You, uh, didn't tell anyone about us, did you?"

"Of course not. I promised, didn't I?"

"Yes. I'm sorry your sister hasn't turned up. You must be going through hell."

"I am."

"Maybe she met a guy . . ."

"No. Donna would never just disappear like that. Never. I went back to the Omelet Parlour. No one even remembers her being there. My brother and his friends have put up over a thousand posters. We've got some money together for a reward . . ."

"Let me help you with that." He opened a small drawer in his wet bar and took out five $100 bills.

"I can't take that."

"It's for your sister. I'm not doing it for you. Please. I want to."

"Thank you," she said finally.

"Let me get you a drink. You look like you've had a long day . . ."

He made them each a vodka. They sipped the drinks and he asked her if she was hungry. She said no.

After a moment she remarked that he seemed distant. He did not tell her he was thinking about what had happened in the Mexican restaurant during the noon hour. Who he had seen. "It's nothing. I'm just tired."

"You look so troubled," said May. "I guess you're mad I came by tonight. I know it's late but I was so worried about you . . ."

"I was thinking about the people who

were hunting me. I'm a little frightened."

"Describe them."

"All right." Who should I describe, he wondered. He could not take a chance on telling her about the computer expert or the reporter. If May talked to them, she would find out too much. There was one man in America who had brought him to Washington. Ivan Tornoff. "He is older than you might think. Maybe 60. He is bald with just a fringe of white hair that forms a narrow white strip between his ears. His walk is determined, aggressive. I've seen him move through crowds. People part, get out of his way. He likes hot dogs. Often I have seen him buy two or three at a time. His English is good but he has a Russian accent. He has killed many men. Oh. There is a little black wart over his eye."

"This was who you saw at the Omelet Parlour?"

"Yes."

"Do you think he knows you are here?"

"Possibly." He did not want to scare the black woman away—she could be valuable. His eyes and ears. She was caught up in the adventure of his life but fear would drive her away. "There is also a chance that this man I saw—Ivan Tornoff—just happened to be in the restaurant. I saw him before he saw me so I think perhaps he does not know about me. After I was on the sidewalk I checked to see if he was following me. He wasn't.

So I am probably lucky this time."

"You still want to defect, don't you?"

"As I told you, I have been arranging to do so but timing is vital. I may have to go underground again."

"And we'll be able to see each other when you defect, won't we?"

"After a month or two."

"When you were out tonight, I thought that you were with another woman. I thought about that much more than your being caught."

"I was with no one, I promise," he said. He wondered how gullible the woman could be. She seemed so bright but women, he had learned, sometimes enjoy being fooled. That was why it was so simple to kill them.

"Can I have another bath here?" she asked.

"You don't even have to ask." He took her glass and kissed her softly. "Whatever is here is yours."

They bathed together and held each other in the black tub beneath the black skylight. He felt at ease for the moment. If he could feel like this always, he knew he would enjoy surviving.

"I'm going to shave," he said.

She stood in the tub and pulled a long fluffy bath towel from the gold-colored rack and draped it over his shoulders. "I'll help you dry off. After you shave, get in bed and I'll come to you. Pretend you are asleep."

Ten minutes later he walked across his thick carpet and slipped between two black silk sheets. He lay on his back and stared at the high beam ceilings. He had chosen her well. He thought of how responsive she had been the previous night. Tonight would even be better. He thought about her warm body pressed against his. The wonderful musky scent she wore. The way she moved and anticipated his desires. The first time they had been together he had been thinking how delightful it would be to have her wake him with kisses and she had somehow sensed his desire. He started to doze, his mind drifting into semi-sleep. He could hear her gentle movements in the bathroom. The gurgle of the water whirling down the drain. The sounds of glass on porcelain. So sleepy, so eager to have her wake him. For a moment his thoughts went back to the Mexican restaurant at noon hour. He could picture Buff Tallons clearly—three piece suit. His tie with tiny blue dots. Oxfords that were perfectly polished. The Russian's master plan had a single weakness, physically *transferring the money.* Now half awake, half asleep, the Russian realized that Buff Tallons could be very useful. But before he could consider his plan further, the Russian felt May get into the bed, felt her nuzzle his neck, felt her fingertips tenderly caress his chest. He could feel the arousal building within him. He felt a wetness on his neck, a sticky wetness. She moaned.

"I know what you want," she said.

"How?"

"I'm a detective. My name—May Grey —like the French detective—Maigret?" Her fingertips froze on his chest.

"You OK?" he asked.

"No."

He flicked on the bedside light and saw to his horror that the bedsheets were drenched in blood. Her body started to shake and she clutched her stomach as the blood spurted from her.

"You didn't use that foam?"

She tried to speak, tried to say something, but her eyes rolled upward as her head jerked back—and she was dead.

He staggered into the bathroom and vomited. The cold rim of the toilet pressed against his forehead as his muscles contracted and spun against him. He could vomit no more. He lurched to the sink and turned on the cold faucet, buried his head under the water. He gulped the icy liquid, then he saw the canister of Kaam on the counter top. He did not understand what had happened. May had been on the pill—at least that is what she had told him.

He dropped to his knees and looked under the sink. At the back of the cupboard he saw that one of the Kaam packs were missing. Obviously May had found them there. Had she believed the rumors that Kaam contained some kind of aphrodisiac? Maybe she had decided to stop using her birth control pills.... He found her purse and shook out the contents. The usual assortment—a few cosmetics and some cash. *Think,* he told himself, *think.* A few minutes later he tipped the bathroom wastebasket upside down—used tissue, a couple of plastic disposable razors, and a small blue compact-sized container clicked onto the white tile. He seized the blue compact. A birth control dispenser—May's name neatly typed on it. All of the pills had been used and there was a notice reminding her to purchase a refill.

So, he thought ... she realized she'd run out of birth control pills. She started looking around for something. At the back of the cupboard, where I had hidden them, she finds the Kaam packs. I had just told her that everything in this house was hers. She used the Kaam. A few minutes later, she is dead.

The Russian cursed. A stupid idea to hide the Kaam packets under the sink. He had been a fool.

He turned the cold water on in the shower and stood under it. The icy jets of water were tiny darts against his skin. He walked back through the bedroom, careful not to look at her body. He moved through his darkened front room. He stood before the coffee table with its mirrored top. He looked down at his image, then he knelt on the coffee table, watching the drops of water splatter from his naked body against its cold surface. After a moment he lay on his stomach, his arms rigid beside him. He could feel the pressure of the table against his head, against his pelvic region, against his bent toes. He opened his eyes to see if he could see his reflection but there was not enough light. The surface of the table was cold. He was aware of puddles of water between himself and the smooth surface.

He forced himself to remain that way for half an hour, trying to concentrate on the problems that whirled about him.

It had been a mistake to kill the first black woman; now a tragedy her sister was dead. It had been unwise to leave the Kaam packages under his sink, no matter how well he had hidden them. It had not been insanity to buy the packages and prepare each of the applicators with the nerve gas he had stolen. That part of his plan had bordered on genius.

He determined the exact moment when things had started to go wrong. It had been after he killed the *safety* from Florida. He had assumed that no one would pay attention to her—no way of realizing that the computer expert, a man who was a criminal, would be so tenacious. Who would have thought that David Cursore would have a set of keys to the old lady's apartment? Who would have thought that Cursore would have entered the old lady's apartment a few hours after the woman from Florida disappeared? Who would have thought the police would have investigated so soon?

If the computer expert had just minded his own business, then the next morning everything would have been all right. There would have been time to remove the suitcases, all of her personal belongings. Life was timing; something was interfering with his timing.

The Russian knew two things must happen if he were to survive. First, he would have to make certain that the computer expert and the reporter died. He had already taken care of that. The trap was set in motion.

After they died he would proceed with step two, and after he had accomplished that he would live easily for the rest of his life.

He must be careful.

He must be very careful. Things must happen in the right order.

21

"Are you awake?" asked Cursore. A strip of sunlight cut through the darkness of the room and etched his ear, a curl of his black hair, and a patch of stubble on his left jawbone.

"Mmm." Jasper pulled a pillow over her head, nestled closer to him, and scrunched her hip against his.

"I thought we were just going to cuddle last night. You ravaged me."

"Mmm."

Cursore flicked the curtain on Mary Lou's guest bedroom window several inches to the right. The band of sunlight warmed her shoulder blade.

"Mmm."

Cursore got up and made coffee. He was careful not to wake Mary Lou. He brought a cup back to Jasper. She opened her eyes and held up a hand to shield her eyes from the sunlight. "Where are my strawberry croissants?"

"Room service didn't answer."

She sipped her coffee. "I'm not going to get pregnant, so don't worry, Mr. Charm."

"You're a little defensive."

"What do you think I am? Some broad who'll nail you with a paternity suit?"

"No, but . . ."

"Look, there's a very good chance I can't have children. OK?"

"How do you know?"

"I'm really in no mood for twenty questions before my croissant. I don't ask much in life. Just a croissant for breakfast, an ocean view . . . and your body."

"I'll do my best. I like you a lot and I feel responsible for anything that happens between us."

"Oh. What does that mean?"

"It means if you found out that you were going to have a baby, I'd help you handle things."

"Stand by me, would you?"

"Yes. Stop worrying."

"I'm not."

"Yes, you are. Tell me what's bothering you."

"Well, for one thing, I'm four days late with the rent and . . ."

"I'll lend you some money."

"You would?"

"Sure."

"It's sweet of you but I'll get the money. One of the minor problems of freelancing."

"I know how it feels to be broke and I'll get the money for you . . ."

"Nope. I'm responsible for my own life.

I like paying my own way. So let's drop..."

The phone rang before Jasper could really warm to her independence.

"Hello," said Cursore, picking up the phone.

"This is Debbie—Dusty's sister—I'm calling from Texas. May I speak to Mary Lou?" said the voice on the telephone.

"This is Cursore, a friend of hers. Can I help you?"

"You live with Mary Lou?"

"No. She was a little worried about staying alone last night, so I slept in the guest room. Have you heard from your sister?"

"No, I haven't. That's why I'm phoning. After we talked yesterday, Mr. Cursore..."

"Call me Cursore..."

"OK. I've called at least a dozen of Dusty's friends and no one has heard anything. I think something bad has happened to her."

"We spent yesterday looking for her. We didn't find anything bad..."

"I was so worried, Cursore, I called the Sheriff's sub-station in the Marina. They referred me to the Detective Detail. I talked to a Sergeant Dartwell."

"Oh."

"He thinks you're a little crazy."

"Maybe I am."

"I have to ask you, Cursore... are you

making some kind of a charade out of my sister's disappearance? It seems like it's a game of Dragons and Dungeons."

"It's no game for me."

"Isn't it a little weird to break into a girl's apartment in the middle of the night and go through her personal belongings if you've only known her for ten minutes?"

"I didn't break in. I had a key to Mary Lou's. We're friends. Your sister's car was missing and it was late. I went into the apartment to water some plants that I'd promised to look after. I noticed your sister's things. I didn't go through any of her luggage until it seemed like she wasn't coming back."

"Sergeant Dartwell said you spent half the night looking for my sister's swimsuit."

"When I met your sister, she was swimming. We made a date for later that night. I got the idea someone must have broken in and kidnapped her. My theory was that her abductor wouldn't give her time to change her swimsuit."

"The police said no one found the suit."

"I know. And I'm sure that what I've done makes you think I'm way out of bounds . . ."

"You think some maniac grabbed my sister and dragged her out of that complex and she was only wearing a bathing suit? My God, what kind of place has it turned into? I was there two years ago. There's security all over the place. Have you done these kind of things before?"

"I know what we're doing might sound unorthodox, but everything that we've done has only been out of concern for your sister's well-being."

"The police said you ruined any chance of anyone every finding fingerprints there. Said you defaced what little evidence there was."

"That's not true."

"Oh? You didn't dust for fingerprints yourself?"

"Yes..."

"If a police crew came in now, would they be able to find any fingerprints?"

"I don't suppose they would but the police refused to do anything when I reported your sister missing."

"That's not what Sergeant Dartwell told me. He said you've hampered his investigation."

"That's simply not true."

"It might be a lie, Cursore or whatever they call you, but my sister never had a problem until she met you."

"I know you're upset..."

"You're goddamn right I'm upset. I love my sister and she promised to call me and the next thing I hear from your girlfriend. Mary Lou has a great many interesting friends... I didn't realize that included criminals..."

"I'm not some drooling crazy. I was charged and convicted of a white collar crime. You can call Sergeant Dartwell and ask him. I got into trouble with computer fraud. I do not, nor have I ever, abducted human beings. Give me a break, all right?"

"I didn't say you were a kidnapper, or . . ."

"You really don't have to. Now, if you'll just try and take it easy, we'll do everything we can here to help you find your sister. OK?"

They said goodbye and Cursore hung up. Jasper finished her coffee.

"What are you staring at?" he said.

"A minute ago, I thought I had troubles," she said. "I'm sorry."

"All I'm trying to do is stay out of trouble until my parole is up. That's all. Now, because I've tried to help someone I met for ten minutes, the police are accusing me of hampering their inept investigation. A woman in Texas thinks I'm a fiend. And you, you won't even let me help you with your goddamn rent."

"It's a conspiracy."

"Don't talk to me about conspiracies. It was a conspiracy that got me in jail in the first place. I am not guilty! Do you understand that?"

"You're yelling."

"You're being unreasonable."

"Wouldn't you be?"

"If you don't stop yelling you'll wake

up Mary Lou. It's only ten minutes to seven."

"What do you suggest I do?"

"I'd like to get a croissant. Then I suggest we go to my apartment. In my apartment is a blackboard. I suggest we write down all the clues we have, and with a cool and calculating approach I suggest we try to find this Dusty lady before we're all arrested."

"Get dressed."

"You could say please."

"I know I could. Would you put your goddamn slacks on? Please!"

By nine o'clock, they had each eaten two more croissants and he was settled on a tubular chair in her apartment.

She cleared several dozen books and magazines from a coffee table so he could have an unobstructed view of a large blackboard she had affixed to her living room wall. It had been covered with a framed tapu cloth from Hawaii. "How do you like that? A beautiful picture and presto—a blackboard." She set the framed cloth on the floor and attacked the blackboard with an eraser. "O.K. Clues." She wrote "clues" at the top of the board.

"First clue is missing car," said Cursore. "Then rubber gloves disappeared. Then a chair had been moved. Bits of adhesive tape."

"Which later disappeared." Jasper

scribbled the information on the board.

"Mary Lou's missing three hundred dollars. Then Dusty's missing swimsuit and the fact that the shower was dry in the master bath."

"I think we could assume that she might have dried the tub out."

"I'll give you that point," said Cursore. "Oh. Someone changed the lining in Mary Lou's wastebasket in the kitchen."

Jasper wrote that down. Then she added: "beach sand" and "sea wheat."

"Death of the old man in Malibu," said Cursore.

"I don't seee how they're connected."

"Write it down anyway."

"OK."

"And there's the transfer of the five thousand dollars."

Jasper printed "$5,000" on the board. Then she added—"Dusty."

Under "Dusty" they wrote several points and by eleven o'clock the blackboard looked like this:

CLUES:
missing car
rubber gloves
adhesive tape
swimsuit
waste basket lining
beach sand
sea wheat
death of Malibu old man
$5,000/Dusty
$300/Mary Lou

A second list was headed *DUSTY* and under that Jasper wrote:

DUSTY
missing
stopped using charge cards
has contacted no one
abandoned suitcases
abandoned car
failed to contact sister or friends
transferred money day she disappeared

"Does it matter that some of the clues overlap?" asked Jasper.
"No. But what about dead end clues?" he asked.
Jasper started a third list. Under *DEAD END* she wrote:

no fingerprints
kidnapper not seen
police uninterested
no report of Dusty's body. Hospital/zip; morgue/zip.

They made some more coffee and studied the three lists.
Finally Cursore said, "OK, let's go over it. I meet a girl at the swimming pool. Dusty. She has heard about me, knows I'm on parole and agrees to have dinner with me. Several hours pass. She mysteriously disappears..."
"Why mysteriously?" asked Jasper.
"OK. She disappears. Late that night I

check the place she is staying. First I discover her car is gone. Next I discover a chair has been moved and it looks like someone had tied her up with adhesive tape. There is wadded-up adhesive tape in the trash can. Her wet—or certainly damp—swimsuit is gone. Now doesn't that sound like she was abducted?"

"Yes."

"I call the police. Oh, Mary Lou's rubber gloves have disappeared. So, I call the police and while I'm doing that— as if by magic the adhesive tape and trash liner are gone. The trash liner has been replaced with something that Mary Lou never uses. The police think I'm nuts."

"OK," said Jasper. "We decide to do a little detective work ourselves. We find that Mary Lou's place is covered with Dusty's fingerprints *and* someone who was wearing rubber gloves. We discover her car has probably been driven to Malibu and back. The day she disappeared all of her money has been withdrawn from her account. And Mary Lou is shy three hundred dollars. I would say your theory that someone broke into Mary Lou's place and abducted Dusty is true. Further, the abductor was after money . . ."

"And it's all circumstantial," said Cursore. "But now let's look at the kind of woman Dusty is. Does she suddenly, capriciously, disappear for a couple of days without letting anyone know where she is? Not according to her sister who thinks I'm behind her disappearance."

"And not according to Mary Lou who is positive you've got nothing to do with the disappearance."

"Thank God for one vote of confidence."

"I trust you," said Jasper. "And that was a cheap shot." She gave him a dirty look. Real dirty. Then a smile.

"One and a half votes of confidence. Now, here we are—Dusty has made no effort to contact anyone of her family or friends that we can discover, and she suddenly stops using her credit cards."

Someone rapped at the door. Jasper opened it.

Sergeant Dartwell nodded to her. "I've been talking to your friend upstairs. Mary Lou. She said I might catch the two of you here."

"OK," said Jasper. "You caught us, I guess. Would you like to come in?"

"Why not?" The policeman walked into her living room and glanced around.

"Coffee?" she asked.

"Yeah. That's fine."

Jasper watched as the cop slumped into a chair and hefted his regulation size eleven boots on her coffee table. "Take your feet off my table, please."

The cop gave her a look like she was a hooker and was overcharging. Then he slowly pulled his feet back and let them fall to the floor. "I checked you out."

"Pardon?" said Jasper.

"I said I checked you out. I do that with people who cavort with felons. Birds of a feather, you know."

"What's he talking about, Cursore?"

"I don't know."

Sergeant Dartwell studied the blackboard. "You people thinking of starting your own little gumshoe business?"

No answer.

He read the notation that said "police uninterested."

"I think I'd like you to leave," said Jasper. "I really don't like you here."

"Yeah. Ran your name through the computer. There's two moving violation citations on you. We're going to have to book you."

"You can come in my apartment and arrest me for traffic violations?"

"That is correct. And, Cursore, old man, I'd like you to come down to the office for an informal little chat. You don't mind do you?"

"What's he done?"

"Many things. For example, his Visa card was found in the possession of a dead woman. She was murdered. Tuesday night. You got an alibi for then?"

"We were together," said Jasper.

"All night?"

"Yes."

"Well, normally that would be enough but your boyfriend here is on parole. The state takes a dim view of someone in that kind of circumstance getting involved in murder."

"Sergeant Dartwell," asked Cursore. "I don't know what's going on. Who was the woman?"

"Did I hear a pleasant voice in this room? Am I to assume that you want to help me—an 'uninterested' peace officer?" He was reading their lists on Jasper's blackboard.

Jasper glanced at Cursore. "We'll go to the police station and I'll pay the goddamn fines if that's what he wants. Don't let him intimidate you."

"You pick some fiesty companions, don't you, Cursore?"

"Excuse me for a second." Cursore followed Jasper into her bedroom where she was angrily hunting for a sweater.

"You really stood up to him, didn't you?" she said.

"We have to be nice to him," he said.

"You mean grovel to him? I'm a journalist and I have friends and no cop is going to treat me that way."

"I know you're mad and you've got a right to be. But you can accomplish a lot more on the outside than you can on the inside. He's got me over a barrel full of snakes if he wants to play rough."

"I am not belly crawling to him."

"Then he is going to make life very

rough on me. I don't know what this murder is all about. I'm a felon on parole. I can't afford to upset him."

"I can."

"Jasper, I'm going to ask you once more . . . Never mind, do what you want . . ."

Cursore walked back into the front room. The cop was reading the information on the blackboard. "How'd you find out about her bank acount?"

"We found some withdrawal slips in her car."

"I'll bet."

"Look, Sergeant, I know you think I'm doing something I shouldn't. But why don't you just take me down to the station. Leave her out of it?"

"She could be an accessory."

"You know she's not."

"I know nothing," said the cop and then he stopped talking.

"I'm sorry I was rude," said Jasper. She was dressed in her sailor outfit and somehow in less than three minutes she had managed to add a blush of rouge to each cheek. "I really don't want to go to the police station. I'll be happy to pay the fines this afternoon. And I'll be happy to cooperate any way you want to."

The cop rocked gently on the balls of his feet. "Maybe I was a little gruff, busting in here. And since you're going to cooperate, I've got better things to do than wade through a lot of paperwork."

"Great. Do you take your coffee with sugar and cream?"

"Please."

She excused herself and went into the kitchen.

"Goddamn," said the cop. "I think you picked yourself a winner there, Cursore."

"I'm more surprised than you, Sergeant."

As he sipped his coffee a few minutes later, Sergeant Dartwell said, "I got a call from this Dusty Bleudell's sister in Texas. She's pretty upset with what's going on."

"We're pretty upset, too," said Jasper.

"The Bleudell family is well connected back east. One of the old men in the family is a great booster of politics in California. Jason Bleudell. He's the guy who arranged for a thousand dollar a plate dinner for the governor. Needless to say someone from the governor's office has already called my boss. My boss is leaning on me rather fiercely."

"So," said Jasper, "if you don't get results quickly, then we're all going to be in trouble."

"I couldn't have put it better myself. That's why I want you two on my side. No secrets."

"We'll work together," she suggested.

The cop glanced at the blackboard again. "I'd say the sum of what we know is nothing. You've been playing with your computer, haven't you, Cursore?"

"No."

"Well, why don't you?"

"You telling me to break the law, Sergeant?"

"No. Maybe you and your damn computers can figure out a couple of things that the police department can't. We don't have the manpower for this one..."

"And if I get caught, of course I go back to jail."

"Of course."

"Cursore," said Jasper. "I left my things in Mary Lou's... Would you mind awfully if I asked you to get them?"

"OK." Cursore got up and walked out.

The cop finished his coffee. "So what do you want to talk about?" he asked.

"Cursore."

"Right. You don't think he's guilty."

"No. I don't." She opened a filing drawer and took out a folder. "I was going to do a story on computer thefts. I spent a lot of time doing research on him. I really think he was framed."

"Look, I'm not here to debate his court case. A jury has already done that."

"Juries can make mistakes."

"Yes."

"Will you at least look at this folder?"

The door opened and Cursore walked back in. He was just in time to see the police sergeant take the folder. The sergeant tucked the folder between himself and the chair he was sitting in.

"Fast trip?" asked the cop.

"I don't like the position I'm getting in." Cursore glanced at Jasper.

"I'm going to spend a lot of sleepless nights over your concern," said the cop. He got up, took the folder with him and headed for the door. "The bottom line is —you two dig up anything on this missing Dusty, you tell me about it, right now."

"Downstairs, Sergeant," said Cursore, "in the office, there's a list of all the people who live here. Tells what their former addresses were, tells how long they lived here, tells what their phone numbers are, who their employers are. If I had that list, I might be able to feed the information into this new computer program I'm working on, and I might be able to come up with some information for you."

"What kind of information?"

"I don't know."

"They don't have to give me the list."

"You're pretty persuasive when you want to be," said Cursore.

The cop reached for the door handle.

"There's one thing more," said Cursore. "Can you get me a list of all the missing persons from this area in the last five years?"

"There's got to be hundreds."

"Is it on any kind of computer files?"

"We don't have anything like that. The FBI does . . . but don't get any ideas about peeking at their computer information."

"Who's the dead woman that has my Visa card?"

"Andria Bevan. A rather carefree divorcee from Idaho. She and her boyfriend checked into a hotel room in Brentwood."

"Did he look like me?"

"We don't know."

"How was she killed?" asked Cursore.

"So far all I've heard is some kind of poison. Look, Cursore, I don't know about your ripping off computers. But I don't see you as a murderer. I told the lieutenant that you probably misplaced your credit card—maybe the killer stole it."

"Thanks. Of course that might mean whoever tried to frame me has access to these apartments," said Cursore.

"It might. I'd watch my step if I were you." The cop thanked Jasper for the coffee, used her bathroom and left.

Cursore and Jasper stood on her balcony and watched Sergeant Dartwell's black-and-white glide into traffic. "What were you talking to him about when you got me out of the apartment?" he asked.

"I had a file on you. I gave it to him."

"Why?"

"Because I think you were set up."

"Yeah?"

"Maybe Sergeant Dartwell can figure out who did it to you?"

"I wouldn't count on it. I wouldn't even count on him looking at that file. Unless, of course, he needed some more information to twist my arm."

"He's not all bad."

"You might think this is a game we're playing but that sonofabitch has got my head in a steel vise and every day he's going to tighten it."

"I think he wants to help . . ."

"You do, huh? I think he's starting to believe my story about Dusty. I think Dartwell is using us as bait."

22

At 1:45 that afternoon, the Russian drove his Jaguar to the Los Angeles International Airport and parked at a two-hour meter across from United Airlines. He slipped a dollar bill in the slot above the "do-it-yourself" baggage carts. One slid out from its compartment. The Russian transferred the two suitcases from his trunk to the cart and wheeled them across the street. At the curb-side baggage check-in, Jon Andrews handed the two bags to a beefy agent.

Sweat glistened on the man's powerful biceps. "These are pretty heavy, man—what you got in 'em? Bricks?"

"Books."

The baggage handler stapled a pair of receipts to the Russian's Washington, D.C. ticket and tossed the cases on a moving belt. The bags disappeared down a chrome chute.

The Russian gave the baggage handler several quarters, then went into the terminal where he found a phone booth and made a collect call to a Washington, D.C. number. The secretary who answered said that the Russian Embassy was not authorized to accept collect calls. The Russian said his code number was JA/15. A moment later he was talking to Ivan Tornoff. They were both aware that the FBI, CIA and the National Security Agency (NSA) were probably recording their conversation.

"Hello, Jon," said Ivan. "How have you been?"

"Fine. You and your wife?"

"She has not been feeling well."

"The reason I called you in Washington was to tell you that the two suitcases are on their way."

"I see. Uh, where do I pick them up?"

"The usual place." That meant the bags would be on the next United flight to Washington, D.C.

"That's very good." Ivan wondered if NSA could figure out what Jon was talking about. He hoped not.

"Also, I want you to contact the man who runs the computer company. The one we had lunch with the day after I arrived. Will you do that?"

"Yes." Why, wondered Ivan, would a renegade operative want me to contact Buff Tallons? Must have something planned. He was a methodical schemer.

"I must go, Comrade. Why don't we talk in an hour? Booth number five?"

"I'll be there." They hung up and Ivan stood and stretched. He was nervous so he opened a tin of Swiss bonbons and ate several. For a moment the chocolate soothed him. Outside, the wind had picked up and dark clouds threatened Washington, D.C. Ivan glanced at his watch. He must hurry to get to the phone booth on time.

As he pulled on his warm jacket, his secretary came in with an envelope. "This just came from Los Angeles. Overnight express."

The Russian diplomat tore it open and a slip of paper floated to the ground. It was an ad for Kaam. His secretary picked it up, smiled, and said nothing. The diplomat read the attached letter with growing concern.

About a block from the Daughters of the American Revolution office is a bank of phone booths. When Ivan got out of his car the last phone was ringing. Booth number five. He hurried to it and picked up the receiver. "Hello."

"Hello, Ivan. You sound winded," said Jon Andrews.

"I got your letter."

"What did you think?"

"Madness."

"Yes, Ivan. But that's what the world runs on. What is your response?"

"I propose that we will give you a million dollars and you forget your scheme . . ."

"I'm sorry, Comrade. The fact is—you cannot get me a million dollars. You cannot even get the front steps of your townhouse redone. And even if Moscow authorized the million dollars they would never rest until I am dead. As a matter of fact, if you told them I was still alive they would recall you to Moscow and heaven only knows what things they would do to you."

"You are wrong. I can get the money."

"No. You can't. And if you do not cooperate with me I shall send a letter to The New York Times explaining what I did and blaming you and the Kremlin for it. Then God help you for deceiving Moscow. You will contact Mr. Tallons and he will do what you say. Do you agree to do this?"

"It is not necessary to kill innocent people."

"Only a few or so will die, at the most. Americans kill a thousand of their people on the highways during a long weekend. They will not miss several more."

"I wish you would reconsider . . ."

"I cannot and I will not. The envelope contained the flight numbers?"

"Yes."

"Good. Then in two hours, simply go to the airport and pick up your two bags."

"I don't have the ticket stubs."

"You don't need them. The luggage has your name on it. Show the guard your ID and tell him that you lost your luggage receipts."

"Considering what you claim is in the

luggage, I suppose there is no other way."

"That is correct. I wrapped the contents well, but in a day or two, after the luggage starts to reek, then . . ."

"Don't paint a picture for me. I really do not understand why you have to be so macabre."

"You talk to me of being macabre, Comrade? What you did to me was more macabre than I could have dreamed."

"I had no say over that unfortunate event."

"Maybe you are right. Have fun at the airport."

When the diplomat was driven to the airport, as Jon Andrews had predicted, there was no trouble claiming the two suitcases.

Ivan Tornoff returned to the Russian Embassy and his driver placed the suitcases in the freight elevator and left. A few minutes later the diplomat came back down and loaded the suitcases into the trunk of his Mercedes. He drove out of the basement parking area and into the street.

Traffic was light and he headed for Georgetown. He realized the grisly contents of the packages was Jon Andrews' way of proving how serious and desperate he was. The diplomat could not really blame Jon Andrews for what he had done—when any man is pressed hard enough, long enough, he snaps.

In the distance Ivan saw the dome of the Capitol Building and past that the Washington Monument. The irony of it all, he thought. He, a Russian diplomat, driving through Washington, D.C. with a dismembered female in his trunk. And all because some fool in the Kremlin had decided to eliminate the Queen. Then last minute changes and the word came —*don't kill the Queen, kill one of our own people to prevent the assassination.* So stupid. If there had been no attempt to murder the Queen, it would not have been necessary to bungle the elimination of Jon Andrews. The Kremlin was run by fools. Washington, too, was run by fools. The entire world was a top that fools tossed back and forth at each other. Just a matter of time before one of them dropped it.

Ivan Tornoff stopped his philosophical ramblings. In his rearview mirror he studied a car that looked suspiciously like a CIA vehicle. A nondescript four-door sedan. Fake radio antenna. Two young and eager agents in the front seat. They had seen his diplomatic plates. They had probably run a routine check and realized that they were on the trail of one of the most important Russian agents in America. He could imagine their conversation:

"Hey, that fucking car belongs to

Tornoff. What do you think he's doing driving around the city by himself?"

"Probably got a body in a couple of suitcases in the trunk."

"Let's follow that sonofabitch and see where he drops it, then we'll bust him."

"Good idea."

Ivan Tornoff made several right hand turns and a few minutes later was headed back for the Embassy. Ten minutes later, electronic doors to the Russian Embassy's underground parking opened and he drove down into the basement. He loaded the suitcases that were becoming increasingly heavy into the freight elevator and took them to the second floor and put them in the bottom of the deep freeze. Then he locked the deep freeze and placed an official seal on it. The cook would be mad, but tough luck.

Ivan's wife, who was recovering from a hysterectomy, was in bed when he walked into their living quarters. "What's wrong, Ivan?"

"Nothing. How do you feel?"

"Fine. The doctor said I would be able to get the stitches out soon."

"That is good news."

"You look so tired," she said.

"I guess I am."

"You can always talk to me, can't you?"

"Of course," he said and kissed her on her cheek. She slipped her arms around him.

They both knew that their two bedroom apartment was bugged by both the KGB and CIA. He did not feel up to putting his wife in the bathtub and turning up the shower so he could explain to her what a predicament he was in. He would tell her later; she didn't need to worry now, so soon after the operation.

23

David Cursore finished swimming the twenty-sixth lap of the Olympic-sized pool. His head broke the surface of the water and he grasped for the smooth tile. The night lights took on diamond-shaped images as he squinted up at them, pulling himself out of the water.

"You're a pretty good swimmer," said Sergeant Dartwell.

Cursore flopped onto a deck chair and continued to breathe deeply, sucking in the cool night air. His body tingled. Then he got up and lowered himself gingerly into the whirling Jacuzzi, a few feet away. There was no one else around as the cop lumbered over and sat down beside Cursore. The cop carried a shopping bag.

"Where's Lois Lane?"

"Oh. Jasper? I think she's over at a medical convention in Century City. Doing a story on replacement organs or something."

"I thought maybe she devoted all of her time to crime solving," said the cop.

"Glad to know she takes a break now and then to earn a living."

"Her rent's overdue."

"Yeah? So is mine. Look, I got the stuff for you—right here in this shopping bag—but if anyone finds out where you got it, know what I'm going to tell 'em?"

"That I stole it out of your car?"

"Very good. You know why I like dealing with white collar thieves? 'Cause they're smart people, as a rule. You're a smart guy, Cursore. I'm impressed with your academic record."

"Where'd you get that?"

"They were in a little file Jasper put together on you. I read it last night."

"The stuff that proves I was innocent?"

"Yeah." Dartwell beamed. "Aren't women wonderful? They got so much faith in us. What would we do without 'em. Look, Cursore, your girl is a damn good reporter. But her notes and observations on your trial are simply her opinion."

Cursore sunk down into the Jacuzzi and let the bubbles caress his body. "Tell me something. Just between you and me . . . you think I'm really all that guilty?"

"I didn't have anything to do with your case. It was all circumstantial evidence—all that means is there were no eyewitnesses. Hell, if I go into a locked room with a shotgun and blast a paraplegic who's asleep and then come out and get arrested—my attorney would scream 'circumstantial.' Just as long as no one actually saw me."

"Lots of innocent people have been jailed or hanged on circumstantial evidence."

"For every error that's made, I'll bet you a hundred guilty people get away with murder."

"Thoreau said that he would rather live in a society that let a thousand prisoners go free than imprison one man unjustly."

"Thoreau was never mugged."

"So you think I was guilty?"

"I don't know. Your girl friend makes a pretty strong case in the stuff she'd dug up . . . but I don't know. I do know you served your time and it's a total waste of energy to devote any more time to proving anything to anyone."

"If I found additional evidence that proved I was innocent, would you help me?"

"I might. Especially if you helped locate this missing Florida broad everyone's on my back about. When you're finished with this stuff, burn it. It's all Xeroxed." He got up to go.

"Sergeant, did you find out how many missing people were reported from this area in the last five years?"

"About a thousand."

"A thousand?"

"You got water in your ears?"

"How many of those people were

eventually located?"

"Fifty or sixty. Look, Cursore, this is California. Half the people who live here are missing. Especially around the Marina—people come here to start a new life. And those kind of people are never satisfied with a new life. They got to have another new life. So we get lots of people who are reported missing from around here. Probably, if we wanted to, we could juggle the statistics to come up with a lot more than a thousand. The Xeroxes of their files are all in that sack. Just make sure you burn it all."

"Thanks. By the way, did you get any more information on the woman who had my credit card?"

The sergeant rubbed his jaw. "Remember the Tylenol killings?"

"Who could forget?"

"OK. This is between you and me. The only reason I'm telling you is something might show up on that computer of yours. It's very hush-hush so far but her murder is tied into some kind of commercial product. I'm meeting with the Assistant D.A. about it."

"What kind of product?"

"Hell. I don't know. Something that's distributed nationwide. The makers of the product are terrified. I get the feeling they're going to pay some God-awful price in blackmail. I got to go." The cop walked toward an exit. A tall black man wearing a UCLA Bruin T-shirt and white jeans intercepted Sergeant Dartwell before he made it to the courtyard exit.

"You a cop, man?" asked the rangy black. He had an Afro haircut and black eyes that blazed in the dark.

"It shows, does it?"

"If you been livin' in Watts, it shows."

"What can I do for you?"

"My sisters have both disappeared."

"You see someone grab them?"

"Listen, man, if I seen anyone grab 'em I wouldn't be jiving with you now. I'll tell you that. Here's Donna's picture, right here." He showed it to Sergeant Dartwell.

"I've seen it on a lot of telephone poles, yeah," said the cop. "Donna Grey. We've got an APB out on her."

"So have May and me. That's my older sister and now she's gone. I mean we were out lookin' for Donna—and wham! May disappears. What the fuck in comin' down, man? Some crazy scooping up black chicks?"

Cursore pulled a towel around his shoulders and moved closer to the two men. "How long has May been gone?" he asked.

"Is this guy with you or what?"

"He lives in the building here. Maybe he's seen one of your sisters," said the cop. No way he was going to commit himself as an "associate" of Cursore's.

"My name is Grey. What's yours?"

"David Cursore."

The black thrust a picture of Donna at Cursore. "Donna. She disappeared last Saturday, then May and I started looking for her. And now some mother has grabbed May. You seen either one of them around because if you *have* . . ."

"Mr. Grey," interrupted the sergeant, "I take it you've reported May's disappearance?"

"Fuckin' A. Told some dude policeman behind a desk over in Venice about it. He said 'yeah- yeah' and took down the information—but no one's done nothing to help us. Donna's car is still up on the roof of this apartment. I know she was here. My sister met a guy who thought he seen her."

"What was the man's name?" asked the cop.

"She didn't tell me."

"Do you know anything about this man?" Sergeant Dartwell's lazy eyes seemed to suddenly come alive. A lion beginning to smell the scent of blood.

"May called me with his phone number but it was no good."

"What was that phone number?"

"I threw it away. No, wait . . . it was on my answering machine. Might still be on it."

"Why don't you and I drive over to your place and see if we can get it. You might also give me a picture of May. Maybe you can remember what else May might have said to you. OK?"

"You going to help me?" asked the black guy. "You really going to help me?"

"That's what I get paid for."

Cursore watched them leave, then he went to his penthouse and changed. On the way down to his car he slipped a note under Jasper's door, then drove over to Integrated Electronics. The night gate guard, an overweight man with permanent scowl marks under bushy white eyebrows, was munching on a ham and cheese sandwich. "You got your pass, Mr. Cursore?"

"I left it at home, Van."

"I'm not supposed to let you in without it." The guard pawed through his lunch box, found an apple and bit into it noisily.

"You're also not supposed to have beer on your breath."

"Why don't I just let you in, Cursore." The guard wiped some apple peel from the corner of his mouth and pushed a botton. The white gate raised.

Cursore lugged the shopping bag of Xeroxes to his office. He turned on the light and locked the door behind him. The light was flat fluorescent and cast dull grey shadows over the interior of his office.

Earlier, Cursore had designed a new program for the company's main frame computer. He'd also made "friends" with the access codes by writing a rather simple code that randomly questioned the central computer—thousands of times per second using progressive permutations and combinations. It was a ploy that could eventually penetrate most computer security. With the right passwords, one could dip into the telephone computer network and not set off any alarms. Cursore's personal computer had already neatly typed out the passwords and counter-passwords for the day. Cursore smiled and started to type. A moment later he was linked to the phone company computer.

There were eighty-eight people occupying his apartment complex, and because of Sergeant Dartwell, Cursore had a list of everyone who had lived in the complex in the last three years. For most of them he had their bank records, phone numbers, previous addresses and a variety of other personal information including drivers licenses. Working nonstop, careful to recheck each person's information, Cursore spent the next three hours dumping stats into the computer.

Finished at last, Cursore leaned back and took a deep breath. His phone rang. The guard was calling to say that a lady by the name of Jasper was at the gate. It was against regulations but did Cursore wish to have the lady admitted? Cursore said that would be great.

"I brought us a chocolate and a strawberry milkshake and two Big Mac's," said Jasper a few minutes later walking into his office, planting a fleeting kiss on his cheek as she set the package of food down.

"Great. Come here and give me a kiss first."

Jasper obliged. This time it was a long meaningful, stupendous kiss—the kind that arouses any normal man at two a.m.

Because it was two a.m. and Cursore was a normal man he became rather amorous and took off her blouse. "Do you always undress women in your office?"

"Yes." He started to undo her skirt. She started to undo his belt. "Hold it," she said.

"What?"

"We have to wait until we go back to the apartment. It's not really safe to do this now. And . . ."

"Maybe it's still safe . . ."

"I had a very interesting discussion with several doctors after the seminar tonight and they said women can get pregnant anytime. They said I was just lucky and I'd better start using something unless I wanted to play against the odds. I never play against the odds . . ."

Cursore glanced at his watch. "We'll run the program tomorrow. Let's go home now."

"Come on. Don't be so impatient."

"Women." He slumped into the chair behind his console. She gave him a sip of malt, and while he ate his hamburger, she put her blouse back on.

"Do you want me to get pregnant?" She munched on her Big Mac.

"I don't know what I want."

"Is that a proposition?"

"What if it was a proposal?"

"I'd run like hell. It's not, is it?"

He took another swallow of his milkshake, wiped his hands off and became serious. "OK, here's my latest theory. The person who abducted Dusty lives in the building."

"Why?"

"First of all—in the last three years, there's been at least thirty-six people within a block of our complex who have been reported to Missing Persons. Eight of those have been from the apartment itself."

"I never heard of anyone. Oh, a year ago there was that waitress . . ."

"Sergeant Dartwell gave me the statistics. Seven of them were women. Only one was located."

"I would think the police would . . ."

"Do almost nothing—they get thousands of missing persons reports every year. Here's an interesting part. You never heard of the women because they were strangers. Of the seven women reported from our complex, five of them were just passing through town. It was assumed that they were just on their way somewhere."

"What about people that no one reported? I mean, if you hadn't met Dusty, do you think Mary Lou would have reported her?"

"Mary Lou probably wouldn't even have known Dusty had stayed at her place after the abductor finished cleaning up. I just caught him in the middle of everything. Pure accident. I say 'he' because I just feel it's a man. Judging by the height of his fingerprints. I also think he'd have to be rather strong to force his way in—even if he had a passkey—which I think he had."

"A person living in the complex would be more apt to get his hands on a key like that."

"Right. Of course it could also be a workman or employees that stole a passkey or had it duplicated. I've included all the employees' names on a list I've programmed into the computer."

"It could also be some crazy mailman or delivery person or service man."

"Maybe, but I think our man lives in our complex. That's why he doesn't get caught. He can approach people easily who are visiting. He knows everything that's happening so he lessens his chances of getting caught. As soon as he met Dusty he probably found out she was just going to be in town for a short time. Might even have found out she had some money. The information she mentioned at the pool would have been all our man needed."

"How do you know it's not several men? For argument's sake it could be a couple—they'd be a lot less suspicious. Right?"

He started to tap commands into the computer. "First, let's try my lone nut theory. From what I've read, nut cases usually don't travel in packs or pairs over extended periods of time like this man seems to be doing."

"Where'd you find that out?"

"Psychology Today."

They both laughed.

"What I'm doing here is I've assumed that at least four of the women who disappeared were grabbed by the same nut. We'll call him Mr. 'X.' Everyone in the complex has a phone and I've just pulled their records for the last three years. So what I'll do is find out how many people were away when each of the women was killed."

"You said killed."

"I think he kills them."

"Oh," she said.

"I know, it's getting grisly. Now you might ask how I know when the tenants were away."

"That was my next question."

"First. If they had their phone disconnected, that would indicate they were on holidays, right?"

"How many people do that?"

"Quite a few, if they're going away for several months."

"What about the rest?" She finished her milkshake and made a slurping sound with her straw.

"I assume that if they did not make a phone call, then they were away from their apartments."

"That's reaching," she said.

"Look at your phone bill someday. What with toll calls and long distance calls and message units, it's pretty obvious that we all use our phones a lot. And I've looked at my bill—when I'm away there's a huge gap in it."

"I don't know. Somebody could be sick. Or they could be at work all day. Or they could have left their phone off the hook. Or they could have a WATTS line or they could have gotten calls but not made them."

"Let's see what happens." Cursore pressed several more keys and in seconds the following appeared on the computer's video terminal:

FOLLOWING IS A LIST OF ALL RESIDENTS WHO MADE TOLL OR LONG DISTANCE CALLS ON THESE DATES:
August 4, 5, 6 one year ago.
August 9, 10, 11 one year ago.
July 8, 9, 10 two years ago.
May 1, 2, 3 three years ago.

"I take it that those dates are when the various women disappeared?" asked Jasper.

"Right. And all of them were women who were just passing through, as close as I can figure out. The middle date is when the women probably disappeared," he said.

The computer found twenty two names of people who made phone calls from their apartments on *all* the days the women disappeared.

He stared at the twenty two names on the video screen—fourteen of them were women. That left eight men.

Cursore looked at Jasper and said: "OK. We've got eight men who made phone calls on each of the days that four women disappeared. We know that those eight men were in their apartments for sure, right?"

"No. We know that somebody was in their apartments. But that's all we know —they could have let a friend use their apartment."

"Good point," he replied. "What I'll do is ask the computer to scan each set of phone calls that was made on our target dates, then compare those calls with the usual length of phone call and the usual numbers that were called. That'll give us a pretty good idea if the tenant was making phone calls or if it was a guest."

The computer quickly detected that on May 1st, three years ago, and August

6th, one year ago, there was a great difference in Mr. Wadeencamp's phone bill. He usually made only local calls and spoke for several minutes. But on the above dates someone talked half the night and phoned all over North America.

"We'll assume then," said Cursore, "that Mr. Wadeencamp was gone. We've now reduced our number of male suspects who were home each time there was a missing person from eight to seven people."

"So if the ladies were abducted or killed on the dates you've indicated, and if the person who did it lives in our apartment complex, then it's got to be one of those names?"

"The odds are very high."

"I don't know. It seems really reaching. Of course I have to admit that every day I'm in my apartment, I use my phone for an hour or two, and if someone looked at my phone bill, he sure could tell when I'd been home and when I'd been away."

"There must be a way to narrow the suspects even further," said Cursore.

"How?"

"It's something the man would do after he kills. He might celebrate—go out for a special victory dinner. He might deposit the money from his victims into a bank account . . ."

"Hold it," she said. "Did all of the victims withdraw large chunks of money from their accounts like Dusty did?"

"Yes. That's exactly why I used those four women. I checked their bank balances before you arrived. A day or two after each one disappeared, she withdrew a large deposit from her savings account."

"It's pretty morbid to go out and have a victory celebration after you murder a woman and clean out her savings account."

"We're dealing with a psychopath. If you would have met Dusty . . . you would have . . ."

"You're right," said Jasper. "OK. You have the banks where each of the seven men have a savings or checking account, don't you?"

"Yes."

"Ask the computer if there's a correlation between the disappearance of the women and large deposits to their accounts?"

"OK." He worked over the computer terminal for ten minutes but the computer could find no correlation. "Just means that one of these men may have an account that he hasn't told the apartment management about. Or our man could simply keep the cash hidden someplace."

They both stared at the seven names on the display screen. Cursore hit a button and a nearby typewriter spit out the seven names on clean white paper. The paper zipped out of its carriage. He made a Xerox for her.

"Let's go home," he said.

"But we're so close..." She stared at the list of seven names. "Can't we narrow the suspects down?"

"Since most people have a Visa or Master Charge at the same place they bank, I could get into the charge card records and see what kind of purchases those seven made close to the date of each person's disappearance. Might help..."

"Let's do it. This is really blowing my mind."

"I'm really tired but if you're game," he said. He sank back into his chair and started to type as she massaged his back.

Across the video screen the following appeared: "Central computer down. Estimated time—one hour."

"What's that?"

"Oh, I forgot. Does this every week or so. Technicians are putting some new hardware in. We'll have to come back in the morning." He got up.

"You didn't hit some trick button so you could have your way with me tonight, did you?" she asked.

"Would you forgive me if I did?"

"Tonight, for some reason, I'm really turned onto you. You are a genius with that keyboard... Let's go home."

"I'm for that," he said, kissing her as they headed out of the factory and back to his place.

When they got in the car he said there was room to do almost anything in the back seat.

"Turns me on just talking about it. But I'll have to make a quick trip to my apartment..."

"Oh, yes... the girl who has control over her life," he said, accelerating his car toward the Marina.

She started to blow in his ear. He was hotter than his engine when they screeched to a stop in his parking space. They were all over each other in the elevator and she would have been embarrassed if anyone came upon them. They ran down the corridor to her apartment and he had her blouse off before she could get the key into her lock.

He carried her to her bed and threw her onto it. She bounced up, ducked under him and pulled off his shirt. "All right, Tarzan," she said. "Get our clothes off and I'll be right out of the bathroom."

He groaned, as she slipped into the bathroom and opened her medicine cabinet. She reached for the Kaam.

"Hurry up," he yelled through the door.

"Keep your pants off." It was 11:47 p.m. Wednesday.

24

Earlier Wednesday, at 7:45, after he had called Ivan Tornoff in Washington, Jon Andrews returned to his penthouse apartment. The day had been hot, too muggy, but the Marina was a pleasant fifteen degrees cooler than Los Angeles. A gentle sea breeze vibrated the sails of the boats in the harbor. The Russian opened his balcony door and stood on his patio, letting the wind caress his cheeks and swirl around his body. He stood that way for several minutes, watching the swimmer methodically move back and forth in the apartment pool. The rhythm of the man's arms slipping in and out of the water had a hypnotic effect on the Russian, but the illusion was broken as the swimmer climbed out of the pool and Jon saw that it was the computer expert.

The Russian felt his skin grow warm, as anger and fear pulsated through his body. The computer expert was closing in on him. Strange, unpredictable bits of irony seemed to focus on him. Jon Andrews rested his arms on his balcony railing, and because the updraft was exactly right, he could make out snatches of the conversation that Cursore was having with the large man who had been waiting at the end of the pool. The Russian heard them talk about a "deal" if Cursore discovered who the killer was. No wonder Cursore was so anxious, so driven. The Russian would be Cursore's pass to freedom.

From his balcony, Jon Andrews watched as the brother of the two dead black girls approached the policeman. He saw the black man motion around the complex, but even before the man pointed to him, the Russian stepped back into the shadows. The computer expert approached the cop and the black. They started to discuss the two black girls in greater depth. The Russian heard the black say that his sister May had phoned him with the number of the person she was visiting in the Marina. The black said he had lost the phone number but a moment later left with the policeman to find it. The Russian relaxed —he knew it would do them no good. He had taken the phone number from a discarded telephone he had found in the garbage. But as he watched the people moving around by the pool, the Russian realized that the phone number might lead them back to his complex because the phone had belonged to someone in the complex. And once the police realized that much, they would begin going door-to-door. They would ask questions, they would look at records, they would be relentless. Who knows? They might get a search warrant and check his penthouse. They would find caked blood in the crevices of the bathroom tile. They would find dried blood on his rug. They would discover him. It was time to disappear again, time to merge into another identity. He was pleased he had already taken the appropriate steps. He had already started the tedious reconstructing of a life, finding another skin to wiggle into. A butterfly in reverse. But before he left Los Angeles he would kill the computer expert and the reporter. And they would become a part of his plan for a final score, as the Americans called it. A big score. One that would allow him to live the rest of his life without having to concern himself with a series of *safeties* that never were as safe as they seemed and never as profitable.

He walked back into his living room and shut the sliding glass door. He turned out the lights and shed his clothing. He lay down on his mirrored coffee table—this time on his back. He felt the cold surface of the glass against his spine and shoulder blades. He was intensely aware of life and death. Of happiness and sadness. Of good and bad. Hot skin against cold glass. It brought things in focus. There would of course be regrets—the Jaguar would be abandoned. His yacht would be abandoned—perhaps he could sell it to some young men he had heard were interested in drug dealing. No. That would not work. That would leave a link. He must walk away from everything as he had planned. On Monday he would go to his bank and withdraw his cash. He would leave the keys in his Jaguar in Venice. It would be gone within the hour. He had already purchased a Mustang in another name. That would take care of transportation. And he had already found a place to live.

The Russian would miss the matched walnut veneer of his Jaguar. He grimaced as he pictured some shop disemboweling his beautiful Vanden Plus. But it had to be done. The Jaguar would be a link to him. He would stay in a motel and from there he would complete his plan. The one that seemed to be falling so perfectly into place. Big Score. Why did the Americans use that kind of idiom? He had set things up almost perfectly. Just a few more phone calls . . . . The Russian sat up on the mirrored coffee table and felt the cold glass against his buttocks. He gazed at his reflection in the blue-black darkness and he could not see where he stopped or his reflection started. An omen of how easily he could merge and blend in this society. He knew his gift was appearing so normal. He stared at the digital watch on his wrist but he could not make out the time. Finally he pushed a tiny button on it and a soft light feathered across its surface. It was 8:20 p.m.

Time to prepare for the phone calls.

There was one item that bothered Jon Andrews. When he had killed the woman from Idaho, he had left a credit card in her hotel room. He had stolen the card from Cursore. He had done this to incriminate the computer expert but for some reason the plan had not worked. Could the police have overlooked the credit card? Could they be that incompetent? The Russian doubted this was the case. He assumed the police had discovered the credit card and were using it to manipulate Cursore. The Russian was annoyed with himself for attempting such a simplistic solution. The only reason he had done it was to confuse the police and agitate Cursore. He cursed in Ukranian, then composed himself.

He dressed in a pair of white slacks and a grey cashmere sweater. He put on soft leather slippers, and by 10:00 he was standing at one of the illuminated blue phone bubbles along the boardwalk. To soothe himself and to kill time he listened to some old radio tapes of The Shadow. An hour later he called "Magic" MacDonal. He dialed the Holiday Inn by the airport and asked to be put through to the executive's room.

"This is Mr. MacDonal," said a voice.

The voice was shaky, filled with uncertainty.

"This is The Shadow," said the Russian. He rather liked that twist. It was working. His plan was working—one of America's top ad executives had flown three thousand miles.

"I read all about you in People Magazine, Mac."

"I'm here like you said. What . . ."

"Hang up, speak to no one, take the elevator to the lobby immediately. Go to the pay phones. You have three minutes. Don't take the policeman who is with you." *Click.*

The New York advertising executive hung up the phone. An FBI agent who was listening on headsets turned off his tape recorder. "You'd better go down to the lobby."

"What if he's down there? What if he . . ."

"He's not down there. He's trying to muddle up our trace. You go down there, and we'll see if we can nail him. Keep him talking."

"Aren't you coming with me?"

"It's OK, Mr. MacDonal. We're on top of this. Just get downstairs." The agent looked like an IBM office manager. Three-piece suit. White starched shirt. Spit-shined shoes. The agent held the door open for Magic and used a reassuring smile to push him from the room.

The phone started to ring in the main

lobby as Magic stepped out of the elevator. Several people glanced at the phone. An elderly lady frowned and tottered toward it. Magic elbowed her aside and picked up the receiver. "Yes."

"You were a little late. Why did you talk to the man in the room with you?"

"There wasn't a man in the room."

"That's not what my people tell me," said the Russian, sensing the other's stress and fear. "Have you talked to Dr. Florence?"

"Yes. I thought you . . ."

"Quiet. What'd she say?"

"She said that the foam contained some kind of nerve gas. She said that there was no antidote for it."

"What was her response when you told her that I was going to place nerve gas in Kaam across the nation?"

"She was upset. But not as upset as I or my employers were. We will do anything . . ."

"Then you have the five million dollars?"

"Yes."

"Umarked bills?"

"Yes."

"Go back to your room. Get some sleep. Since you've talked to the police about this, I'm going to punish you. I'm going to kill two people at random tonight."

"I didn't talk to the police."

"Don't lie to me. I know your every

move. At 6 a.m. Thursday you will return to this phone. Have the money in a case. I'll tell you what to do with it. If you follow my instructions, I'll tell you where half the contaminated Kaam packages are. Two hours later, if all goes according to my requests, you'll find the remaining packages. Good night."

The Russian hung up. He was certain that Magic MacDonal had contacted the police. The executive would have had no other choice when the Russian had called him a week earlier. The Russian dialed another number.

"Hello," said Buff Tallons.

"Good evening, Comrade. This is The Shadow."

"What?"

"I want to spare you the pain of being electrocuted for treason."

"I'm afraid I don't understand . . ."

"Yes, you do. I can prove that you worked with Ivan Tornoff of the Russian Embassy in selling classified computer secrets to Iron Curtain countries. I have tape recordings, pictures and names of your contacts. If you do exactly as I instruct you for two hours Thursday morning then you will never hear from me again. Do you agree?"

"What do I have to do?"

"Pick up an attache case from the Holiday Inn by the airport. Deliver it to me. If you are caught, then you can say I forced you to act at gunpoint. The police will assume I was nearby watching with a high-powered rifle. Do you agree?"

"How do I know you are not bluffing?"

"There is a man who works for you. His name is David Cursore. Is that so?"

"Yes."

"His friends call him Cursore."

"Yes." The industrialist's voice grew weaker, frightened.

"Two Russian agents were working with you, approximately four years ago. They defected with a great deal of money. Mr. Cursore was blamed and went to jail. The only way you could have proven him innocent was to admit your conspiracy with the Russian Embassy. You kept your mouth closed, didn't you?"

"Where did you get that information? No one knew . . ."

"Be still. I want you to be ready to leave your home at 6:30 a.m. tomorrow. Understand?"

"Yes."

"All right. Contact no one and be ready for my call. If you do as you're asked, no one will ever hear from me again. Pleasant dreams, Comrade." The Russian hung up.

He walked around the Marina for awhile, bought a soft drink, then waited some more. He expected that Cursore and the reporter would spend the night together. He had heard enough of their conversation through the bugs he had planted in their apartment to realize that when they made love that night they would use the Kaam foam. Then they would be dead. He had twice visited her apartment to make certain that the contraceptive foam was in order. He had used a slightly different formula—it would take at least ten minutes for the nerve gas to work. Time for them to begin making love and also contaminate him.

A random killing. He—or at least a man called Jon Andrews—would never even be tied to a random killing. Yes, Jon Andrews would disappear in a few days. As usual he would be several moves ahead of the Americans—and this time he would have five million dollars in cash. He had already made complete plans for Jan Country to assume ownership of a beautiful home in Big Bear Lake. Clean and fresh. The perfect place for a man to start anew. Two hours and a lifetime away from Los Angeles.

The Russian looked at his watch under a street light. Almost midnight. Soon the computer expert and the reporter would return. Everything was going with amazing luck. The frightened ad executive had the five million dollars. A small price to pay for a billion dollar product. Buff Tallons would do exactly as he was told, caught in the steel trap. Besides, Ivan Tornoff had already talked to the manufacturing executive. The diplomat did not want Jon Andrews exposed. And Comrade Tornoff had a magnificent gift for persuasion. He would do an excellent job of persuading Buff Tallons to play along.

The Russian was beginning to think he had broken his chain of bad luck. Things were falling into place. He was thinking clearly, lucidly. Perfect planning, and his luck was running strong. He could feel it in the crisp night air. Good feeling.

25

At 10:20 p.m. Thursday, as arranged, Magic MacDonal opened the door that led to the adjoining room of his suite in the Holiday Inn. Waiting for him was a tense group composed of two FBI agents, one of whom was Assistant Special Agent in Charge (ASAC) of the L.A. FBI office; Dr. Jane Florence; an assistant from the District Attorney's office; Deputy Chief of West L.A. Police Department; Assistant Sheriff from L.A. City Sheriff's Department; and Sergeant Dartwell.

"Would you like some coffee, Mr. MacDonal?" asked Dr. Florence, indicating the tray of half-eaten food on a large coffee table in the suite.

"I haven't eaten all day. And I don't think I'll be able to until this is all over. When I talked to that madman on the lobby phone downstairs, I could feel him watching me."

Special FBI Agent Kruger, a lean, methodical individual, allowed, "Mr. S' wasn't watching you and it's doubtful if anyone working with him was either."

"When did we start calling this lunatic 'Mr. S'?" asked the assistant from the D.A.'s office.

"First time he called me on the phone he said he was 'The Shadow'," said Magic MacDonal.

"I don't think we should play to his ego, Mr. MacDonal," said the Assistant D.A. "The man is a terrorist and he should be dealt with as such. Now the first thing the District Attorney instructed me to discuss was how seriously can we take this character. Any thoughts, Dr. Florence?"

"I'd take him seriously. He called our office and told us the exact components of his nerve gas, half an hour before anyone got the lab reports. He described the victim in detail."

"Christ," said the Assistant D.A., "what's the FBI's assessment?"

"We recorded his voice the second time he called Mr. MacDonal in New York, and we got him again when he called a few hours ago. We've analyzed Dr. Florence's lab reports and examined her notes. I think this man will go ahead with his threat to contaminate the product if we don't satisfy his demands."

"You think he's in this alone?"

"I have no way of knowing that."

The Assistant District Attorney glanced at his watch, then addressed the assistant L.A. Sheriff. "Anything to add?"

"If we call this sicko's bluff, and we should, then we better start notifying the public about the dangers of this baby eradicator," said the assistant Sheriff.

"It is not a baby eradicator," snapped Magic MacDonal. "It is a contraceptive foam and has nothing to do with the fetus . . ."

"Please. Let's not argue," said the Assistant D.A. "The purpose of this meeting is to plan a course of action that meets all the contingencies as well as staying within the law."

Sergeant Dartwell, who had not been briefed about anything, listened. He knew he was there only because of his involvement in the case. If anything went wrong he would probably end up being crushed in the political free-for-all that his bosses would play.

"With all due respect," said Magic MacDonal to the assistant Sheriff, "a course of action has already been developed with the help of the FBI. As you know we want to pay the man off and that will be the end of our problem."

"What happens when he puts the bite on you again?" asked Dartwell.

"We'll face that when it happens. But we all feel that the five million dollars will allow this individual to go away and live the kind of life he obviously is trying to gain."

"You get one terrorist off, you'll have fifty more standing in his tracks the next day." Sergeant Dartwell picked up some cheese and stuffed in into his mouth.

"The FBI," said Special Agent Kruger, "has prepared a number of studies on these situations, and if the extortionist is non-political, as this man seems to be, there's an excellent chance he'll take the money and disappear. You'll never hear from him again."

"Another federal program to buy criminals off?" snapped the Deputy Chief of West L.A.

"Give it a rest, Chief," said the Assistant D.A. "We *are* all on the same side. And we're trying to save lives."

"I don't think that would be much solace to the poor lady he tested his concoction on," said the doctor.

"You're right, Doctor," sighed the Assistant D.A. "But if we don't go along with the demands and he carries out his threats, we're going to have a lot more dead people on our hands."

"So . . . Just going to give him the money and that's it?" asked Dartwell.

"Of course not," said Special Agent Kruger. "From the moment Mr. MacDonal leaves here we'll have surveillance coverage. We're going to use twelve of our men. We'll need fifteen of yours for backup including the West Side Major Crime Violators Task Force."

The assistant Sheriff glanced at the Assistant D.A. who nodded.

"I have a question," said the doctor.

"This extortionist has made it clear that he'll contaminate other containers of Kaam if we don't pay the ransom. In the event that something goes wrong, how are we going to alert the public? We only have about twelve hours before the drug stores open in California?"

"Amen," said Dartwell.

"We're ready to go on television and radio," said the assistant Sheriff. "We've got a network of people standing by to go door to door in areas where we think people won't get the message."

"Maybe we should alert them now," said the doctor.

"No."

"Why not?" she asked.

"I'll tell you," said the assistant Sheriff. "Consolidated Medicines is a multi-national company. I bet they employ twenty or thirty thousand people in California alone. The public gets scared . . . you watch Consolidated Medicines stock tumble."

"Hold on," said the Assistant D.A. "There's nothing political about our procedure. On the other hand, we've got one nut out there. Maybe you think we should allow one nut to destroy a major American company? That company helps pay our salary."

"Suppose he's already contaminated Kaam?" asked the doctor.

"He's given his word he hasn't," said Special Agent Kruger. "We have to try to figure out what that's worth. As long as he thinks he's getting what he wants, I doubt if he'll play hardball with us."

"We are going to try and grab him, aren't we?" asked Sergeant Dartwell.

"Absolutely," said the ASAC agent. "But we'll only nab him if we can make a clean collar. We're not going to take any chances that he'll get away. Our psychologists feel that he could turn lethal if we made him angry or indicated to him we weren't going to hold up our end of the bargain."

"Well, for God's sake, let's not do anything to upset this poor, confused terrorist," said Dartwell.

"Sergeant," snapped the Assistant D.A., "we're trying to save lives. I don't think anyone in this group particularly is amused by your sarcasm."

"I'm not amused with it," said the doctor, "but I certainly see the Sergeant's point of view. We're really handing this terrorist, who is a murderer, everything he wants on a silver platter."

"If you want to put it that way, Doctor, fine," said the Assistant D.A. "But he's got us by the short and curly—we either go with him, or we fight. If we fight we're going to destroy a company. We're going to put the same kind of crazy notions in every nut's head in this country. And a lot of people are going to end up dead."

"Chief," asked Magic MacDonal. "What are you officers concerned about? The money? The insurance will reimburse us. And it's a lot cheaper for them than watching a billion dollar company fold."

"I don't give a rat's ass about the money," Dartwell said. "I'm just sick and tired of being pussy-whipped by every two bit hood that yells boo from the closet." More dirty looks from the senior officers.

"I don't know if I agree with the word pussy-whipped," said the doctor. "But he's right. If we don't take a stand then we're going to be pushed into corners we'll never get out of."

"Hold it," said the Assistant D.A. "Just hold it. I understand all of your feelings. We're not trying to coddle criminals. Lord knows, the D.A. has more convictions than any of his predecessors. But it has been determined by the FBI, the Sheriff's office, the D.A. and the LAPD that we keep a low profile on this. We're trying to save lives; we're thinking of the public's safety. We have an alternative plan in the event anything goes wrong. Now I want the cooperation of everyone in this room. We have to have a united front."

The only two people who had any eye contact with each other were Dartwell and the doctor. The rest were looking at the crumbling wedge of cheese on the coffee table.

Sergeant Dartwell was thinking about

the bureaucratic mess he was in. Coddling an extortionist. The man had obviously killed the woman from Idaho as a test of the nerve gas. The man had tried to frame Cursore. The reason was simple. Cursore had stumbled onto the psychopath. Connections were clicking into place in the cop's mind. He had an overwhelming sense that Cursore and the girl were in terrible danger. A very specific danger, but he did not know from what.

"I have a question," said the Assistant D.A. to Dartwell, "about this man David Cursore. I understand a credit card of his was found in Andria Bevan's room."

"That's right."

"Do you think this Cursore has anything to do with The Shadow?"

"I don't know. I doubt it."

"Well, we invited you to this meeting because of your special knowledge of this case. You must have an opinion."

"I think this fellow who calls himself The Shadow may be connected with Cursore. But I don't think Cursore knows anything about it."

26

Ivan Tornoff arrived at the Los Angeles Airport shortly after 11 p.m. Thursday. He rented a car and drove to 315 Marguerita Street in Santa Monica. The houses were in the million dollar category, set behind swaying palm trees and sweet-scented oleander bushes that towered above the wide sidewalks.

He got out of his car and walked to the front door. The sound of a Bach fugue washed through the clear night, and he pictured mothers and fathers putting children to bed in the two and three-story homes that he imagined were hidden behind walls of bushes and wrought iron. Ivan tried the door and found that it was open. He walked inside and had the impression of great wealth and taste. Elaborately designed oriental rugs covered a chocolate flecked carpet that stretched wall to wall in the living room. On either side of an enormous wood-burning fireplace, he saw shelves of leather bound books. There was a six or seven-piece sofa with fine oak furniture: a long sleek dining room table, a perfectly restored, wind-up Victrola, a twelve foot highback bar, complete with a mirror that ran the length of the room.

He could hear the sound of someone moving around on the second floor. Ivan walked up the circular staircase that descended to the main foyer.

In the master bedroom, Buff Tallons opened a drawer in his handmade Swedish bureau and tossed several freshly laundered shirts into an overnight grip. He scooped up a bottle of aftershave and was reaching for his razor when he saw Ivan standing in the doorway. Buff Tallons' Chanel cologne clattered to the floor and smashed, sending slivers of glass spraying across the peg and groove floor.

"What the hell are you doing here?" asked the industrialist.

"I took a plane as soon as we finished talking today."

"There's nothing to talk about."

"On the contrary," said Ivan, sitting on the queen-sized bed that was covered with a llama skin comforter, "there's a great deal to talk about."

"Does anyone know you're here?"

"It's quite safe, and I'm certain that if neither one of us does anything foolish, all will continue to be safe. As I understand it, you have certain things you must attend to tomorrow morning." He glanced at his watch.

"It's impossible for me to act as a

courier for anyone," said the industrialist. "Absolutely impossible."

"You're frightened, aren't you?"

"If you want to know the truth, I am. First some person from our past calls me and tells me I must act as a courier. Then you call from Washington and tell me that the man is a renegade spy and I must do what he says. Wouldn't that frighten you?"

"It would frighten any intelligent man," said the Russian diplomat. "That is why I've flown here. There were certain things I could not discuss with you over the phone. First, let me tell you about the man who called you up. His name is Jon Andrews—at least that is the name he goes by now. His real name does not matter. At one time he was one of our finest field agents and . . ."

"Just say spy, OK?"

"Yes. Unfortunately, after he came to this country, a decision was made to eliminate him. I was against such action; nevertheless, an attempt was made. The attempt failed, as I feared. We had trained this man to survive rather well by developing his taste for a very high lifestyle. It seems he's developed a plan to extort several million dollars from a large American drug company. The extortion was not that difficult. But of course the physical transfer of money between Mr. Andrews and the American company is the difficult problem. He needs someone that the FBI will trust and someone that he can trust. Since you are well connected with the community..."

"He knows I've worked with you. He's blackmailing me. You said our arrangement would never be discovered."

"I apologize," said the Russian. "The positive side is that he will probably succeed with his plan. And he'll disappear and none of us will hear of him again. Of course, should someone bungle his plan, he will probably tell what he knows to the authorities. I will be deported—and you, of course, will be dealt with."

"I'll go to prison."

"Yes."

"This isn't fair," said the industrialist.

"It wasn't fair that a friend of yours, an innocent friend, went to jail instead of you. But that is the way things work out sometimes."

"I have gone through hell over what happened to David Cursore."

"I'm sure you have. But you also became very rich from what happened. And if you want to stay rich and out of jail, then it is imperative you comply with Jon Andrews."

"There must be an alternative."

"Certainly. Refuse to cooperate and tell the authorities about your involvement with me."

Tallons slowly began to unpack his bag.

"Cheer up my friend," said the Russian. "Your friend is out of jail. You have given him a good job. And after a few hours' work tomorrow morning, then you will be—what do they say here—home free? Yes, you'll be home free."

"And suppose something goes wrong tomorrow?"

"This ex-field man of ours is very clever."

"But something could go wrong?"

"Something can always go wrong. But don't worry—Jon Andrews is a brilliant person and this situation is child's play for him. Look at how clever he was to choose you. He knows you must do everything to help him, and it is in all of our interests that you protect him from the police. And you and I are only tiny pieces of his puzzle. I wish we had more men like Jon."

"What does he have on you?"

"Not much. Probably he realizes that I reported he was killed to Moscow."

"What if they find out that he is alive?"

"If all goes well, no one will find out anything. Now, since you're all unpacked, why don't I help you clean up that cologne. Then perhaps you would have a small glass of spirits and then I should really be getting back to my hotel."

"Yes. I don't suppose it would do to have anyone see the two of us together, would it?"

"No. And speaking of precautions, do you always leave your front door open? That's inviting trouble, you know."

The industrialist pulled some Kleenexes from a box of tissues and started to mop up his spilled cologne.

27

At three minutes past midnight, Jasper opened her bathroom door. She was wearing a lovely black peignoir and her hair spilled across her shoulders.

Cursore was in bed, waiting for her. He did not know if he loved her—he was not certain if he could ever love her—but for a moment he weighed what life would be like if he never saw her again. He felt emptiness. It was not an overpowering emptiness but he was aware that a part of her life was beginning to blend with his. If they stopped seeing each other he knew he would miss her. And that, he supposed, was the start of love. . . .

"Are you OK?" he asked.

She did not reply.

"Hey, you OK?"

She opened her mouth to speak and then suddenly moved her slender hand to cover her full lips. It was as though she was going to become sick and was trying to stop.

He swung his feet to the ground and moved to her, held her. "It's OK. What's wrong?"

He could feel her stomach muscles contract suddenly against his body. "I . . . I know who the person that we're looking for is."

"You do? Who?"

"That man we saw outside the elevator. He has the penthouse down the hallway from you. His name is Russ something. He's a banker. The man with the Jaguar."

Cursore dug into his pocket and pulled out the paper with the names from the computer on it, scanned it. "There's a Russ here . . ."

"I remember he was at the pool when you were talking to Dusty. He was watching her. I didn't pay any attention to him at the time. But the way he looked at her. Not like a man watching a woman. Like a hunter stalking an animal. He had that same look when he saw us in the elevator. I can feel it."

"What do you think we should do? I mean, just because you have a feeling . . ."

"I think we should go to his penthouse and confront him. What if he has Dusty with him?"

"Knock on his door and barge in there?"

"First we'll call Sergeant Dartwell. He'll talk to him."

"Maybe we should do it in the morning." He kissed her, nuzzled her neck.

"You might feel a lot differently in the morning . . ."

"Stop kissing me like that. I can sense that man is dangerous. We *have* to call the police."

Cursore realized how adamant she was. "OK. I guess Sergeant Dartwell can't get much more peeved than he is."

"Thank you," she said. "This is giving me a headache. I'm sorry. I'm really wired." She stepped into her bathroom, found an aspirin and washed it down with a glass of water. She put away her cold cream and the unopened package of Kaam. "I just keep seeing his eyes. Cold like fish eyes."

Cursore started to dial Sergeant Dartwell's home number when he felt a cold pressure on his neck. He turned around and saw that the pressure was coming from the business end of a .38 handgun. Its vented silencer dug into his neck. The Russian, his eyes gleaming in the dark, held the .38. Cursore had the impression the man had handled a firearm before. "Hang up the phone," he said.

Cursore set the receiver back on its cradle.

"Honey?" asked Jasper, walking back into the bedroom. "Why aren't you phoning . . . my God!"

"Come in here, and sit down in the chair by the dresser," said the Russian.

Obediently, terrified, Jasper made her

way to the chair. Her eyes never left the gun that was pressed against Cursore's head. "W-what do you want?"

"What have you told the police?"

"N-nothing," she said. "We don't know anything about the police."

"If you lie, I will kill this man," said Jon Andrews. "You must not lie to me again. I had a listening device in both of your apartments. I know you've talked to a Sergeant Dartwell on several occasions. Have you told anyone else about your theories?"

"No," said the woman.

"And you?" demanded the Russian, nudging Cursore's skull with the muzzle of the handgun.

"No. No one else." Cursore had the strong impression he was going to die. The inside of his mouth felt like dry leaves and he was aware of each of his breaths. Inhale. Exhale. He wondered how many breaths he had left.

"I am surprised you did not discover the body of the Florida woman in the bottom of the Malibu sewer drain."

"That's why you killed the old man?" asked Cursore.

"God," said the woman. "God. No."

"Do you have any adhesive tape?" asked the Russian.

"Yes."

"Get it."

Cursore caught a glimpse of the man in the bedroom mirror. He could see that the intruder was wearing rubber gloves. Cursore realized that if the man tied them up, it would be the end. He thought he might as well make a stand. He would have a better chance with his hands free.

Jasper brought a roll of adhesive tape into the bedroom and tossed it on the bed beside the Russian. "No," said the man. "Pick it up and tape his legs to the chair."

"How'd you get in?" asked Cursore.

"A key."

"You have a master key, don't you?" said Cursore.

"Yes."

"Is that how you got to Dusty?"

"Yes."

"And you tied her up, too?"

"You're a good detective," said the Russian. "Too bad the police won't believe you."

"A pity," said Jasper. She knelt in front of Cursore and wound the tape around his legs, then around the legs of the chair he was sitting in.

"Make it tight," said the Russian.

"What are you going to do with us?" said the woman.

"Hopefully, nothing."

Cursore could feel the tape straining against his shins. He looked at Jasper and smiled.

Suddenly there was a knock at the door.

The man with the gun held a finger to

his lips.

Another knock. Then Mary Lou's voice said: "Jasper, I know you and Cursore are in there. I've already checked his apartment. Open up." She banged on the door.

"Talk to her, but I'll kill her if she finds out what's going on," whispered the Russian.

Jasper went to the door. "Hi, Mary Lou. We're kind of unpresentable."

"I know. Did you hear the news?"

"What?"

"There's some kind of problem with Kaam. The manufacturer has asked everyone to return it for a new kind."

"Oh."

"You don't mind me telling you, do you? They won't say what's wrong but I didn't want you to get into trouble."

"Thank you, Mary Lou."

"OK. See you two for breakfast. I made some croissants. That puff pastry'll be the death of me."

"OK. See you in the morning."

The Russian picked up her phone and dialed a number. "Let me speak to Mr. MacDonal . . . hello . . . why'd you tell? You said you wouldn't tell . . . oh . . . we still have a deal, then. All right. If you don't have the money, you'll regret it. You better." The Russian hung up.

Cursore and Jasper watched him.

"What's wrong with that foam?"

"It contains a topical poison."

"My God," she said. "Is mine poisoned?"

"It doesn't matter now," said the man with the gun. "What matters is that they're lying to me, and you might be more use to me alive than dead."

"What . . ." she started to say.

"It's an extortion scheme. Our friend here has obviously poisoned some of those Kaam packages. Tested the poison too, haven't you?"

"I don't think we need to continue this discussion," said the Russian.

As the Russian's finger tightened on his handgun, Jasper grabbed a vase and threw it at him with all of her might. At the same instant, Cursore twisted around and smashed his fist into the Russian's arm. The gun slipped from the Russian's hand as it went off. There was a soft splat as its slug tore through the headboard of the bed.

Jasper grabbed a paperweight from her dresser and hurled it at the Russian's head as Cursore got him by his leg. The Russian was a blur—a series of lightning-fast reflexes—as he twisted away, regained the gun, and fired. Cursore felt a hard thud, and the impact of the shot propelled him halfway across the room as he crunched into the bathroom door. He saw the ceiling spinning, felt warm blood gushing from his head, then everything went black.

The Russian grabbed the woman as

she reached a shoe tree. He backhanded her, sending her sprawling across the room. She landed in a crumpled heap against a footstool.

She covered her mouth to stop the fear and revulsion. "You've killed him. He's dead. You've killed . . ."

The Russian dragged her to her feet. "Come or I'll kill you also."

She could not tear her eyes away from Cursore. One moment he had been alive and alert and full of vitality. Now he was a rag doll, his legs still tied to the chair. His face was a mask of blood. There was a hole in his cheek and the blood was gushing out of it. She started to cry, hysterically. The Russian slapped her and dragged her to her feet.

"Do you want to die, too?"

"No."

"Then come with me. Make a false move, I will kill you." He found a long coat for her and ordered her to put it on. As she tied the buckle in place he said: "Wipe your tears away."

She brushed the tears away and looked at Cursore again. He was no longer breathing. Blood was everywhere. The Russian took her by her arm and led her away from the apartment. He locked the door behind him.

28

By one a.m. Thursday the entire West Coast news media had the story about the contaminated Kaam. Somehow it had been leaked. All-night disc jockeys warned of the possible recall, and after The Tonight Show, a special news bulletin was telecast. Of course, no one realized that the contraceptive foam contained a deadly nerve gas that could kill within minutes of exposure to it. This was due to Magic MacDonal's expertise with news releases. The release said: "The makers of Kaam in the western United States have discovered that a contaminant may have been introduced into the latest shipments of their product. If you have an unopened package, please return it immediately to the company and it will be replaced with two packages. Kaam will also refund your full postage. Again, anyone who has a new package of Kaam is asked to return it unused to the manufacturer. Do not open the package."

Magic sat in the hotel suite in the Holiday Inn with the two FBI agents,

Sergeant Dartwell, Dr. Florence and the assistant District Attorney of California. They watched a reporter on Channel 7 deliver the news bulletin. After it was over the assistant D.A. turned down the volume. "What do you think?"

"I think sales are going to go all to hell, that's what I think," said MacDonal.

"Maybe not," said Dr. Florence. "A number of products have been recalled —and when it was done by the manufacturer, the public responded rather well."

"We're talking about a new kind of roulette here," said the ad man. "Fucking roulette. That's what one of my contacts at UP called it. He said, 'Magic, you mean to tell me that this batch of Kaam could do you in? Sounds to me like fuckin' roulette.' And then he laughed."

"If you want my opinion," said Sergeant Dartwell, "I think we should have told the public just how lethal this Kaam could be."

"Look," said the assistant D.A., "we have no evidence that *any* Kaam on the shelves has been contaminated. We simply have the threat that it might be, and since the extortionist is going to be paid off, I don't think there's all that much to worry about."

"I agree with him," said FBI Agent Kruger. "We start telling the public that a crazy is extorting cash from one of the largest drug houses in America, we're going to be swamped with copycat criminals. Half the felons in America will be poisoning everything from dog food to Tootsie Rolls."

"And of course," said Magic, "if anyone thinks that Kaam contains a nerve gas, that'll be the end of one of America's largest companies. I think we've managed to handle this problem with foresight and wisdom. I just feel awfully nervous about delivering the money. Awfully nervous."

"Mr. MacDonal, if you wish, my offer to have one of our agents substitute for you still stands," said the FBI representative.

"I appreciate that, but I really feel that I'm responsible for a part of what's happened. If there had been no ad campaign, then there would have been no product for this extortionist to use. I'll deliver the money as I promised."

"You sure you want to do that?" asked Sergeant Dartwell.

"No. But the fellow who calls himself The Shadow probably knows what I look like. I'd hate to mess up things by not keeping up our end of the deal."

"That's very commendable," said the FBI agent.

"I keep thinking that he knows we're talking," said Magic.

"No. He doesn't."

"He said he was going to kill two people at random tonight to punish me for discussing what's happened with the police."

"I hope not," said the FBI agent. "I hope he's just trying to frighten you. He would have assumed that you would report any kind of extortion attempt to the authorities."

"But he's going to kill two people tonight. What about them?"

"There's not much we can do," said the deputy Police Chief, "until he does something. We can't panic an entire city. That's what this psycho wants."

The doctor finished off a Perrier water. "From what I've seen, this psycho is a very clever man. But like Mr. MacDonal, I can't help but feel shock at the two random victims he intends to select. There's millions of people out there and two of them are going to die just so that idiot can make a point."

Five miles away in Jasper's apartment, Cursore stirred. The glare from the bathroom light hurt his eyes. He was aware of the sound of his heart, or maybe it was a headache. Something was pounding in his mind. He tried to get up and realized his right hand was covered in blood. So was his left. Both of his ears were ringing. The front of his shirt was soaked in blood. His face was numb but the fact that it felt numb proved he was not dying. He remembered the man with the gun. He remembered Jasper and the distant popping sound the gun had made. Jasper's room floated in and out of focus. Cursore knew he would lose consciousness again. He had to find Jasper. Something about a news bulletin. Poisoned Kaam. What was that all about?

He pulled the telephone off the hook, dialed Mary Lou's phone number. After it rang several times she said: "Hello."

He wanted to say hello and tell her what was wrong but he couldn't make the words come out. Blood was everywhere and the light from the bathroom was starting to grow dim.

"Who is this?" asked Mary Lou.

He wanted to tell her about Jon Andrews, the man who lived down the hall from him. Finally he said: "Shot."

"What?"

"Shot." He had at least a dozen other things to tell her but he couldn't make the words come out. What the hell was going on with his brain? Must tell her about Jasper. Jasper was in trouble.

"Is that you, Cursore? That you?"

"Shot."

"You're shot? You at home?"

"Jas . . ."

"You at Jasper's?"

He thought he should tell her about Jasper guessing who the killer was. Thought he should tell her about the killer being in her apartment. But all Cursore could do was try to figure out why the phone slipped from his fingers.

Yes. The blood was making the plastic slippery.

He realized a part of him was on another planet or maybe the far side of the moon.

He heard Mary Lou banging on the door, then he was aware of the security guard opening Jasper's door. He heard Mary Lou screaming.

After awhile he heard the dull wail of sirens and he felt the vehicle he was in drifting around a corner. With considerable effort he deduced he was in an ambulance. He congratulated himself for being such a fine detective.

There was the sound of people around him. A bright light was glowing over him. People in green gowns and masks peered at him. One of the men with the masks wore little rectangular glasses. He had black eyes with long white lashes. Must be their leader, thought Cursore.

He heard sounds of machinery. Something was gurgling in his throat. A rubber gloved hand pushed a needle into his skin. He wondered if the rubber gloves were stolen. Do doctors wear gloves so they won't leave fingerprints?

He said, "Fingerprints."

"It's OK," said a female voice. "You're in a hospital. You'll be all right."

However, he thought they had surrounded him in masks and they were all wearing rubber gloves. Going to finish things off. All of them were criminals.

He heard voices. Someone said something about sinuses filled with blood. Another deeper voice said it was lucky that the bullet missed his brain. Someone said he had a hard head.

Everything ebbed. The bright lights went to soft grey. The voices started to fade. I'm dying, he thought. He focused his attention to one of the criminal's eyes. Between the bushy eyebrows was a cleft, a wrinkle. As long as he could keep the wrinkle in focus, he would be all right. The wrinkle got larger and larger and then everything went velvet black.

Goodbye, he said to the world. So many things to tell people, probably too late now.

29

By 3 a.m. Friday morning, the story of Kaam's recall was in the first edition of The Los Angeles Times. One of the newspaper's trucks rumbled through the semi-darkness of Westwood and stopped at the corner of Ohio where a man in faded blue overalls tossed several bundles of The Times to a teenager in a stained pea jacket. The boy loaded two hundred and thirty papers into a pushcart and headed westward to begin his route. He tossed a copy of The Times onto the doorstep of Martha Kringle.

Inside her two room apartment, Martha was still up. Martha was wearing a sky blue nightgown that covered her supple body. She smoked her twenty-fifth cigarette of the night and drained her fifth cup of black coffee. She brushed her jet black hair from her high cheekbones and, checking the peephole in her door, made certain no strangers were lurking on the landing. Martha slipped on her oval reading glasses and picked up the paper, then locked the door behind her.

She started to read the lead story about a group that had set off a bomb in Beirut. The world seemed a tragic place to her as she gazed at the picture of a man who had been blown apart by a terrorist explosion.

Then she lit her twenty-sixth cigarette and realized that her life was not all that bad. She was twenty-eight and lived in America and her door was locked and she was reasonably safe from terrorists. So what if she was heartbroken? Time heals all wounds. Or wounds all heels. She tried not to think of him. The bastard.

A few minutes later, a tap at the door startled her. She considered the cracked paint on the back of the heavy oak chair. Another soft tap. She stared at her well-used brown sofa and her worn green carpet and the matching avocado appliances in the bachelor kitchen. The section in front of the stove needed new linoleum.

"Martha," said a voice on the other side of the door. "It's Scotty."

She stubbed out her cigarette, ran her slender fingers through her disorganized hair, and scowled. Why had he come back? Damn him.

"Open the door, OK?"

She folded her arms and spoke to the empty room. "Why?"

"Because I love you."

"Sure you do. Now go home to your wife. I'm asleep."

"You're not asleep. All your lights are on."

"I don't want to talk to you."

"I couldn't sleep and neither could you —and that means a lot," he said.

"It means that I'll be half asleep tomorrow."

"You got any coffee?"

"No."

"I can smell it."

What the hell, she thought. If I keep talking to him, he'll start yelling and wake up the neighbors and I'll be looking for a new place and there's nothing available that's any cheaper than this. She was trapped with her $433 a month apartment and her married boyfriend—and she didn't know which one was worse, so she opened the door.

"You look like a dream in that negligee," he said hurrying into the room, sweeping her backwards, kissing her hungrily on the neck.

"Set me down, you big lumox." Martha headed toward the warm coffee pot and poured him a cupful.

Scotty shuffled across the room and took the coffee. He was a large man who walked like a large man. She had often read stories about large men who moved like cats. Scotty did not fall into that category. He was anything but graceful.

Awkward. "Why are you staring at me that way?" he asked.

"You're clumsy and inept."

"Don't talk to me that way, darling," he said. The coffee slipped from his hand, and he desperately grabbed for it. He somehow managed to break the handle of the mug as it smashed onto the floor. Hot coffee splashed along his leg. She finally found a dish cloth and mopped it up. He watched her with what she thought was pure dumb love.

"You want me to tell you how inept you are?" she asked.

"No."

"You're so inept you could screw up a wet dream."

"Don't talk to me that way," he said. "You and I have something special . . ."

"Bull. We have a certain amount of fun in the sack—that's it. Nothing else. Go home and entertain your wife."

"She's away, I told you."

"She'll be back tomorrow and if you're not there, she'll be angry and tell her Daddy and you'll be out of a job."

"You know that's the only reason I stay married to her. I promise you when I save enough money, I'll be . . ."

" . . . able to start your own business?"

"Right. Like I been telling you. And then I'll get a divorce and you and I can be truly happy for the rest of our lives."

"You really believe that, don't you?"

"Yes."

"I wish I could believe it. I really wish I could. But you and I don't have a chance. Not a rat's chance."

He put his arms around her.

"For someone so damn clumsy, you can be gentle," she said. She realized where the empty night was headed. She hated her quandary. Despised it. But she needed strength to get out of it and she was too tired to do anything except fall asleep in his arms. She was not happy he had come back, on the other hand . . . "Where have you been all night?"

"Just driving around, along Mulholland, listening to music. Thinking about you. Wishing we didn't have to fight so much."

"Oh."

He carried her into her bedroom and laid her gently down on her bed and kissed the nape of her neck.

"That feels good," she said.

"I love you."

"We can't make love now. I don't have anything."

"You had some last night, a fresh container of it."

"I threw it out."

"You always do that when we fight," he said.

"I guess I do." She was sorry now she had tossed out the Kaam. She wanted him but there was no way she was going to take a chance on getting pregnant when he was married to another woman

—and it didn't matter what he said. She was the bright one and he was the dumb one and she had no compulsion to change roles.

"I got some more from the store." Scotty reached into his jacket and took out a purse-sized container of Kaam. "I figured that you might have tossed the last one out."

She sat up. "So you just drove over to your father-in-law's drug store and opened it up in the middle of the night . . ."

"Yes."

"For an inept guy, you really amaze me."

"Hell, sometimes I amaze myself." He kissed her. She felt her body begin to tingle.

He kissed her again.

Martha sighed. She was beaten for the night—tomorrow with the sun would be a different day. Then she could be strong, but she wanted him and he knew he had her and maybe that was part of the fun of being with him. He could always find a way to have her; she could never really find a way to have him. She swung her legs to the floor and, picking up the canister of Kaam, walked to the bathroom. She flicked the light on. He watched her.

When she came out of the bathroom a few minutes later, she was naked. They fell into each other's arms and within seconds they were making love.

As they started to build to a climax, Martha suddenly screamed. Scotty couldn't understand what was wrong, then he saw that the bed sheet was drenched with blood. The woman was strangely inert. Then the convulsion hit him and he knew he was going to die. He tried to push himself away from her. But he couldn't.

He tried to breathe but his lungs were choked with blood. He couldn't figure out what the hell was happening. He tasted his own warm blood. And that was his last recollection of life.

30

He remembered that nothing is carved in stone until you're dead. And he realized if he could think that, he was alive. But David Cursore still did not know where he was until he smelled the acrid scent of hospital disinfectant. For a moment he did not even remember who he was. He thought about his name. *Cursore.* He remembered his biology teacher at the University of Texas who had talked about a New Zealand bird known as an Apteryx —a creature the size of a small goose, nicknamed a Kiwi. The Kiwi belonged to a class of birds called *cursores.* They were wingless and sometimes tailless and relied on their ability to run for survival. At the university, David Cursore had met a girl from New Zealand and she had bought him a gold tie tack of a Kiwi when he had told her about *cursores.* Then the woman found another lover when she grew tired of sharing him with computers. Through his twenties, Cursore had felt like a wingless bird— scampering about life, spending so much time with theoretical mathematics. Meanwhile many of his classmates were flying high—securing good jobs, earning gobs of money, raising families, traveling. They were eagles, soaring. Cursore felt like a wingless bird, scuttering through windowless rooms, pecking away at computer keyboards. For a while things got out of balance as he immersed himself, *hacking,* fascinated with the networks of computers that mushroomed around him. Nothing else mattered for Cursore. The computer became his mistress; he offered no resistance. Computers had seduced others. All one really needed for the mystical process to transpire was a highly logical mind, loneliness and an offbeat mathematical curiosity. Before Cursore was aware of it, he had almost enslaved the computers while they had totally enslaved him.

Then a few days before his thirtieth birthday, Cursore met Buff Tallons. Elegant, sophisticated and urbane, the older man radiated style. He always knew the right wine to order, always sensed the correct thing to say, always knew where the great plays were before they opened. Buff perceived unlimited potential in David Cursore. David Cursore was awed by him, for the older man embodied all the things that baffled David—power, prestige and charm—and all of these things were a direct result of Buff's relationship with electronics. The pair became friends. This was inevitable—for Buff, who was childless, recognized in David the raw energy that he had once possessed.

Their friendship quickly changed to mentor and apprentice, and the two found themselves locked in parallel courses, separated by two decades. That was the only difference that seemed to exist between them. Twenty years. Yet without those years, they would never have been drawn to each other; they would have been fierce, perhaps hostile, competitors.

As he lay in the hospital bed, all these thoughts pulsated through Cursore's mind and he knew he was alive. The problem was he was trapped in his body. He could hear and smell. But he could not speak or move. He could barely feel anything with his fingertips. Once he had spent an hour in a "salt water" isolation tank that had completely deprived him of contact with the outside world. No sound. No sight. A dark, windowless womb. That is how he felt now—cut off. He was aware only of his breathing; it was slower than he remembered.

Hospital? More pieces of the puzzle floated into place. He remembered Jasper coming into her bedroom. And then Russ.... Now the images of the last twenty four hours cascaded rapidly through his mind. Russ was the psychopath that they had been looking for.

Cursore had not been crazy or even confused—there had been a nut on the loose and that nut was Russ. It was Russ who had kidnapped and probably killed Dusty. It had been Russ who had returned to Mary Lou's apartment and destroyed the evidence. It had been Russ who was behind the disappearance of the missing women.

Why, wondered Cursore. And why couldn't he move? What was going on? What had happened to him? Something to do with being shot, something to do with the operation and the bright lights. Jasper was gone. He had to tell the police, had to tell someone that a nut had taken her. Cursore wondered if she were still alive. He tried to move again but couldn't. His limbs were frozen. The only thing he was aware of was his breathing. He could hear the hum of some kind of a machine. Then he heard footsteps approaching. The steps stopped. Another set of footsteps approached also, then stopped.

"I think he's going to be OK," said a man's voice.

"*You* think?" said the deeper voice. "You ain't no doctor. You're a dumb orderly like me. We don't get paid to think."

"When they finished with him in surgery I heard old Doc Adams say he had a crease down his skull like a plow done it. How'd you like to have a furrow in your head? Heh-heh."

"What I want is to get home. It's damn near five a.m. and I'll miss the bus if you don't snap it up. You gonna finish that mopping or what?"

"I'm almost done."

"How long this boy going to be out?"

"What do I know? I ain't no neurosurgeon. If he's like that guy down in B ward, he could be out for years."

Years? Cursore struggled to speak, but couldn't.

"On the other hand, this dude could be waltzing out of here by noon. You just never know about them bangs on the head."

Their voices faded as they left the room.

Cursore silently screamed for them to come back, but no sound escaped. He could hear the words echoing through his head, crashing against his aching mind. Aching. That was good. Feeling was coming back from somewhere.

A little while later, or was it a lot later, a nurse came in and he heard her moving beside him. He felt her warm hand on his face, felt her brush the perspiration from his forehead with a warm cloth. "I don't know if you can hear me, Mr. Cursore, but the reason you can't see is that we've put some bandages around your eyes. If you can her me, raise your hand, OK?"

He willed his right hand to raise. Nothing.

"OK. Look, maybe you can hear me and can't respond. That's all right. You were shot but the wound was not serious. No brain damage, as far as I know."

I'm lucky to have someone like that, thought Cursore. Lucky. Keep talking, lady. Please.

"As the doctors say, there was quite a bit of commotion to your temporal area. A concussion just means you get your brains rattled around a bit. You get a lot of tiny multiple bleedings and sometimes, like now, that interferes with areas of speech and movement. You might be able to hear everything I'm saying . . ."

"That's very doubtful," said a man's voice.

"Oh, Doctor . . . I didn't see you . . ."

"You finished changing his blood serum?"

"Pretty much. But . . ."

"Come on," said the doctor. "I need some help with Mrs. Dunlop."

Cursore heard them leaving and attempted to scream again. Couldn't. He *had* to tell them about Russ. He had Jasper. Had to tell someone. Cursore struggled to move his hand. He felt his thumb dig into his thigh. Feeling and motion were coming back. But so slowly.

31

At 6:30 a.m. Buff Tallons strolled through the lobby of the L.A. Airport Marriott Hotel. The inviting aroma of freshly perked coffee made him pause. A lady, wearing the distinctive brown jacket of a hotel chain, was serving hot rolls amid a group of sleepy-eyed businessmen. The men, seated in a sprawling conversation pit, were waiting for the bus to take them to their various planes. They smoked and talked in small groups. Tallons headed for a bank of elevators and three minutes later knocked on the door of suite 889.

A beady-eyed man of about thirty opened the door.

"Are you Mr. MacDonal?" asked the industrialist.

"Yes."

"I'm here for The Shadow," said the older man. He could feel his heart quicken when he glimpsed a heavy-set man at the far end of the suite. The industrialist wanted to turn and bolt for he could sense that the large man was a policeman.

"Yes," said Magic MacDonal.

"Please come in," said the heavy-set man, getting up. "You're Bluff Tallons?"

"Who are you? Police?"

"Yes. You'd be with the computer company. The president . . ."

"I was instructed to pick something up here. I was told that only Mr. MacDonal would be present."

"May I see your ID?" said the heavy-set man.

Buff Tallons pulled out a sleek wallet and wiggled out his driver's license, passed it to the large man who studied it and then stared directly at him. "Everything seems to be in order, Mr. Tallons. Thank you." The large man with the penetrating eyes smiled and returned the driver's license. "My name is Sergeant Dartwell, I'm with the Los Angeles Sheriff's Department . . ."

"I was told that no police would be involved," said Buff. He fought an overwhelming urge to race out.

"We are involved though, because a person who calls himself The Shadow is perpetrating a scheme to extort five million dollars. What has he told you so far?"

"I was to come here and pick up a briefcase from Mr. MacDonal. Then I was to go downstairs and wait by the third telephone booth off the lobby."

"But how did he get you to cooperate?"

"Cooperate?" Tallons' mouth felt dry,

like it had been stuffed with cotton.

"Yes."

"He said that if I did not cooperate he would kill my grandchildren in Pittsburgh." He hoped the policeman could not tell he was lying.

"What else did he tell you?"

"He said if I told anyone, especially the authorities, he would kill my grandchildren."

"I'm sorry you're in the middle of this, Mr. Tallons, but we still have a few minutes before you're due in the lobby. So I'll give you a little background and what we know. This man, this Shadow, intends to release highly toxic containers of a birth control contraceptive called Kaam—it's a copycat scheme of Tylenol."

"My God."

"The company that Mr. MacDonal represents has decided to acquiesce to this extortionist's demands." The policeman picked up a wide black leather attache case. "Now if you want we can have a man take your place, act as the courier . . ."

"Does that briefcase contain the ransom money?"

"Yes."

"I'm a little frightened. I don't mind admitting it," said the industrialist. "But I feel I should do what the terrorist wants." He was more than frightened, but he knew that any slip-ups and he'd be facing treason charges.

"We've had people watching you since the terrorist said you'd be acting as a courier."

My God, thought Tallons, the police must have seen Ivan Tornoff at my home. How long will it take for them to put two and two together? What else do they know about me? I bet the CIA will be in on this. A Russian diplomat in my home while the police watched. This is a nightmare.

"When the extortionist notified us that he was going to use you as an intermediary, we immediately placed you under surveilliance."

"Why didn't you tell me or call me or something?"

"Because the extortionist cautioned us not to. And for all we know, you could have been working with him. Why didn't you call us?"

"You don't think I am working with this terrorist?"

"We ran a check on you. It's not every day that we discover someone with your level of priority clearance. But I suppose since you deal with military computers, you almost have to have one, don't you?"

"Yes, but you haven't answered my question. You don't think I have anything to do with this man who calls himself The Shadow?"

"Of course not. You make almost as much in a year as the total ransom demand. Your net worth is many times that. We feel you were probably chosen because of your high priority security clearance. The Shadow knew we would check you out and he realized we would trust you with the money. Perhaps he has something on you. That is of no concern to us, however."

"He has the lives of my grandchildren," said the industrialist.

"We'll have them placed in protective custody immediately," said Dartwell.

"They're in another state . . ."

"That's no problem for us," said Donald Neechman who had opened the adjoining suite door and was watching them. "I'm Special FBI Agent Neechman. We'll make sure nothing happens to your grandchildren."

"It might not be a problem for you, Mr. Neechman, but I'm worried about them."

"I understand your concern, sir. Could you write their names and addresses on this notepad?" asked the agent, producing a pencil and paper.

As Tallons wrote down the names of his daughter, son-in-law and two grandchildren, he tried to figure out how many people were involved in extortion. "Can you tell me the number of police officers who will be working on this?"

"Enough. You'll be protected every moment, Mr. Tallons. If you'd rather not act as courier, as Sergeant Dartwell suggested . . ."

"No. I'll go through with this."

"Do you think that there's a chance that the extortionist knows you personally, sir?" asked the FBI agent.

"I have no way of knowing if this madman knows me or not. But if your man failed to fool him, that would be a terrible risk." Not for my grandchildren, thought the executive, for *me.* I don't want to hang for treason. Or get electrocuted or gassed or anything. My God!

The elevator ride to the lobby floor seemed to take days. Tallons checked his watch. It was exactly seven a.m. as he made his way toward the row of chrome telephones on the west side of the spacious lobby. He was aware of nothing but the soft leather handle of the attache case as the third phone started to ring. He picked up on its second jingle. "Hello."

"Hello, this is The Shadow—testing one, two, three. If you're listening from the FBI, you better let me go free."

"There's no one from the FBI," said Tallons. "What do you want me to do with this case?"

"Does it have the money in it?"

"Of course." Damn, he thought. I didn't even look. If I give him this case and it's empty . . . .

"Did you look, Mr. Tallons?"

"Yes. What do you want me to do with it?"

"Basically," said the voice on the telephone, coming from God only knew where, "I want to make certain that both of us end up . . . happy."

Tallons knew what that meant. One slip-up and he, Tallons, would be facing a court for treason.

"I want you to go to United Airlines and buy a ticket to San Francisco and go to Gate 80. Don't let the money out of your sight." *Click.*

Buff Tallons rode an airport shuttle bus to the terminal. Ten minutes later he was heading toward Gate 80 where the San Francisco flight was scheduled to depart in half an hour. At the security gate, Tallons handed his briefcase to the guard and she slipped it on the conveyor belt that took it through the X-ray. He walked through the metal detector. There was a *peep*—his gold GMT Rolex. He slipped the watch off, put it on a plastic dish and walked through the detector again. No sound. He tugged his watch back on, picked up the five million dollar briefcase, and headed along the tiled floor toward the escalator. People thronged around him and he tried to figure out where the police were. He wondered how close he was to The Shadow. He wondered how the man was keeping track of him.

"Buff Tallons," said a loudspeaker. "Please pick up a white courtesy phone." The message repeated itself.

At the top of the stairway, he turned to

the right, spotted one of the paging phones, and lifted the receiver. "Yes."

"You sound like you're out of breath."

"A little."

"Did you know there's a radio transmitter in your briefcase?"

"No."

"I saw it on the security guard's monitor when you went through baggage inspection. I'm glad to see you weren't wired."

"I didn't know about the radio transmitter—honest."

"Go to the washroom to your right. Last stall by the urinals. Lock yourself in. Behind the dispenser for toilet seat covers, you'll find a nylon flight bag. Folded up. Transfer the money to that, then leave the case, locked, in plain sight by the wash basins. Got it?"

"Yes."

"Then go to the far end of the wash room and wait until someone steals the briefcase. As soon as they take it, go back into the terminal. To your left is a door that's marked Employees Only. Take the flight bag, walk through the door and down the stairs. Got it?"

The money transfer to the bag took less than three minutes, but Tallons only had to wait two minutes for a man in a dirty white trench coat to spot the unattended briefcase. He casually grabbed the case and hurried out the door, clutching his prize.

Buff Tallons went out of the washroom as several large, undercover men pounced on the character in the trench coat. Tallons ducked through the door marked Employees Only. A custodian carrying a portable trash container and a broom casually moved toward the industrialist and said: "Step this way, Mr. Tallons."

Tallons realized it was the same voice he had heard on the phone. The Shadow. The older man froze as the "custodian" handed Tallons a nylon flight bag that looked exactly like the one he was carrying. Then the man took Tallons' bag and stuffed it into his garbage sack.

"OK," said the Shadow. "Go back out there now and walk past the man who stole your briefcase."

"I've done my part, haven't I? I swear I didn't know about the radio transmitter."

"You've done your part. Now go."

Relieved that it was almost over, Tallons hurried back into the main terminal. He could see that the FBI agent —what was his name? Neechman—had collared the character with the briefcase. The shabbily dressed thief was spread-eagled against a grey wall. People—all in a hurry to get somewhere —moved by, hardly breaking their pace. Apparently it was rather common to see a scene such as this, or so their placid expressions would lead one to think.

As Buff moved past Neechman, there

was a muffled roar. And then all hell broke loose as the muffled explosion turned into a white flash of light that ripped Buff Tallons' nylon bag apart. He felt his legs skid across the tile and was slowly aware of a dull pain somewhere. The pain was coming from him; his head scrunched against the tiled floor. Blood was everywhere and one of the placid watchers of a moment ago screamed, clutching his broken arm. Neechman tried to get up to say something but sank back to the ground. He felt energy leaving his body. Out of the corner of his eye, Buff Tallons glimpsed the huge policeman—what was his name? Dartwell, that was it. Well, Dartwell didn't dart very well. He plowed his way through the carnage and knelt by Tallons' side.

"Sonofabitch changed cases. Where is he?" asked Dartwell. His voice was much softer, more distant than Tallons remembered it. Everything was becoming softer, more blurred.

"In the employees' entrance," said Tallons. His voice was a distant roar.

The cop gently set Tallons' head on the floor as a man edged through the crowd. The man knelt by Tallons. "I'm a doctor. I'm going to try and help you."

"Sergeant," said Tallons.

The cop paused. He seemed to be moving so slowly. Why was everything slowing down?

"I framed David Cursore. He didn't break any laws. I set him up. I know I'm dying."

"You framed Cursore? Why?"

"Ask Ivan Tornoff . . . FBI must have..." And that was the last thing Buff Tallons ever said.

"You want a priest?" asked Dartwell. "There's a priest here."

No, thought Tallons, *no. Not even a Catholic. On the other hand, maybe a priest wasn't such a bad idea.* And that was his last cogent thought.

Then out of the darkness he heard a man start to say something about absolution. That was the final thing Tallons heard.

32

Jon accelerated along the Ventura Freeway as the sun, a great golden ball of fire, bubbled out of the east.

On the steering column of his 1968 Shelby 350 was his vehicle registration and his latest name: Jan Country. He liked that name, fit him well. He depressed the accelerator and the car leapt past a chrome tanker, sparkling in the early morning light. The driver of the rig glanced down at the jet blue 350 hurtling along the dark asphalt.

A warning light on his oil gauge blinked. The Russian coasted off the freeway and stopped next to a Mobil station pump. "I'd like some gas, and would you check the oil level?" he asked the attendant.

"Sure will. Fine car," said a thin dark man with the name "Efram" stenciled across his clean white overalls. Efram had large warm eyes; they looked like they belonged on a cocker spaniel puppy.

"Thanks. Does that phone work over there?"

"Did last night," said Efram, unlocking the pumps. "She takes high test?"

"Yes, please." The Russian strolled to the phone booth. He dialed a toll free number connecting him to an agency where one could report crimes anonymously.

A lady's voice said, "Crime Stop. Your confidential number is YY-34. What would you like to report?"

"There's three containers of deadly nerve gas. They are at the following locations: Alan's Drugs, Westwood, California. Tim's Drugs and Surf Drugs—both in the L. A. Marina. The nerve gas is in Kaam."

"I didn't get all that, Sir."

He repeated the information slower, then added: "The person who you should contact is Sergeant Dartwell at the Marino del Rey Sheriff's office, California. I'd say you had about half an hour before the stores open. Tell him that there are no more containers and tell him thanks for the money. Got it?"

"Yes, sir, but . . ."

"I have to go." He hung up the receiver and walked back to his car. He'd kept his part of the bargain. He had the money and the Kaam would never be sold if the police moved with dispatch. He smiled to himself as he visualized Sergeant Dartwell getting the information. There was no way anyone would be able to trace him with the toll free number. He'd won.

Efram had the 350's hood open but he was lying on his back under the car. He popped his head out and held up a forefinger covered with oil.

"Lucky you stopped, Mister. Your oil plug came out. You only had about a pint of it left when you drove in here." Efram pulled out a polka dot handkerchief and wiped his moist eyes.

"Today must be my lucky day."

"You can say that again. Another ten miles you'd have started to burn out the engine. Fifty miles, you'd need a new one."

"I take it you've worked on these vehicles before."

"Used to have a Mustang shop. Got a few tools in the back and I think a block plug that will fit this."

Jon watched as Efram finished work on the car. The Russian liked the sure, efficient way Efram went about his task, wasting no extra motion. He knew what to do and he did it. Five minutes later, he tossed the empty cans of oil into the trash and smiled. "Do you live around here?" asked Efram.

"I'm afraid not."

"That's too bad because I'd love to work on this baby. Why'd you paint out the racing stripes?"

"I don't like the Highway Patrol to pay much attention to me."

Efram meticulously filled out an itemized bill and presented it to Jon. "Good thinking. I'm not charging you for labor. First time is free."

Jon gave the mechanic his Visa card and watched the man run it through a special touch tone validator that was programmed to locate stolen cards in microseconds. All was fine because the electric circuits of the American Express III closed and hummed, and Efram spun the card around for Jon to sign. "How far to Big Bear from here?"

"Hour and a half. Roads are real good this time of day. God, I wish I lived above the smog belt. Thank you, sir."

"Thank you. I appreciate your help."

Jon was almost to Big Bear when he realized he had given the mechanic a credit card with Russ—his Marina name on it. He cursed in Ukrainian. As he continued driving up the tortuous road, he opened his wallet and found his Visa card with Russ Smith embossed on it. He bent it back and forth, breaking it in half. Then he broke it into quarters and dropped the small squares into his ash tray.

The Jefferson and ponderosa pine rose above him as he turned off the main road and down Viewridge Lane. The two story A-frame with the diamond-shaped picture window sparkled in the mountain sunlight. He found the remote garage door opener and pressed it. The overhead door opened; he drove in and the door closed behind him. He cut the ignition and leaned against the leather seats and smelled the wonderful aroma of new cowhide mingling with the scent of fresh ponderosa pine.

He admired the workmanship of the garage. Clean, white concrete floor. Several solid work benches hewn from two-by-eights. A dozen built-in cabinets over the work benches.

He opened his trunk and took out the nylon flight bag. Jasper squinted at him from inside the small trunk. She was twisted like a sad rag doll. He leaned over her and pulled a two-inch strip of white adhesive from her mouth. She whined in pain and he realized the injection he had given her was wearing off. He carried the nylon flight bag and a brown leather suitcase up the carpeted stairs and then walked up one more flight to the master bedroom. The Russian returned to the car and lifted the woman over his shoulder, then carried her to the main floor. He set her down on a leather sofa. He paused and glanced out the bay window at the lake that stretched out below his home. Around the edges of the large window were several stained glass panes in the shape of dancing angels. They were in muted yellows and blues. He took a deep breath of the air, heavy with the scent of oiled oak. All of the room's trim was custom oak, including the crown molding around the tops of the high vaulted rooms. There was some dry wood in the fireplace, and he found a match and lit it. The fireplace was made of large slabs of stone that matched the color of the stained glass window. The chimney had a terrific draught and within seconds the fire was roaring above its black metal gratings.

Jasper moaned as he picked her up and carried her upstairs to a guest bedroom. There was a fireplace with stacked wood in it by the bed. He laid her limp body on the king-sized bed, then checked to make certain that her arms and legs were still securely bound with inch wide adhesive tape. Satisfied, the Russian gently patted her cheeks. "Wake up," he said.

No answer.

He shook her gently. "Wake up." One of her eyes squeezed open and she coughed slightly. Then the other eye fluttered open. He could tell she was frightened. "I'm not going to hurt you, I just want some answers. Don't pretend to be asleep."

"Mmm," she said.

"What did you find out about me? You and Cursore?"

"Nothing."

"Don't lie to me. It's very important that you tell me exactly what you know about me."

She said nothing. She frowned, trying to bring the moment into focus. She was disoriented, and before he could talk to her anymore, she drifted off into sleep. Despite his shaking her, Jasper's eyes remained closed.

He had time. He could hear some kind of gull squawking across the water. He remembered that a part of the lake was designated a game and bird preserve. A light haze of snow started.

He spent the next half hour walking around his five bedroom, three bath home. He opened his nylon flight bag and stared at the bundles of hundred dollar bills. There would be time later to count it. He was enormously pleased his plan had worked so well. There would be no need to risk changing his identity again. Jan Country. He liked that name—it was a great name.

When he checked on Jasper, she was still sleeping. Didn't matter. He had time now and soon she would tell him everything he needed to know—and then he would kill her. He hoped she would be the last person he would have to kill for a long time.

In his suitcase he found a children's nursery rhyme book. He sat down next to the fire and started to read the story about the Three Little Pigs. As he reread the story, the wind picked up on the lake, rippling the water, forming tiny troughs of waves on it. A little more snow darkened the day.

He was glad that he had a warm fire inside his new house. Big Bear was so close to subtropical Los Angeles and palm trees, but the City of Angels seemed worlds away. Worlds away.

After a moment he set the book aside and looked out at the lake. In the distance he could see a pier that jutted out from the other side of the water. He picked up a pair of fieldglasses and discovered that a small area was cordoned off. Bubbles burst along the surface of the water. That was the area of the lake that was being revitalized with oxygen. The process would kill the algae and the fish would come back. They were coming back—he saw several leap out of the water.

Made perfect sense to him. Coming to this lake, a lake that had once been lifeless and now was returning to life. He was like the lake, and after he killed the girl, he would shake the dead thoughts from his mind and everything would be all right. Life would surge through him again. Already he could feel vital forces starting to creep through him.

33

At nine a.m. Cursore's eyes snapped open and he scanned his hospital room. Sleek, green machines took up most of a wall. Sunlight filtered in through gauze curtains, creating dappled shadows across the foot of his bed. A plastic I.V. tube snaked from an opaque container and disappeared under a bandage on his forearm. He watched clear liquid drip into him.

A nurse in a green shift that whispered against her pantyhose came into the room. He thought he recognized her perfume. "Hello," she said, "welcome back to the planet." He did recognize her voice. She was part of the sounds that had reassured him in the night. "We took your bandages off. Can you see OK?"

He nodded, tried to speak, couldn't.

She took his pulse, smiled at him. "I don't know if you remember me from last night." He nodded his head quickly. "Good. Well, there's no permanent damage to your head, but you're still in the midst of recovering from a rather bad concussion . . . I guess I shouldn't be telling you all these things. That's doctor's job. It's just so frightening to wake up and not know what's going on."

He wiggled his right hand. The feeling had almost returned to his shoulder but his fingers were still numb.

"I'm babbling on too much..."

He shook his head. Then he raised his right hand and made a gesture as though he were writing.

"Pencil?"

He nodded and smiled. Damn, it was difficult to communicate like this.

The nurse put the pad under his hand and slipped the pencil between his fingers. He scrawled: "Get police."

"You want me to get the police?"

He nodded.

"There's a Sergeant Dartwell who's on his way here right now," she said.

"Stop Smith," he wrote in letters two inches high.

"You mean Dr. Smith?" she asked. "He's your doctor... how'd you know that?" Before she could continue, an orderly passing by called her name. "Mr. Cursore, gotta go but don't worry about Dr. Smith... he's the best. And don't tell him I told you anything... doctor is supposed to explain everything to you. See you later." She was gone in a flurry of green smock and clicking heels and perfume.

What had she been going on about, he asked himself. Had Russ Smith become a doctor? Or was it a coincidence? Had to be a coincidence. A shadow fell across him. Thank God! Sergeant Dartwell loomed over him. The big man scrunched up his brow and looked down at Cursore.

"They tell me you can't talk," said the cop.

Cursure shrugged.

"You're lucky you and Lois Lane ain't dead. We found a canister of Kaam with nerve gas in it at her place."

Cursore tried to talk, but no sound came out. Just an angry grunt. He tried to hand the cop the note about Smith.

"Take it easy. Your boss is dead . . . Tallons . . . gave a dying declaration. Said he set you up. What do you think of that?"

What am I supposed to think about it, thought Cursore. Tallons—couldn't believe that. Couldn't. Yet—Cursore couldn't waste time thinking about that. Jasper was in trouble. Had to get the cop to understand!

"Jasper's missing. You know anything about what happened? Because whoever tried to kill you is The Shadow . . . don't laugh at the name . . ." The cop read the note.

Russ Smith took her, Cursore wrote. He tried to will his speech back, tried to make the letters move faster out of the pen. Couldn't. He thought of Jasper with the man who had shot him. He felt the anger pulsating through him. Had to get her back. Had to.

"This guy live in your building?" asked the cop.

Cursore nodded his head, affirmatively. Good. At last he was getting somewhere. He watched the cop reach for the phone, heard him call his office, heard him sending officers to find Russ Smith at the apartment complex. He kept calling Smith the "probable Shadow." The cop hung up and explained what had happened. "OK . . . we got people looking for him. I'm meeting a team at your complex. We'll get her back."

Cursore grunted, shook his head. Then he wrote. *Russ gone.*

The cop read the note. "Do you know where?"

Cursore shook his head.

"Did he harm Jasper?" asked the cop.

Cursore nodded. He had to get out of the hospital, had to find Jasper. He was losing her to a madman. Some guy who called himself The Shadow. Why would Smith call himself The Shadow? Maybe it was too late. Didn't want to think about that. Didn't want to think about the things this psychopath would do to the woman he loved. He realized at that instant he loved her. Funny time to come to that conclusion.

Dartwell was back on the phone, explaining to his office that he was going to stay and try to talk with Mr. Cursore, find out more about Smith. That was the first time Cursore had ever heard the cop refer to him as "Mr." without a sarcastic inflection.

The cop hung up the phone and then stared out of the window. Cursore sensed Dartwell was having trouble putting his thoughts together. "Look," said the Sergeant, searching painfully for the right phrases. "I'm really sorry about this . . . but we both know that about ninety-nine out of one hundred, hell . . . I, I guess there's not much for me to say." Dartwell dug his thick fingers into his jacket pocket and paced around the hospital cubicle. He almost knocked over a bed tray at one point, then sat down in a straight-backed plastic chair and crossed his legs.

Cursore fumbled the pencil into his hand, and printed: *Tell me about the Shadow.*

Sergeant Dartwell nodded. "OK. This guy you call Smith is into extortion. He must have figured he could top the Tylenol thing. What he did was get himself some nerve gas. Then he put it in the dispenser that comes with Kaam. The dispenser is like a fat syringe made out of plastic. You probably know . . ."

Cursore nodded his head vigorously.

"Well, this character Smith starts calling himself The Shadow. He tested the concoction out on a lady, a divorcee, and maybe on the girl from Florida.

Makes you bleed to death in seconds.

Cursore winced.

"Then he contacts the ad agency that markets Kaam and tells them he's going to release the poisoned contraceptive foam if they don't pay him five million. It's a billion dollar company . . . they agreed. Candy-asses. Somehow this Shadow gets your boss to act as courier for the cash. The FBI had a radio transmitter in the briefcase that contained the five million. But this Shadow was too smart for them. He blew them up after he switched cases. Killed one of their best agents this morning at the airport. I was there. It was awful. That's where I ran into Tallons. Now, looking back over the last week, what I figured happened is that this nut, Russ Smith, realized you were on his trail. So he tried to make you look like a dope. That failed, so he tried to frame you with the death of the woman from Idaho, and that didn't work out so well, so he found out who your boss was and somehow got him to act as courier. You must have really annoyed this psycho, wrecked his plans that you probably knew nothing about. So when he got the chance, he killed you. Or tried to. You weren't being very cooperative, Cursore. Real inconsiderate."

Cursore tried to sit up, willed his body to. His body wasn't listening.

"Thing I still don't understand is how in hell Smith got Tallons to cooperate.

Tallons said something about a threat to his grandchildren's life. I didn't buy it then, and I don't buy it now. The FBI is questioning some guy named Tornoff in Washington."

The phone rang and Cursore shivered. His tactile feelings were returning, but not fast enough. He could feel his toes tingling. He moved his head a little to the right. As the cop talked on the phone, another nurse came in and checked dials and readouts. There was a young doctor with her who read some charts and left. The nurse took the needle from the I.V. feed out of Cursore's forearm. "You were really out of it for awhile," she said. "You feeling better?"

Cursore nodded, tried to listen to what the Sergeant was saying. The nurse made some quick notes on a clipboard and left.

" . . . then, throw up a roadblock and have the airport covered. It's only three miles from his apartment," said the cop and hung up. He sighed. "You were right, Cursore. Russ Smith sure is gone. They found all of the paraphernalia for the nerve gas in his place. Definitely The Shadow. But there's not a trace of him . . . or the girl. He is one smart sonofabitch. He called me and told me where the Kaam packages that contained the nerve gas were. Bastard used a toll free WATTS line so we couldn't trace him. We got his voice on tape . . . a lot of good it'll do us."

Cursore watched the monitor that linked his room with the central hospital computer. He picked up the pencil again, scribbled: *Get me to the hospital computer.*

The cop reread the note. "OK," he said. "I'll see what I can do." He left and came back in a few minutes with a young doctor. They were arguing about Cursore's condition.

"But you said he's getting better," insisted the cop.

"Right . . . but we start wheeling him around, we're going to have problems with him. The man has a concussion . . . several concussions, that's why he can't move . . ."

"Doc, there's a computer terminal at the end of the hall. Surely to God we can push him that far."

"I don't think it would be a good idea."

"Doctor, there's a nut loose somewhere who gets his jollies off by placing nerve gas in Kaam. He's going to kill a woman he's got with him if we don't find him. Mr. Cursore might be able to do it if we can use the computer."

"I'll have to check with some people," said the doctor. "I can't be responsible for this. You're not allowed to use our computer unless you have clearance. You sure there's someone who's poisoning birth control foam?"

"Positive."

"I'll see what I can do," said the

doctor. He hurried out of the room.

Cursore's left arm tingled and he lifted his hand. He rubbed his face. Feeling was coming back.

"You're not paralyzed anymore. You're OK," said the Sergeant. "Or almost OK."

Cursore shook his head. He still had a long way to go. He beckoned for a nearby wheelchair. The Sergeant wheeled it over and helped Cursore into it. His entire left side buzzed. His right hand hung beside him and he had the feeling for a moment that the fingers belonged to someone else. His left side was becoming stronger. As the cop pushed him down the hospital corridor, Cursore picked up his right hand with his left. Damned if it didn't feel totally foreign to him. At one level he sensed that it was his hand, his arm, his side. But in his mind that frozen side of his body seemed like it was no longer part of him, never had been. A limb belonging to another person?

They came to a door at the end of the corridor and Sergeant Dartwell opened it and wheeled Cursore in, stopping within a few inches of a keyboard. Using his left hand, Cursore flicked several switches, and lights started to blink. A green monitor became bright, as the phosphorus warmed up behind it.

A few minutes later, Cursore had linked the hospital computer to his computer at the factory.

Sergeant Dartwell watched a series of

numbers flash onto the screen. The display showed the vital statistics of Russ Smith plus all of his credit cards and bank statements. "Son of a bitch," said the sergeant. "He's got no money in his accounts. Really cleaned everything out, didn't he?"

Cursore kept tapping keys. He was pulling out data on the credit cards. Three or four times Cursore fumbled with his hands and had to start again. The images of Jasper's face kept flooding his mind. He didn't want to see her dead. Had to stop it—if it hadn't happened already. Didn't even want to think about that possibility.

"I bet you're cussing a lot," said the cop. "Just take it easy. You're doing fine. Lookit, your right hand is starting to move. But I bet you're cussing. But that's your name. Curser."

The computer expert continued hunting through the information that the green screen displayed. He was probing and questioning entries. He realized a lot of what he was doing was guesswork—he had to find the man who had called himself Russ Smith. Had to.

"What the hell are you two doing in here?" demanded a hulk of a woman. She looked like a matron and there was a nametag on her that claimed that she was.

Cursore continued tapping the keys. He could feel his right toes. He wiggled them, experiencing the same sensation he had with frostbite after skiing. All the nerves in his toes and fingers were on fire. He had a headache. Didn't matter.

"This is police business," said the cop.

"I don't give a damn what it is, buster," said the matron. She was around two hundred pounds and she looked like steam would start to squirt out of her flat ears. She crossed her arms. "First, get this patient back to his bed. Second, leave that computer alone."

The cop nodded. He was about to say something, when Cursore reached up and tugged at his sleeve. Displayed on the terminal was a transaction for $29.90 at Efram's Mobile Station in Upland. The purchase had been made that day and the buyer had been Russ Smith.

"Bingo." said the cop.

"What," snapped the matron, "kind of games are you playing on that thing? I'm warning you . . ."

"I have to use this phone," said Sergeant Dartwell. He reached for a nearby phone and, with firm and gentle pressure, he pushed the matron back into the hallway and locked the door.

Cursore felt the adrenalin course through him. Despite the violent headache, he had almost all of his feeling and locomotion on his left side. Nearly all of his feeling was back on his right side—although his strength was still haphazard. He traced the Visa card backwards and a read-out of Efram's station appeared on the screen.

Sergeant Dartwell went through Information to get the number of Efram's station and two minutes later had the owner of the station on the line. Cursore discovered that there was a conference line on the phone and turned it on so he could hear.

"Hello, Efram Mobil."

"Yes. This is Sergeant Dartwell. This is police business. I'd like to ask you some questions."

"Sure."

"Did a man make a credit card purchase of $29.90 at your station today?"

"Yes."

"Was his name Russ Smith?"

"Yes. I think it was. Russ something."

"What time was that?"

"Oh, little after I opened. Around seven. He had a Shelby Mustang . . . about a '66. Fine car. Oil plug came out. I fixed it up for him. How'd you find out?"

"We were lucky, sir. Did the man say anything about where he was going?"

"No, I don't . . . oh, yeah, Big Bear. He said he was living up there. Said he liked it up in the mountains. Can't say as I blame him."

"How far are you from Big Bear?"

"Couple of hours. He should be there by now."

"Did he leave a phone number or address or the receipt for the purchases?"

"I'll look."

Cursore and the cop waited anxiously.

"You there?" asked Efram.

"Yes."

"Nothing on the receipt. I ran it through our American Express telephone link. Everything was OK and in cases like that all I put down is the license plate number."

"What was it?"

"Didn't bother. His Mustang had a new license sticker on it. Lovely piece of machinery."

Cursore scribbled a question on his writing pad. The cop read it and asked Efram if there was anyone with Russ Smith.

"No. All alone. What's wrong?"

"We'll tell you as soon as we can. Appreciate your help," said the cop. "Bye." He hung up and the matron returned. This time she had a large, beefy security guard with her. "Those cars have trunks . . ."

"Arrest those men, Charlie," she snapped. "They've taken over the computer."

Charlie was getting ready to give them problems.

"Look, Charlie," said Sergeant Dartwell. "We both know you're not a peace officer. You don't want to mess with us."

"I don't?"

"The last time I tangled with a rent-a-cop, he had to rent a neck brace," said Dartwell.

Charlie eyed the .45 hanging on the sergeant's side. Charlie backed off. By this time Cursore was standing. He started to limp along with the cop. "You better get back to bed..." said Dartwell.

Cursore's eyes blazed and he grabbed the cop's shoulder and shook his head urgently from side to side.

"OK," said the cop. "You look kind of funny in that nightshirt and head bandage. Look like an Arab... but if you're game..."

After they picked up Cursore's pants and shirt, the two of them walked out the front entrance. Patients and doctors stepped aside.

In his squad car, parked in the doctor's spot, Dartwell called Dispatch and ordered a helicopter. While he was calling, Cursore found a sheepskin jacket and put it on. The dispatcher told Dartwell that all the choppers would be tied up.

"Shit," said Dartwell. "This is an emergency."

"Sorry, Sergeant, you've got seven more emergencies ahead of you and only three choppers we can use. You can try the Malibu..."

"No time. Thanks. Ten-four." He hung up.

Overhead a hospital ambulance helicopter fluttered toward them. It landed and the pilot got out of it. Several orderlies scurried forward with a stretcher, keeping their heads low to avoid the slow-turning rotor.

"I'm going to get that pilot to do us a favor," said the Sheriff. "You better stay here, though."

Cursore shook his head violently.

"You sure you're up to it?"

Another violent nod.

"OK, but I hope you can start speaking pretty soon. I'm getting tired of having a dummy on my side." It was the first time the two had ever smiled at each other.

The helicopter pilot listened to the cop and then said: "I'm sorry, fellows . . . I can't . . ."

Cursore reached into his pocket and took out his wallet. He found three one hundred dollar bills and unfolded them.

"But if an emergency comes up . . ."

"Then you'll still keep the three hundred dollars and I'll pay for any more expenses you run up," said Cursore. His speech had returned.

"I don't know."

"Take the money," ordered the cop.

A few minutes later the three of them were moving across the city in the silver and white Bell helicopter toward the San

Bernadino Mountains and Big Bear. It was almost eleven a.m.

"I wonder what this Russ Smith is calling himself now?" asked the cop.

"Don't know," said Cursore. "I bet he changes names faster than Zsa Zsa Gabor."

"You're full of jokes, Cursore."

"I'm just frightened for her. I really am. I don't know what I'd do if . . . We got to find her!"

34

At 11:30 a.m. Jon Andrews alias Russ Smith alias Jan Country, saw the glowing logs in the fireplace needed restoking. He finished reading The Cat And The Fiddle, yawned and got up. He walked down the back stairs and into his beautifully appointed garage. He noticed that a bird had made a mess on the roof of his Mustang. This offended his sense of order and cleanliness. He pressed a button and the electric overhead opener hummed. The garage door swung up, and he settled into the reupholstered leather in his car, switched on the ignition and backed out onto his large driveway. Mammoth ponderosa pines formed a circle around most of the driveway, screening the garage from the road which led to his home. He was less than twenty yards from the shore of Bear Lake where his sleek new jet boat, a Thunderbird Formula 20, was docked at its floating aluminium pier. The pier added seventy thousand dollars to the cost of the property. Doesn't really matter, he thought. I'm never going to sell this place. Everything I want—time to relax and enjoy. For months he had considered getting married for he liked children, and as his mother had said, no man is complete until he is a father.

He turned on the tap and ice cold water spat into the bucket. Even though the air was sixty-five, the water in the outside line was near freezing. He must remember to shut it off in the next month or so as the original owners had suggested. Didn't want a bunch of broken water lines. He found a sponge and washed the roof of his car. The new metallic blue paint glistened in the sunlight. The dirty water ran onto the driveway and he splashed the rest of the bucket against it, washing everything into the four inch tall grass bordering his home.

He walked down to the boat and started it, then switched it off. The jet boat's top speed was fifty-five miles an hour and had come with the house. He glanced back at the road, pleased with how well hidden he was from any curious locals who happened by in passing cars. Something wet hit his face. He touched his nose—a snow flake had fallen on it. To the west he could see clear skies over the Pacific, less then seventy-five miles away as the crow or ICBM flew. So this was what the natives called a sun blizzard. It was beautiful—a great way to begin his first day at Big Bear. He debated on whether to leave his car outside or back it in. He decided to leave it out—there was still work to do.

The Russian walked inside the garage, up the stairs to the main house, then up the flight of steps to the guest bedroom. Jasper Garner's red hair was splashed across her chest and her blue eyes never left him as he entered the room. Her legs and arms were still securely bound.

"I need to know some things," he said. He noticed that her chin had a streak of grease on it from the Mustang's trunk.

"Have you thought of joining the Hare Krishnas?"

"I'd like to know what you told the police about me."

"Everything."

"I think if they knew everything about me, I would be in jail by now. Your lover was a fool. I hope you won't be."

"I don't want to die."

"You won't." He wondered if she could tell he was lying. He had seen other people in similar circumstances. Even when death was inevitable, they always denied it—until it happened. He would have to kill her; there was really no other way.

"We told the police what we suspected," said the journalist. "They'll be looking for you."

"They'll be looking for Russ Smith. He no longer exists," said Jan Country.

"So now you'll kill me?"

He thought it might be bad luck to begin his life in the new house with a total lie. "That would be too bad," he said. "You are a very beautiful woman."

"Big deal."

"Pardon?"

"I said . . . big deal. Look where it got me."

"Yes."

"Why did you murder all those women?"

He knew she was probing, trying to find a weak spot. Why not tell her? She was an inquisitive reporter who had become a part of the puzzle. She deserved at least to know *why* she was dying. So he told her about how he had come to America—and how he had killed Dusty. How his name had been Jon Andrews, then Russ Smith. And now Jan Country. Then he told her about the Kaam. "I was quite disappointed that you and the computer expert did not use the container I left in your bedroom bath."

"You were going to watch us make love and die?"

"Yes, I suppose I was."

She looked away and tears glowed on her cheeks. "You don't have to kill me. It wouldn't do any good."

"We both know I can't let you live," he said, injecting her with sodium pentothal; she sobbed her way into unconsciousness. When he was certain she was sleeping deeply, he rolled a blanket around her, tore the tape from her wrists and carried her downstairs, out past his Mustang. Snow fell around him—great clusters, like soft leaves. Already the roof and trunk lid of the car had turned white—only the hood, still warm from the journey, glistened. Soon it would change to white as the snowflakes splattered and cooled its slippery metal. The Russian carried the woman's body easily on his shoulder, and when he reached his jet boat, set her on the floor of the craft. He glanced back at the road behind his house—it was translucent through the snow. Occasionally the sun broke through, hurting his eyes.

He started the 3300cc engine. It roared to life, vibrating the fiberglass hull. The snow made the Russian think of his own country, the Ukraine. He was sorry about the things that had happened. He missed his family and his mother. He still felt the hurt when he thought of his own people trying to kill him. Life was such a disillusionment. If his own people had only played fair. But they hadn't, so why dwell on it? He would do what he had to in order to survive.

He used an aluminum paddle to push off from the dock. Then the engine coughed to a stop; the tank was empty. Curious, he thought, for he had left the boat with a full tank. Maybe the kids had drained it. He was grateful for the snow that whirled around him, camouflaging him as he made his way past the Mustang and into his garage. He found a five gallon container of gas and carried it back to the boat. His footprints were already starting to fill in.

The Russian frowned as he thought of the credit card that he had used with the name of Russ Smith. Worse, he had told the gas station attendant that he was going to Big Bear. That had been a mistake—for now there was a link to a man named Russ Smith and Big Bear. The Russian poured the gas into the boat's tank and realized he was being too paranoid. No one knew that Russ Smith had anything to do with the Kaam extortion. No one except the journalist knew about him. And in a few moments she would die. When the authorities found her decomposed body in the spring, they would assume she had simply drowned. It would be doubtful if they could figure out who she was. He had even called Sergeant Dartwell and kept more than his part of the bargain by revealing where the deadly Kaam containers had been left. No link between that and himself. He looked down at the girl wrapped in the blanket. A link who in a few minutes would be dead. David Cursore was another link. But he was dead. Of course there was still Ivan Tornoff. He was still alive but there was no way for the Russian to trace a man called Jon Andrews—a person who did not exist—to the San Bernadino Mountains. So the Russian felt safe in his new identity as the snow swirled around him.

He finished filling the Formula 20's tank then started the engine and guided the boat carefully through a series of small channels, past several tiny rocky islands where people had built outlandish cabins. The lake was the result of a dam that a developer had built many years ago. It was several miles wide and ten or fifteen long. The snow eased a bit but it was still difficult to see more than a quarter of a mile.

The visibility from the Bell 206 drifting over the treetops was better. David Cursore pointed down to the Shelby sports car that was parked outside the open garage.

"Might be our man out there," said the policeman, indicating the jet boat headed toward the middle of Big Bear. He leaned toward the pilot. "Can you take us over that boat?"

"No problem," said the chopper pilot. He tipped the nose down and zeroed in on the boat.

Cursore had a pair of binoculars pressed against his forehead. "It's Russ Smith. He's got something wrapped up in a blanket. He's pushed it over. We got to get down there . . ."

The helicopter moving against the wind suddenly floated out of the snow shower, not more than fifty yards from the Russian. Jon Andrews was busy watching the heavy anchor he had attached to the blanket suck the woman beneath the water. He squinted up at the helicopter—where the hell did that come from?

Bubbles snapped to the surface from the sinking woman who had disappeared beneath the choppy waves.

"This is the police," boomed a loudspeaker from the chopper. "Stay where you are. Do not move."

The helicopter bucked the gusting snow as the Russian pulled his .38 revolver from beneath his jacket and fired at the glistening bubble of the Bell. The plexiglass shattered as a slug ground through it and a shard from the bullet tore into the pilot's arm. The Bell seesawed crazily downward through the swirling snow; the wounded pilot wrestled with his controls.

The Russian yanked a lever, jerking the jet boat into drive. But he was too anxious and his engine sputtered to a stop. He started it again, blasting another shot at the chopper. The Russian smiled, as overhead the pilot clutched his side, trying to wrestle the whining machine back to a horizontal flight path. The chopper's flat blades beat unevenly at the falling white chunks of snow.

The cop grabbed the controls and

stopped the pitching; however, the craft continued toward the lake. The tip of its rotor slashed the water, sending up a thirty foot spray. The helicopter shuddered crazily. Dartwell poured the juice to the engine . . . the chopper rose in jerks.

The icy wind and snow cut Cursore's face as he crouched in the doorway of the craft. "Take it down," he screamed over the grinding engine.

"This is worse than Nam," yelled back the cop. The engine revved madly.

"Take it down!" Cursore felt a searing pain along his temple as the wind rasped across the bandage. For a moment his legs buckled.

"We got to get out of here!" The cop shielded his face as another slug from the Russian's weapon ricocheted off the plexiglass bubble.

"He's drowning her!"

The cop took a deep breath of the hot air that was rushing past him from the controls and tried to knock the Russian into the water with the chopper's undercarriage.

There was a micro-second as the Bell hung five feet above the jet boat. A silly thought went through Cursore's mind as he leapt. Something Shakespeare said about the better part of valor being discretion. . . . Too late, the snow engulfed him, sucking him downwards.

Jon Andrews stared in disbelief as the

sun momentarily pierced the snow flurries and then a falling man blotted out the light.

The man's feet slammed into a cushioned seat and the boat listed wildly. In the same instant the helicopter's engines sounded ready to explode as they ripped the craft upward. Iron and glass and plastic rattled against fluffy flakes. The snow seemed to fall so effortlessly, while the machine made a tremendous commotion as it fought its way upward, disappearing into the white umbrella.

The Russian saw the man was wearing a turban. No. It was a bandage and long strips of it were loose, fluttering around the man's face, obliterating it. The Russian swung his automatic at the lurching figure. It looked more like a mummy than a human being.

The wind tugged the bandage away from Cursore's bleeding forehead and the Russian's action halted for an instant. How could the computer expert still be alive? This was impossible. In that fraction of time, Cursore hurled the empty five gallon gasoline can at the Russian.

Jon Andrews, regaining his balance, stepped easily to one side, deflecting the can with his arms. And with that Cursore was on the Russian. He realized he had been a fool to take on the killer without a weapon.

The Russian coolly moved the pistol

under Cursore's swing and squeezed the trigger. Cursore's hand clutched the barrel and his thumb caught the safety catch of the weapon. The Russian kicked Cursore in his stomach and snapped the safety off. As he was about to pull the trigger again, the helicopter—Goddamn it, he had forgotten about that—darted out of the swirling snow and forced him to duck. He fired at the craft but it had disappeared, swallowed by snow. The Russian remembered a children's story he had been reading. Chicken Little and the sky falling in—and then Cursore attacked again.

They struggled, and the Russian felt Cursore sink to his knees. The American was weak, his strength draining quickly.

The Russian brought his knee as hard as he could into Cursore's chest but Cursore saw it coming and twisted away. All the while Cursore was somehow able to maintain his grip on the Russian's gun hand, keeping the weapon pointed away. It suddenly discharged into the snow flakes.

The echoes had not died, as the Russian pulled free. Cursore scrambled for the aluminum paddle, brought it down on the Russian's arm, smashing the gun to the deck of the boat. They both fell against each other, clutching for it. The Russian's hand closed on the gun as Cursore got his knee on the weapon and seized Jon Andrew's throat.

Their eyes were only inches apart as the Russian fought for breath. His fingers closed on the butt of the weapon and slowly, ever so slowly, he pulled the pistol free. His neck throbbed but the pain would only be temporary.

The gun's front sight tore through Cursore's pants and ripped his knee. Cursore realized he could not maintain his grip on the man's throat and in seconds the .45 would be free.

Cursore thought of the woman he loved on the bottom of the lake, felt the metal sight tearing across his knee, smelled the coffee breath of the Russian.

Cursore let it go. And pushed. Pushed with all his strength and the Russian fell backward and Cursore was on him. The one thing Cursore thought about was the gun. He had to get to it before the Russian could react. Had to. His fingers closed on the barrel, twisted, twisted with his last reserve of strength.

There was a soft *thud* as the weapon went off. The Russian stared into Cursore's eyes. Cursore's eyes remained wide, frightened, then the white flakes settled on the Russian's cheeks and he sank backwards. He clutched his stomach and his face ground against the cold plastic seat.

David Cursore pulled off his coat and dived into the water. It was about twenty five feet deep and he could see quite clearly. There were bubbles everywhere but he did not know where they were coming from.

Finally, on the bed of the lake, he spotted Jasper. She was looking up at him, her red hair floating in the water, swaying seaweed. An anchor chain was twisted around her legs and stomach, and she could not escape because everything was tangled in some kind of polyethelene tubing that seemed to be growing out of the lake bed. His lungs were bursting. He realized no person could survive for more than sixty seconds under the water. He estimated she would have had to have held her breath for at least ten minutes, perhaps more. Nevertheless, he swam down to her.

When he reached her, his lungs were ready to explode. She was dead anyway; she'd have to be. He turned and swam to the surface, gulped in several lungfuls of air and dived back down.

The second time he swam directly to her. He tried to pull the anchor chain from her waist but couldn't. Her eyes were open and she was staring at him. His lungs burned and his face stung where the bandages had covered his wound. He was aware of the ribbon of white gauze floating away from his head. He tugged at her anchor chain. He had to go back to the surface again, but as he swam away, her icy cold hand reached out, holding him. She was alive. How could that be? He needed air, needed it desperately. He pushed away, and she handed something to him—he realized it was a plastic hose as air bubbles squirted his face. He put the tube in his mouth. The air was coming from somewhere—she had been breathing it. Must be OK to breathe. He took a tentative gulp, then another. Definitely air from someplace. He passed the hose back to her, and she clamped it between her teeth. A few moments later, he freed her from the anchor chain and they tumbled upward to the surface.

The helicopter was only a foot or two above the water. The air was so cold that he could hardly work her head through the life preserver that dangled next to the chopper's door. Finally he got her shoulder through. She clutched him and the helicopter rose several feet as the winch attached to the life preserver hoisted them level with the door.

Dartwell pulled them inside.

"You got to get us to a hospital," sputtered Cursore.

"Fine by me," said the pilot, pointing the Bell toward shore. His shoulder was red with blood but he seemed to be OK. At least he was conscious.

Dartwell turned on the heater and wrapped them each in blankets. Cursore looked at Jasper. "Thanks," she said.

"You cause me a lot of trouble," he said.

"Why don't you two shut up until we get you to a hospital," said the cop.

35

Mary Lou did herself proud when she whipped up her world famous southern fried chicken with all the trimmings.

"This is the best cole slaw I've eaten in my life," said Jasper. She and Cursore were seated beside each other in Mary Lou's apartment. The sun had set and Mary Lou had turned on the stereo—an old Hoagy Carmichael tune, "Stardust," was playing.

Mary Lou smoothed her hands on her apron and sat down at the table. "I got the recipe from The Pantry. The secret is garlic and mustard."

Dartwell helped himself to a second bowl. "Sure is good. You know, looking at you, Mary Lou, I would never have thought that you were the kind of person who spent much time in The Pantry. Not a very class place, although the food is good . . ."

"Listen, Sergeant, if you were ten—make it fifteen—years older, I'd show you some things about me that would make your head swim." Mary Lou smiled, then considered Cursore. "Speaking of swimming heads, how's yours?"

Cursore touched the small bandage along his temple and nodded. "Takes more than a bullet to slow him down," said Jasper.

After the four finished the chicken and creamed potatoes and apple dumplings, Mary Lou opened the bottle of brandy that Dartwell had brought and poured them each a healthy snifter of Courvoisier.

Cursore and Jasper drank steaming hot coffee with their brandy. Mary Lou smoked a Virginia Slim. The cop asked if anyone minded if he had a cigar with his cognac.

"I don't like cigar smoke," said Mary Lou, "but if you tell me a couple of things, I'll let you."

"It's your place. I won't smoke 'em," said the cop. "And if you want some questions answered . . . try me. I couldn't say no to anything after a meal like that."

"After you took these two to the hospital, why didn't you keep the five million you found?"

"I was afraid someone would tell on me," said the cop. "Too bad we all didn't know each other as well as we do now."

"A pity. I'm still not clear how this little redhead survived being dumped on the bottom of Bear Lake for damn near a quarter of an hour."

"I told you," said Jasper. "There was an air hose down there!"

"Come on," said Mary Lou. "That was an hallucination..."

"No," said the cop. "Bear Lake used to have a lot of fish in it until the boats polluted it. All the algae died, then the fish died. Couple of years ago, some biologist got the idea of aerating by running air hoses along the bottom. She was lucky enough to end up near one."

"I was pretty scared, though," said Jasper.

"*You* were scared," said Cursore. "I thought you were dead and a corpse was hanging onto me when you grabbed me down there."

"I wasn't grabbing you, I was trying to goose you..."

"Will you two save the mush for later?" said Mary Lou. "My last question is... how come we haven't heard anything about this whole episode?"

"That's one reason I'm glad you invited me over tonight. You see, this Russ Smith... he was a spy."

"Really?" asked Mary Lou.

"Yes. And I shouldn't really be telling you but I kind of got permission. Smith or Andrews or Country—whatever he called himself—was a killer. Certain Russians were very embarrassed so the State Department agreed to keep the incident hush-hush."

"My God! To think I was living in the same apartment complex as a spy," said Mary Lou.

The cop took another sip of his coffee. "I understand how you feel and there's a man from the State Department who's going to stop by later and debrief you. He should be here pretty soon."

"He isn't going to try any strong-arm tactics with me, is he?" she asked.

The cop scratched his chin. "No. See ... through what's happened they've discovered certain people who can be of great help to the State Department. One is an older Russian diplomat who I can't mention. Seems he's going to cooperate with the government. His testimony has also cleared Cursore of the charges that sent him to prison. But if any one raises a stink, I'm afraid the D.A.'s department may not go through with its intention to grant Cursore a full pardon."

"Sounds like blackmail." Mary Lou washed down a grape with some brandy. "But who am I to fight the government? And since the man who killed poor Dusty is dead ... what's the point?"

"I appreciate that, Mary Lou," said Cursore.

Before she could reply there was a loud knock on the door. She opened it. And there, his face flushed with anger, sucking on a dirty cigar was Parole Officer Gwilliam. The fat man pointed the wet end of the cigar at Cursore. "You. Get out here in the hall!"

"Pardon," said Cursore, setting down

his brandy.

"You heard me, asshole. I told you to meet me at your place last Friday."

Cursore started to get up, Dartwell leaned across the table and whispered: "I'll handle this guy. You take it easy. You've been through too much."

"You, big man, you sit down," roared Gwilliam. "This is none of your concern."

The women watched Dartwell move toward the fat man who tried to grab the sergeant's collar, missed and seized the small gold crucifix that hung from the policeman's neck. Wrong thing to do. Dartwell's powerful fingers seized the cussing Gwilliam under his chin and pushed the obese figure back into the hallway. Dartwell pulled the door closed behind him.

"Maybe I should help," said Cursore.

"Maybe we should just help with the dishes," said Jasper. "I want you all in one piece tonight." She placed a gentle palm on his chest and he settled back down. "Finish your drink, darling."

Cursore lifted his cognac to his lips as the muffled sounds of a fat man being thrown into a service elevator echoed through a corridor. There were several thuds and assorted curses. A moment later Dartwell, breathing heavily, sauntered back into the apartment. He adjusted his tie and sat back down at the table. "You sure have some wacky friends, Cursore. Who was that fat guy?"

"My parole officer," said Cursore.

Dartwell sucked in his breath and crossed himself. "Mother of Mary."